Praise for previous books by Karen Toller Whittenburg

Nanny Angel

"Karen Toller Whittenburg's contemporary spin on *Mary Poppins* is whimsical and amusing. Love is all around in this charming book."

—*Affaire de Coeur*

"This is a wonderful fantasy, with soft, human characters.... A delightful story."

—*Rendezvous*

The Pauper and the Princess

"Karen Toller Whittenburg writes some very tender, very sensual scenes."

—*Affaire de Coeur*

"Well-told tale that will hold the reader's interest due to strong-willed, dimensional characters."

—*Rendezvous*

Wedding of Her Dreams

"Karen Toller Whittenburg bets that clever characters, fast pacing, and wonderfully witty dialogue will delight readers, and wins hands down."

—*Romantic Times*

"A delightful romance packed with witty characters, humorous situations, and sensuous dialogue that will keep you smiling long after the last page is turned."

—*Rendezvous*

Dear Reader,

Magic, like love, is in the eye of the beholder. So who's to say that magic, along with love, can't be stitched into the seams of a wedding dress...an antique gown that changes the lives of three special brides and their unsuspecting bridegrooms. I imagined just such a dress and the predicament of a bride who avoids putting on the dress for fear she'll find herself falling in love with the wrong man. In *Two-Penny Wedding*, Gentry Shaw convinces her bridesmaids to try on the wedding dress, but as each of them succumbs to love as a result, Gentry comes face-to-face with magic in the form of her first and only love, Jake Daniels.

Daydreamer that I am, I believe it could happen, and as you read about Gentry and Jake, I hope you will believe it, too. After all, isn't there a touch of magic, a gentle twist of fate, any time a man and woman fall in love?

Karen Toller Whittenburg

Karen Toller Whittenburg

TWO-PENNY WEDDING

Harlequin Books

TORONTO • NEW YORK • LONDON
AMSTERDAM • PARIS • SYDNEY • HAMBURG
STOCKHOLM • ATHENS • TOKYO • MILAN
MADRID • WARSAW • BUDAPEST • AUCKLAND

Jolie, Debbi, Crystal, and Bonnie
This one's for you.

ISBN 0-373-16648-6

TWO-PENNY WEDDING

Chapter One

While her three bridesmaids waited in the bedroom, Gentry Elizabeth Northcross adjusted the neckline of her wedding gown and checked her appearance one last time in the dressing-room mirror. The gown left one shoulder bare and angled from the other in a slim, formfitting line that draped completely over one breast and not nearly so completely over the other. From there, the sequined fabric nipped in at her waist, mapped the curve of her hips and flared to a scooped and scalloped hemline, which struck her mid-thigh in front and mid-calf in back. Attached to the swath of material at her shoulder was a diaphanous, cathedral-length train, which floated behind her, its sequins shimmering like a river of rainbows with every move she made.

The gown was one-of-a-kind, avant-garde, very chic, and every time she looked in the mirror, the neckline seemed a little lower and the hemline a little higher. Resisting the impulse to tug on one or the other, she opened the dressing-room door and stepped into the bedroom.

Three women—two brunettes and a blonde—turned their heads in her direction. Three pairs of curious eyes—blue, brown and gray—looked her over from head to toe. Three startled expressions and a shared silence confirmed Gentry's worst fears. She smiled anyway, and did a slow pirouette for her audience. "Well, what do you think?"

"Oh, Gentry, it's so...unusual." That, from Heather, the doe-eyed, diplomatic friend.

"Isn't it a little tight for a wedding gown?" Hillary's eyes were blue, but she saw the world in practical black and white.

Gentry pulled the gossamer train into a glittery circle around her feet and waited for her best friend and maid of honor to comment. Sydney Ryals examined the gown from sequins to scallops before she lifted skeptical gray eyes. "Where did you get that? The Fairy Godmother's Thrift Shop?"

"Sydney!" Heather scolded softly. "It's not that bad."

"Yes, it is. She looks like she was standing on the wrong end of the magic wand when it backfired."

"Sonny had it made for me," Gentry said defensively. "One of his artist friends designed it."

"Whoever created this must think he's Salvador Dali." Sydney wrinkled her nose as she studied the dress again. "Well, you absolutely can't wear it."

"Of course I'm going to wear it." She smoothed the sequins covering her hips, uncomfortably aware of the way the fabric clung to her skin. "I wouldn't dream of hurting Sonny's feelings by rejecting his thoughtful gift."

"What about *our* feelings?" Sydney's gesture included the other two. "Our reputations as women of style are at stake. And if your gown looks like that..."

She gave a delicate little shudder. "Your fiancé didn't have his protégé design *our* dresses, did he?"

Gentry pursed her lips, annoyed with Sydney for being honest. "No, he didn't."

"He did choose the color." Hillary settled on the bed and opened a bottle of nail polish. "Gentry selected the style, sent a picture to me, and Heather and I ordered all three of them from Harrods. If you hadn't been so busy, you could have voiced your opinion. As it is, the dresses will be delivered tomorrow and I can only hope you haven't put on any weight since you sent your measurements."

Sydney dropped onto the chaise longue, picked up a magazine and began flipping through the pages. "Unlike you, Hil, I don't have to worry about every mouthful of food going straight to my hips. What color did the artistic Sonny select for our ensemble?"

Hillary looked up from her nails. "Pink."

"Rose petal," Heather corrected her. "That's the color listed on the order form."

"Pink?" Sydney made a face as she looked to Gentry for confirmation. "You let him talk you into *pink?*"

Gentry was beginning to wish she hadn't asked her bridesmaids to spend the entire week before her wedding with her. "He likes the color contrast with my hair."

"It's a visual thing." Hillary resumed polishing her nails. "You know how artistic men adore contrast."

"No, but I know how awful I look in pink. And it isn't exactly your color, either. If Sonny wanted to see Gentry's long red tresses against a Pepto-Bismol background, why didn't he make *her* dress rose petal pink?"

"Who can explain the artistic mind?" Hillary gave her head a dramatic toss. "Face it, Syd. Not everyone has your knack for making a fashion statement with sweatpants and flannel shirts."

"Play nice, girls." Heather stepped around the gauzy trail of the wedding train and moved to the window seat, her favorite spot in the room. As children, the four friends had spent hours in this bedroom—Heather sitting in the window seat, knees drawn to her chest, Sydney draped lazily in the chaise longue, an open book or magazine in her lap, Hillary and Gentry lying across opposite ends of the canopied bed—planning futures that had never materialized. "The four of us haven't been together for ages. We only have seven days and, frankly, I don't want to spend any of them listening to you two pick at each other."

Hillary held out a newly polished fingernail to check the color. "It was only two years ago, Heather. That really doesn't qualify as *ages.*"

"Well, it seems longer than that to me. I don't know why we can't see one another more often."

"It would be too taxing for Gentry," Sydney said. "I don't think she should get married any more often than every two years. These weddings that don't happen are trying for all of us."

"Not to mention the length of her engagements," Hillary added. "Do you realize, Gen, that, counting both engagements, you've been engaged to Sonny longer than it took you to get your art degree?"

"Does that exclude the brief interlude she was married to someone else?" Sydney asked. "Or do we add in those few months as a bonus for going the distance?"

"Sonny and I believe a long engagement is the best foundation for a long and happy marriage."

"What were you aiming for...a century of wedded bliss? Wouldn't that require about a decade of engagement?"

"I think it only calls for a little more than eighteen months, exactly what Sonny and I have had."

"This time," Hillary clarified. "Last time it was a full two years."

"And that wedding didn't happen. What does that do to the long-engagement theory?" Sydney asked.

"Not a thing," Gentry said with unruffled confidence. "This wedding will happen as planned. Nothing can stop it from being absolutely perfect."

"Correct me if I'm wrong, but isn't that what you said two years ago?" Sydney flipped a page in the magazine. "Just hours before you left Sonny Harris at the altar to elope with another man."

"I'll thank you not to remind me of that embarrassing lapse in sanity."

"Oh, my." Hillary's eyebrows rose in alarm. "I hadn't thought of that. Syd's right, Gentry. You can't be married in a white dress. You've been married before."

Sydney noisily turned another page. "That tradition went out when Elizabeth Post took over for Emily. Since there aren't many virgins left, brides can wear white as a symbol of their pure hearts."

"Who says there aren't any virgins," Heather protested from the window seat.

"I said *many,* not *any.*"

"You're misinformed," Hillary stated flatly. "The fact is, Gentry has been married before and she should wear an ivory or cream-colored bridal gown, not white."

"That marriage was annulled." Gentry's tone posted a warning that this subject wasn't open for discussion. "Wiped from the records. It didn't count. It didn't even exist. I can wear white if I want to."

"I don't see how you can say it didn't count." Sydney idly turned a page in the magazine. "Most of the guests you've invited to this wedding were here for the last wedding, when you took off with a man you'd known less than two weeks. The smartest thing you ever did...in my humble opinion."

There was a moment of stilted silence while Hillary, Sydney and Heather focused on nail polish, a shampoo ad and looking out the window, respectively, to avoid meeting her eyes. Gentry positioned the oval mirror to give herself a view of the room, then stepped back to look at her reflection. "A week from today I'm going to marry the man I should have married two years ago, and I expect my friends to be happy for me."

"I'm happy for you." Heather, always the peacemaker, paved the way.

"Of course we're happy for you," Hillary said. "But I still say you shouldn't wear a white gown. It just isn't the correct thing to do."

Sydney's gray eyes met Gentry's green ones in the mirror. "If you're happy, I'm happy."

"Good, because I'm very happy."

"Hooray," Sydney said dryly. "Now all we have to do is find you something else to wear. Has Sonny *seen* that dress?"

"Only a sketch. He says it would be bad luck to see it before the wedding."

"Doesn't he think it would be in bad taste for you to get married in a *white* gown?"

Gentry, Sydney and Heather turned a common frown on Hillary, who shrugged. "All right, all right. But I still don't think a pure heart is an adequate substitute for a time-honored and tasteful tradition."

Sydney shook her head. "Honestly, Hillary, if I didn't know better, I'd think you were raised in a convent. You act like you've never even been introduced to the concept of sex."

"I'll have you know I've been introduced plenty of times, but I fail to see what that has to do with anything."

"It means that, according to your time-honored and tasteful tradition of virginal brides, Heather is the only one in this room entitled to wear a white wedding dress."

"Hey, just because I haven't met the right guy..."

Hillary dismissed Heather's protest with a wave of her hand, fingers splayed so as not to muss the nail polish. "It means, Sydney, that Gentry is the only one of us who *shouldn't* wear white. She's been married. We haven't."

"It's women like you, Hillary, who kept the ERA from being ratified."

"A feat for which you should be thanking me. Equality with men would be a step down for some of us."

"Please don't start that," Heather said quickly. "Gentry told you her first marriage was annulled. And she eloped then, anyway. So, technically, this is her first wedding and she can wear any color she wants."

"May I suggest rose petal pink?"

"No, Syd, you may not." Gentry smoothed the front of her dress and tried to find some redeeming beauty in its uniqueness. "Is this really that bad?"

"Yes," Sydney said.

"It's awful, Gen." Hillary wrinkled her nose for emphasis.

"I've seen you in more flattering outfits," was Heather's tactful comment.

With a frown, Gentry checked her reflection again. "Don't you think you could grow to like it?"

"Not in this lifetime," Sydney said.

"We're your best friends." Hillary relaxed against the headboard of the bed. "Would we lie to you?"

"I wish you would." In the mirror, Gentry sought Heather's diplomacy... and received an apologetic shrug of consensus. She lifted her chin. "It's Sonny's opinion that matters," she said stubbornly. "I'm wearing this dress."

"It's your funeral." Sydney dropped the magazine onto the floor and cupped her hands behind her head. "But then, in my humble opinion, that's true no matter what dress you wear."

Hillary threw a pillow, hitting Sydney's elbow. "Shut up, Syd. Just because we think she should have stayed married to Jake—"

A startling, self-conscious silence filled the room, leaving the name echoing in the stillness. All three of the women shot a guilty glance at Gentry, looked away and then began talking at once.

"Did you guys know that Lucy Pendrax is pregnant?"

"Let's listen to some music."

"What time is it? I thought we were going to swim before dinner."

"Jake." Gentry raised her voice over their forced chatter and pronounced the name with deliberate casualness. "See? You can say his name in front of me. It doesn't affect me in the slightest. I hardly even remember what he looks like."

Sydney picked up the pillow and propped it behind her head. "Tall, darkly good-looking and sort of mysterious, along the lines of Antonio Banderas, with the body of Schwarzenegger, eyes like Brad Pitt's, the charisma of Harrison Ford, and a smile that stops your heart."

"Don't forget the way he looks in a pair of Levi's."

"Heather!" Sydney's tone held surprised admiration. "Don't tell me *you* noticed Jake's butt?"

"Hips," Hillary corrected her. "The other term is simply too crude to be used when speaking of one of the finest examples of masculine derrieres I've ever had the pleasure of gazing upon."

"I'm sorry I asked you three to be in my wedding." Hands on her hips, Gentry turned to look at her friends in disgust. "If you'd give Sonny a chance, you might discover he's twice the man Jake Daniels is, and he's much more handsome."

"Depends on which way he's facing," Sydney said.

"Sonny is gorgeous," Hillary agreed. "But I'll take that wild, rugged, sexual quality that Jake has, any day."

"Me, too," Heather said. "In a heartbeat."

"You'd live to regret it, too." Gentry picked up the pillbox hat with matching sequined netting and put it on her head. "Wild and rugged sexuality is not a component of a long and happy marriage."

Sydney's brow furrowed in confusion. "You're kidding, right?"

"No, I'm not."

For a moment, Sydney was speechless. "No wonder Jake kicked you out after only three months."

"He did not kick me out. I left him."

"But why?" Heather asked. "You two were so insanely in love."

"*Insane* being the operative word." Gentry adjusted the bridal headpiece and the netting, uncomfortable with the memory of that time in her life. Jake Daniels was in the past and that's where she meant for him to stay. "I sometimes wonder if I didn't imagine the whole episode. And now that Sonny and I are back together, it's really like Jake never existed at all."

"Does he still go on those weekend fishing trips with Ben?" Hillary asked. "They were good friends once."

"I wouldn't know. My brother never said anything to me about Jake one way or another. Now that Ben's married, I doubt he'll have much time for fishing with anyone. Unless Sara takes up the sport." Gentry gave an indifferent shrug and hoped that would put an end to this particular topic.

"I may never forgive Ben for falling in love with her." Hillary sighed as she recapped the bottle of nail polish. "He swore he would wait for me."

"There you have it, Hil," Sydney said. "He knew there was no danger you would ever grow up."

"Ben's married. I still can hardly believe it." Heather leaned her head against the dormer wall and looked out the window. "Honestly, Gentry, weren't you flabbergasted when he told you he was married?"

"Stunned," she answered. "I was beginning to think he'd be a bachelor for the rest of his life, but I understood the moment I met Sara. Ben's always been afraid that marriage would be boring, but life with her will keep him on his toes, that's for certain.''

Heather jerked upright in the window seat. "Have you guys ever heard of a superstition where if someone's name is mentioned, it means they'll show up?"

"Superstitions are nonsense." Sydney repositioned the pillow beneath her head and closed her eyes.

"I always thought you had to say the name three times really fast." Hillary held out her hands to examine the new shade of her fingernails. "Or maybe three people say the name once at the same time."

Sydney yawned. "Three people have to say the name three times while spinning in a circle."

"However it happens, we did it." Heather sat up on her knees and pressed her hands against the windowpane.

"Ben's out there?" Gentry stopped trying to make the hat on her head appear less gaudy and took a step toward the window. "But he and Sara are in Hawaii on their honeymoon. They won't even be back until just before the wedding on Saturday."

"Not Ben." Heather tucked her knees under her and leaned closer to the glass for a better view. "I haven't seen him in a while, but it certainly looks like Jake getting out of that truck."

Truck had a ring of truth, which sluiced down Gentry's spine with the chill of winter...even though it was almost July. Just the thought of seeing him again froze her in her tracks. Jake had been out of her life longer than he'd been in it. Their marriage had lasted three months. A turbulent, traumatic, passion-filled three months, the memory of which she had safely buried under a mountain of denial. She would die happy if she could forget she'd ever set eyes on him.

"You're imagining it, Heather," Hillary said. "We were talking about Jake and you just thought you saw him."

"I usually don't imagine men in this much detail." Now her nose was flattened against the glass, and she had both hands pressed against the panes. "And they never look this good, even from a distance."

"Let me see." Hillary was off the bed, her blond hair swinging in perfect unison around her shoulders as she strolled to the window. "Scoot over, Heather."

"I was here first." Heather moved over only slightly. "And don't fog up the window with your heavy breathing, either."

As the two women bumped hips, vying for a view of the front driveway and the steps leading to the front doors, Gentry fought a swelling wave of emotion. Panic. Anticipation. Disbelief. Curiosity. Jake wouldn't come here. Not the week before her wedding. She hadn't seen or heard from him since the day she walked out of the Two-Penny Lodge and out of his life. If he'd had any desire to see her, he could have come after her then. She'd really expected he would follow...or at least make contact. But he hadn't. Not unless she counted that one card...and since he hadn't bothered to sign it, she didn't bother to count it. She couldn't believe he'd show up now. He couldn't. He wouldn't dare. "Did you figure out who it is?" she asked as if the answer was of no concern to her. "A deliveryman, maybe?"

Hillary glanced over her shoulder at Gentry. "Only if you're expecting someone to deliver a big black dog."

Cleo. Ben had asked her to keep the dog while he and Sara were gone. "Oh." Gentry released a tiny sigh of relief. "That's only Arthur. He said he'd bring Cleo over sometime this afternoon."

"Who's Arthur and who's Cleo?" Hillary asked, still craning her neck for a better view.

"Cleo is Ben's black Labrador retriever and Arthur is Ben's new butler. I'm keeping the dog while Ben and Sara are on their honeymoon. Arthur's having some kind of butler reunion at the house, and he didn't want Cleo around. She's something of a troublemaker."

"What I'd like to know is why Ben's new butler looks just like your ex-husband."

"He doesn't. Arthur is tall, thin, fiftyish. You'd never mistake him for..." The panic took precedence, and in a sparkle of sequins, she moved to the window and pushed between Heather and Hillary. "Let me see."

"He's at the front door now." Heather wiggled backward and off the window seat. "You won't be able to see him from the window."

Gentry swept the view with a narrowed gaze. The truck was really a utility vehicle, one of those four-wheel-drive affairs some people preferred to rent when visiting California. It was exactly the kind of vehicle Jake liked to drive. Whoever the driver was, though, he was already out of sight, blocked from view by the porch overhang. She heard the faint chime of the doorbell downstairs. And with the sound, it occurred to her that at least one of her bridesmaids didn't seem the least bit interested in verifying the identity of the delivery person.

Gentry turned, protecting the dress with her careful movements. "Sydney? Aren't you the least bit curious who's at the door?"

Syd looked up from her magazine and didn't even have the grace to look guilty. "Can't say I'm especially anxious to meet Ben's butler. He sounds a little old for me."

"But you'd be anxious to see Jake, wouldn't you?"

"Sure, but you said it wasn't Jake."

Gentry fumed, unable to believe she'd fallen for such a shameless pretense. "It isn't Jake. I'm on to your little joke now, and I don't find it very funny."

"Am I laughing?" Sydney asked evenly. "Are Heather and Hil convulsed in giggles?"

"You're waiting until I rush downstairs and make a fool of myself."

"I wish I'd thought of that, Gen, but I didn't. I don't know who those two—" she gestured at the other two women "—think they saw, but, frankly, I can't imagine why you would believe for a second that Jake would come all the way from Arkansas to play a rather tasteless joke on you, the woman who hardly remembers what he looks like."

"It's not a joke," Heather said sincerely. "I really thought I saw him."

"Sorry, Gen." Hillary shrugged. "I thought it looked like him, too."

Sydney picked up the magazine again. "Look on the bright side, Gentry, Jake probably wants to avoid seeing you as much as you want to avoid seeing him, which means he wouldn't step foot in this house if he thought you were in it. And if, by some wild, fantastic chance it is Jake, it can only mean he's come to attend your wedding, which will make it the event of the season."

"Over my dead body."

Sydney shrugged. "I, for one, would consider that a noble sacrifice."

"There's going to be a sacrifice if I find him in this house." Taking the longest steps allowed by the tight fit of her dress, Gentry walked across the room, flung open the bedroom door and paused to listen, trying to distinguish an identifying tone or pitch in the murmur of voices below.

"To come inside . . ." That, obviously, was Teresa, the housekeeper.

"Ben . . . reunion . . . dog . . . couldn't stay . . ."

The words drifted up, without context or meaning . . . except that after all this time, and even at this distance, she recognized his unhurried midwestern drawl. Without conscious effort, she visualized his expression simply by the tone of his voice. His lips were curved in that slightly lopsided smile and his eyes held that down-home, a-word-is-as-good-as-a-handshake twinkle that had first captured her attention. There would be a strand of dark hair drooping onto his forehead, and every so often, he'd reach up and push it out of the way. A gesture she had always found endearing and inexplicably sexy.

Damn Jake, anyway. What was he doing here? Now? Just when she least wanted to think about him.

"Jacob!" Pop's booming bass rattled the chandelier as he entered the foyer below, and Gentry tiptoed out to the bannister rail to peek over. "How in the hell have you been, stranger? And why haven't you been to see us before now? Just because our daughter divorced you, doesn't mean Frannie and I did."

From her lofty viewpoint, Gentry saw her father slug Jake on the upper arm in one of those male-bonding rituals she'd seen so often among her brother's friends and her father's comrades. Why couldn't Pop treat Sonny that way, she wondered, although she knew it would be an exercise in frustration for both men. Her father intimidated the hell out of practically everyone. He was a boisterous, blustery eccentric, who said what he thought when he thought it and made no apology for it afterward. He, like Sonny, was a self-made man who had seized opportunity at every turn, rising from the ranks of movie extras to the height of stardom as a hero of the silver screen. Known to most of the world as Charlie North, former actor, director and producer, Charles Bennett Northcross was still a disciplined mass of energy and enthusiasm. Few men could look him in the eye with complete candor. Few women could resist the vitality of his genuine admiration for their gender. No one, man or woman, could match his lust for living.

Whatever Jake replied to this boisterous greeting was lost in the Jolly-Green-Giant boom of Pop's laughter. Gentry seethed. Did he have to act quite so pleased to see his former son-in-law?

"Yes, Ben got bitten by the lovebug and we haven't seen him since. Supposed to be back for Gentry's wedding, though. Hey, it's great to see you, Jake. What are you doing here, anyway? Did you come for the wedding? Gonna be quite a dog-and-pony show, if you know what I mean."

Gentry kept quiet as the other women tiptoed out to join her.

"*That's* Jake," Hillary whispered, pointing...as if Gentry might not have noticed.

Gentry put her finger to her lips, warning them to be silent.

"He's still a fine specimen of manhood." Sydney's voice was low but not inaudible, and Gentry gave her an immediate frown.

"Will you be quiet?" she mouthed. Jake was talking again and she strained to eavesdrop.

"Cleo couldn't . . . wasn't feasible . . . Arthur didn't know . . . and here I am."

"Well, lucky for us, I say. The guest house is empty and you're welcome to it. As I said, there's all kind of nonsense going on in this house lately, but it'll be over Saturday and you can enjoy the rest of your vacation. Frannie's out this afternoon at some committee meeting or other, but she'll be delighted to see you. In fact, we'll be glad for the company, what with both of the kiddos marrying and taking leave of their senses . . . so to speak."

Jake's protest, if indeed it was a protest, sounded weak and ineffectual.

"Don't be silly," Charlie's voice boomed. "Gentry won't care. Will you, sweetheart?" He made a grand gesture, revealing her hanging over the balcony rail, shamelessly eavesdropping like a twelve-year-old. For a moment, her panicked eyes met Jake's startled ones, and then she set her jaw with determination. Her ex-husband meant nothing to her now. She could afford to be polite. Coolly polite.

"Hello, Jake," she said.

"Hello." His slow, I'm-in-no-hurry drawl pulled at her, luring her back to a time and place she chose not to recall. "Who's up there with you? Sydney?"

"Here." Syd shoved past Gentry to lean over the bannister rail. "It's great to see you again, buddy. Where've you been keeping yourself?"

"The Two-Penny Lodge," he said. "You know where it is. Why haven't you been to visit?"

"I'm afraid you'd make me catch my own food."

"Cook it, too. The lodge is still pretty rustic."

"Hi, Jake. It's Heather."

"And me." Hillary waved.

He stared up at them from the foot of the stairs as his engaging grin took possession of his lips ... and stopped at least one heart in its tracks, despite the silent protest of its owner. "The Four Horsemen, as I live and breathe," he said. "I thought you all would have disbanded long before now."

"We're in Gentry's wedding," Hillary explained. "We weren't invited along when you two eloped, so this time we're making sure the ceremony goes off without a hitch."

"No one could do it better." He scratched his chin and just stood there staring as Gentry scowled at him. "I was just telling Charlie that Ben invited me to spend my vacation at his house. That was pre-Sara, though, and when I arrived, I discovered there wasn't room for me among all the starched white shirts gathering at Ben's house for some kind of butler reunion. So I'm just dropping off the two things he asked me to bring by, then I'll be on my way."

"Oh, no you don't." Sydney leaned farther over the bannister rail for emphasis. "You can't walk in here, turn around and walk out again. We have to catch up on what you've been doing with yourself the past couple of years."

"He's staying." Pop used his there-will-be-no-argument voice. "I invited him to spend the rest of his vacation in the guest house. No one's using it. Sonny and his friends are staying across town at a hotel. His uncle rented a whole floor for the out-of-town relatives and a suite for Sonny and his groomsmen... gotta keep the engaged couple honest until the wedding. Makes no sense to me, but Sonny insisted on preserving Gentry's honor...or some such thing. He's a strange bird. Hard worker, though. Built his own business from the ground up. Portable johns. I call him the *Can King*. Let's have a drink, Jake, and you can tell me fish stories.''

"Well, I..."

"No excuses. I'll have someone get your things and take them out to the guest house for you."

"But I don't think Gentry..."

"Forget about Gentry. This is my house and she's got nothing to say about who stays and who doesn't." Pop dismissed all possible objections with a wave of his hand. "Besides, she won't know who's here and who isn't this week." Pop looked up and cupped his hands around his mouth, as if his big mouth needed amplification. "It won't bother you if Jake stays here, will it, sweetheart?"

Before she could weigh the phrasing of the sentence against her very real, very positive knowledge that it would bother her very much indeed, Pop had taken her agreement for granted. He clapped his arm around Jake's solid shoulders and bent his head to say something in private, then laughed heartily after he'd said it. Jake laughed, too. A warm, husky rumble of humor that strummed her heartstrings with memories. This had to be stopped, she thought. "Wait just a minute."

The men turned and looked up at the landing again. "What is it?" Pop asked with a frown.

"I want to talk to you. Stay there." Looping the sequined train over her arm, she moved down the stairs, pacing her steps to keep the scalloped hem from creeping any higher on her thighs. When she reached the bottom of the stairs, her knees were shaking...which was totally ridiculous. Her brief marriage to Jake had been annulled in the eyes of the law and the church. It had been wiped from her heart. She wasn't afraid to face him, damn it. She'd just pretend he was a friend of Ben's whom she'd never liked.

That idea carried her across the foyer and right up to the moment when Jake's eyes met hers. At this proximity, she had little protection against the tender humor that always seemed to be in his eyes, the little twinkle of laughter that made her think he never took anything seriously. Okay, so maybe she once had liked him a little. His gaze dropped, measuring her from sparkling train to bare shoulder, and there was a faint but noticeable quirk at the corner of his mouth...as if he were fighting back a chuckle. She went back to the idea that she'd never liked him at all.

"Hello, Liz," he said. "You look particularly *sparkling* today."

He was the only one who'd ever called her Liz and lived to tell about it. She must have been crazy to think it sounded sexy when he said it. Her temper rose in direct correlation to his lazy and all-too-seductive smile. "Don't call me Liz."

"Still as touchy as always, I see."

"Only when I'm annoyed."

"I've never seen you when you weren't...Liz."

A lie, of course. She knew it as well as he. And the very fact annoyed her further. "That could be because you're so annoying, Jake."

"Me?" His eyebrows climbed with innocence. "Nah. I'm the same easygoing guy I've always been. Your nerves must be on edge."

"She always gets this way before her weddings." Sydney tucked her hand in the crook of Jake's arm. "It's so good to see you again. You're not planning to run off with our bride this time, are you?"

"Only the bridesmaids." His tone was definite and Gentry's temper rose another degree. "Are you still available?"

"You can't afford her, Jake." Hillary moved closer, edging Gentry aside. "Take me. I'm much more reasonable."

"Heather?" Jake singled her out for a smile. "Don't tell me you're still waiting for Mr. Right."

She blushed and nodded. "Afraid so. And don't pretend you want to apply for the job, because we both know better."

He shrugged. "It's true. You're all too good for me. I could never choose among you."

"You did once," Hillary pointed out.

His bedroom blue eyes swung unerringly to Gentry. "We all make mistakes."

"True," Sydney agreed. "Take Gen's wedding gown, for example. Someone made a big mistake with that."

"What wedding gown?" Pop's voice boomed into the conversation, his forehead furrowed with the question.

"What you see is what you get," Hillary said matter-of-factly.

Pop's disbelieving gaze surveyed Gentry's attire from pillbox to sequined train. "What kind of costume is that? Some kind of a joke?"

Gentry seethed with misplaced irritation. "Sonny had this bridal gown designed and made for me as a wedding gift, and I wouldn't dream of offending him by not wearing it at our wedding."

"Well, it's a good thing I don't mind offending him, because you're not wearing that to any wedding in this house."

"It's my wedding and I'll wear any dress I please."

"It's my house, and nobody wears anything that hurts my eyes." Pop nodded, cutting short the argument. "Now, Jake has been nice enough to bring this present to you, and I think you ought to be a little more grateful."

"You didn't have to go to the trouble of getting me a wedding gift, Jake," she said, with a cool frown at Pop. "Your continued absence would have been more than enough present for Sonny and me."

He smiled. "The gift is from Ben. He asked me to deliver the dog and the box personally, since he couldn't be here to do it himself. It seemed like a small-enough favor to do for a friend."

"Ha!" Gentry lifted her chin. "You and I aren't friends."

"Ben and I are."

"Ben couldn't have asked you to deliver anything, because he's on his honeymoon."

Jake's laughter was a low rumble in his throat. "I realize that you and I didn't know there was anyone else in the world on our honeymoon. But Ben remembered how to use the telephone."

"They do have telephones in Hawaii." Hillary seemed pleased to be able to corroborate the information.

"I've heard they even have a phone in some of the better hotels." Sydney added her support.

"Ben sent you a present?" Heather sounded impressed. "Even though he's on his honeymoon. I think that's sweet."

"I told him to do it." Pop nudged the cardboard box toward Gentry. "Open it. See what's inside."

"Good idea," Sydney urged.

"Curiosity killed the cat." Hillary eyed the package with interest. "Syd's dying to see what's inside."

"Right, Hil. Like you don't want to tear into it yourself."

Gentry bent to the box, puzzled by the knowledge that Ben had gone to the trouble to buy a gift before he left on his honeymoon. He had to know it wasn't necessary. She had a feeling he'd left it for Jake to deliver for reasons other than his hurry to be alone with his wife. Ben had minced no words telling her she was an idiot for leaving Jake in the first place, and then reiterating that she was an idiot to marry Sonny. It would be just like her brother to have blackmailed Jake into delivering this gift . . . for her own good.

"I'll take it upstairs," she said, wanting to escape the audience. Or at least one member of it. "And open it later . . . when Sonny's here."

"If you had to wait for him, we'd be knee-deep in unopened presents. Now, open the box, Gentry," Pop commanded. "We all want to see what's in there."

"You don't want to cart that big box up the stairs." Sydney leaned down and pulled off the bow. "Open it, Gentry. Come on."

"Yes," the others chimed in. "Open it. Let's see what he sent."

"Yes," Pop agreed with a grin. "Let's see."

She had a bad feeling about this. But it was a little too late to back down now. She was outnumbered and terribly aware that Jake was watching her with a question in his eyes. She would meet his inquiry with indifference, she decided. His gaze with cool rebuff.

She tore the wrapping paper and opened the large cardboard box. As she lifted the tissue paper, she saw a folded sheet of stationery, a square of blue against a sea of ivory satin and lace.

"Oh..." Heather edged closed to peer into the box. "Whatever it is, it's beautiful."

Gentry closed her eyes, knowing she had just opened Pandora's box. "It's a dress," she said. "A million-dollar wedding dress."

Chapter Two

Gentry slapped the cardboard flaps over the top of the box and held them in place. "I'll just take this up to my room and look at it later."

"The hell you will." Sydney leaned down and grasped the corner of one flap. "If there's a million-dollar dress in there, I'm going to see it."

"Me, too." Hillary stepped forward to lend support.

Gentry leaned across the box, thwarting their attempt to reopen the flaps. "You can see it some other time. Besides, it isn't even from Ben. It's from Pop." She shot a meaningful glare at her father. "He was just too chickenhearted to give it to me himself, weren't you, Pop?"

"Absolutely," Pop drawled in cursory agreement. "And Ben was too lily-livered to deliver it in person, so he got Jake to do it for him. Now, are you going to get that dress out of the box, or shall I do it for you?"

Nothing like the support of a loving parent, Gentry thought in disgust. "Do you really want all these people to know you were foolish enough to spend a million dollars on a ridiculous old wedding dress?"

"Won't bother me. Just think how foolish I'd look if I'd spent a million dollars on that outfit you're wearing now."

"There's nothing wrong with this gown," she said tightly. "Sonny had it designed especially for me."

"Now, that doesn't surprise me." Pop shook his head, and from the corner of her eye, she saw Jake grin. "Looks just like something he'd display in one of his art galleries. Now, open that box and let's see what a real wedding dress looks like."

She raised her chin and held on to the box. "I won't."

"Oh, come on, Gentry." Hillary pulled on her corner of cardboard. "It's just a dress."

"That's right." Sydney tugged harder on her end. "Give it up. You're outnumbered."

"You don't want to see this dress," Gentry warned the bridesmaids. "Trust me. It's a joke."

"Then let us in on it." Hillary got a grip on an inside flap. "Don't be stingy."

Pop frowned down at her. "Show them the magic dress, Gentry."

"Magic?" Heather's voice rose with interest. "Did you say *magic?*"

"Okay. Move aside or I won't be held responsible for the damage." Sydney ripped at the box with Hillary's able assistance.

Gentry stopped trying to prevent the inevitable and moved back, meeting Jake's amused gaze with sincere irritation. "My brother put you up to this, didn't he?"

He cocked one eyebrow in denial. "Ben asked me to deliver this box to you and that's what I've done."

"Oh, of course. How could I have forgotten? You always manage to be an innocent bystander, don't you."

"Oh, look, there's a note from Ben." Hillary drew the single sheet of blue stationery from the box and held it out of reach. "Here, I'll read it.

Gentry,
Can you believe it? For once, Pop wasn't exaggerating. There is magic in the world. Put on this wedding gown and find out for yourself.

Love,
Ben."

Sydney lifted a handful of ivory satin. "Imagine a dress like this showing up just when you need it."

"I don't need it. I have a wedding dress." Gentry indicated the dress she had on, but no one paid the slightest bit of attention. They were all mesmerized by the satin and lace unfolding from inside the cardboard box. It was unfair that she couldn't turn back the hands of time for just a few seconds. All she wanted was to seal this box back up and pretend she'd never set eyes on it. Damn Ben. And Pop. And Jake, too... for good measure.

But Pop was grinning like Sylvester the Cat, completely unperturbed by her irritation. And her friends already had their hands on the gown, shaking it free of the protective tissue, oohing and aahing over the richness of the fabric. Jake's eyes never strayed from her face, watching and gauging her reaction to the situation. He probably found the whole thing vastly amusing.

Under his scrutiny, a subtle and familiar discomfort stirred in the pit of her stomach and set her shifting from one foot to the other. The moment she recognized the nervous movement, she stopped, only to find that she had clenched her hands in turn. Jake had no business being here. He had to know that showing up now, just before her wedding, exactly the way he had two years ago, would cause an upset. Of course, he would enjoy nothing more than upsetting her wedding a second time. He undoubtedly had had just this effect in mind when he agreed to come here for Ben. It was entirely possible he had planned the whole thing. Mr. Innocent. Ha!

"I can't believe you don't want to wear this, Gentry." Sydney's droll expression spelled out just how much she was enjoying the situation. "How often do you get a chance to wear an expensive gown like this?"

"Maybe this is the wedding dress Sara wore when she and Ben were married." Heather, the fanciful, touched the ivory lace on the sleeves with reverence. "Look at the tiny buttons on the sleeves and all down the back. I've never seen such delicate lace. It must have been made by fairies."

"It was made by hand." Hillary offered a seam as evidence. "Look at the stitches. They're tiny and uneven, but perfect."

Gentry didn't want to look. She didn't even want to be this close to the stupid dress. She straightened, gave the hem of her dress a yank, discreetly hitched up the neckline and arched a suspicious eyebrow at her father. "I'm not wearing it, Pop," she stated firmly. "You can forget that idea right now."

"It's an expensive dress, Gentry," he replied. "And a special one. You should at least try it on."

Her jaw set with determination. "Not a chance. There is no such thing as magic, and this is not, I repeat, *not,* a magic wedding dress."

"Then, try it on." Pop issued the challenge like the sly old dog that he was. "If it isn't magic, what have you got to lose?"

"My dignity."

"Oh, like you're a bundle of dignity in *that.*" Hillary pointed at the sequined train of Gentry's dress. "Wouldn't you at least like to see what you'd look like in a million-dollar dress?"

"No."

"Liar, liar, pants on fire." Sydney shook the satin skirt to loosen the wrinkles. "You're as curious as the rest of us and don't bother to deny it."

"If you're so curious, why don't you try it on."

"Maybe I will."

"You can't, Syd." Heather frowned in protest. "It's Gentry's wedding gown."

"No, it isn't. I'm wearing my wedding gown." Gentry's denial was ignored by all.

"I only want to try it on," Sydney said. "You can, too, if you want."

Heather's objection faded away. "You think it would fit me?"

"Since it's a magic dress, it might even fit me." With a whimsical smile, Jake stepped forward and cupped one of the dress's sleeves in his hand. Contrasted against his palm, the ivory lace looked delicate, fragile and somehow sensuous.

Gentry couldn't seem to stop staring at it, as an odd restlessness seeped through her.

"Okay, Charlie, what makes this wedding gown so special?" Jake directed his inquiry to Pop. "And, more to the point, why were you willing to spend a million bucks to get it?''

"I thought you'd never ask.'' Pop's chest puffed up with importance, and his voice shifted into the deep, silky tones of a born storyteller, one of his favorite roles.

"Please don't tell that ridiculous story again.'' Gentry rubbed her forehead, wearied by the nonsense her father was about to pass off as truth. "It's embarrassing.''

"What is?'' Pop asked. "The fact that your father believes in magic? Or the fact that he likes to entertain his audiences with a little drama?''

"It's embarrassing that you admit to being in love with a woman other than my mother.''

"Oh, for the love of Pete...'' he said roughly. "That was twenty-eight years ago. Before you were born. Get over it. Your mother did.''

An assertion Gentry found difficult to believe, considering she knew that he had never once admitted he was in the wrong. "I'm going upstairs,'' she said. But if she'd hoped anyone would go with her, she was disappointed. They all stood like good little children waiting for their bedtime story. Her footsteps marked her retreat, which slowed to a stop as Pop began his story.

"I met Libby Kirk on the set of *Easy Street*. She was already a star with huge box-office draw, and like every other one of her leading men, I fell passionately in love with her. I was obsessed with her beauty, driven mad by her indifference and determined to know everything about her. She found me mildly amusing, I believe. At least, she tolerated my adoration and occasionally rewarded me with stories of her past. I was a worshipful listener, and when she told me about the wedding dress, I drank in every word as if I could consume this part of her history and make it a part of my own.

Her great-grandmother, Elizabeth, had been an actress, also. She was quite famous in Europe and caught the roving eye of a high-ranking and very-married member of the British royalty. He wanted her as his mistress and meant to have her no matter what he had to do to get her. She was engaged to marry a brilliant young actor named Gentry Donovan, who subsequently met with an inexplicable, highly suspicious fatal accident."

With unerring timing, Charlie North paused for the suspense to build in his audience. "Elizabeth had been given a special gift, a wedding gown by Worth, who was a dressmaker of some renown. She had just finishing putting on the gown in preparation for the wedding when she learned of her lover's death. And at that very moment, his image appeared next to hers in the mirror and she vowed she would never love another."

"But she must have." Hillary stated the obvious. "Otherwise, how could she have had a great-granddaughter?"

"I told you it was nonsense," Gentry said, aware that Jake had stepped closer to her during the story-telling session. The heat from his body was warmth at her back, the scent that clung to him was of fresh air and summer storms, and it evoked a memory of standing naked in the rain with him. She had never been so uninhibited before...or since. "There's no such thing as magic."

"Let me tell the story, please." Pop resumed his narrative, as superb an actor as he had always been. "When His Lordship arrived, opportunely, to console her in her loss, he found nothing except the wedding gown—the very one you're holding there—and the hazy image of Gentry and Elizabeth in the mirror."

"Did they vanish?" Heather asked in wide-eyed wonder. "Were they really in the mirror together?"

"How could she have had a great-granddaughter if she vanished?" Hillary was far from convinced. "And people can't appear in a mirror if they've vanished . . . or died."

"Ah, but that's the magic, isn't it?" Pop smiled with his enjoyment of the spotlight. "She did vanish, that very night, leaving the country and everything she owned. On a ship bound for America, she met a gentleman of business, a banker, and married him, even though she never loved him. They had several children, one of them Libby's grandmother, Gentry Elizabeth."

She could feel Jake's sympathetic gaze on her as she waited for the next bit of mortifying confession.

"You named Gentry after some other woman's grandmother?" Sydney asked, clearly surprised that she had never known this interesting fact.

Pop shrugged off any hint of impropriety. "Frannie and I liked the story and wanted to give our daughter a name with a romantic history."

Jake's blue eyes offered her another hint of compassion. He knew how she hated the idea that her father had named her after the grandmother of Libby Kirk, an actress with whom he'd had a well-publicized affair. Jake knew the resentment that seethed inside her every time Pop insisted he'd done no such thing... that her namesake was some long-forgotten woman with a romantic past.

"So how did you end up with this dress?" Heather asked. "And how do you know it's magic?"

Pop warmed to his subject. "Libby told me that her great-grandfather recovered the dress and presented it to his daughter, Gentry Elizabeth, on the occasion of her marriage. When she put on the dress right before the wedding, she discovered the magic...the image of her true love appeared with her in the mirror. It frightened her, though, and she refused to wear the dress, afraid that if she did, something would happen to her fiancé. Her father stored the gown in a bank vault for safekeeping, and it didn't see the light of day until a few months ago when the old bank building was sold and a remodeling project begun. The discovery made a small special-interest article in the newspaper, and the gown was purchased by a bridal shop owner in Kansas City. Someone connected the gown to the Kirkpatrick family and, subsequently, to Libby, whose real name is Gentry Elizabeth Kirkpatrick. When I heard about it, I contacted the new owner and bought the dress for my own Gentry Elizabeth."

"So what does it do?" Hillary asked. "If Gentry puts it on is she going to see Sonny in the mirror?"

"If Sonny is her true love, she will. The wedding dress can only reflect the image of two people who truly belong together. That's the magic."

"And if you believe that, I'll sell you my interest in a prosperous diamond mine in Iowa." Gentry frowned on her friends and family. "Honestly, Pop, I can't believe you told that with a straight face."

"But Ben said the dress was magic," Heather pointed out. "In his note."

"He's in on the joke, too. Don't you see? This is all a hoax. Just another example of the Northcross humor at work." Gentry looked from one bridesmaid to another...and watched as they silently took sides against her. "All right. Believe Pop's nonsense if you want. I'm going upstairs."

"Take the dress with you." Sydney tried to hand her the gown without success. "I know you really want to try it on."

"I want to try it on." Hillary looked at Pop. "Will it work for any bride or only ones named after the first Gentry Elizabeth?"

"Ben assured me this is an equal opportunity bridal gown. It's how he and Sara came to fall in love."

"Really?" Heather's brown eyes went wide and soft with the possibility. "Did Sara try on the dress?"

"That's what I understand."

"Did she see Ben in the mirror?"

Pop shrugged complacently. "They're married, aren't they?"

"Wow."

"That's amazing." Hillary turned to Jake. "Did Ben tell you the dress had *magic* powers?"

"He didn't even tell me what was in the box."

A likely story. Exasperated beyond belief, Gentry slipped past the bridesmaids and started up the stairs to her room. Five stairs up, the front door opened and Cleo bounded inside, followed closely by Sonny Harris, returning from his afternoon golf game.

In white shorts, white polo shirt, white sport socks and shoes, and with a handsome smile that revealed even, white teeth beneath his clipped-to-quarter-inch-perfection Don Juan mustache, Sonny Harris looked like an ad for a sporting goods store. In a glance, he took in the gathering in the foyer and moved forward to join them.

Realizing that he hadn't noticed her poised halfway up the stairs, Gentry stooped behind the bannister rail. If he saw her in her wedding gown, Sonny would probably call off the wedding. He believed in all the superstitions surrounding matrimony... something old, new, borrowed and blue, a penny in each shoe, no communication between the bride and groom before the ceremony, and absolutely no glimpse of the bride in her wedding gown until she started down the aisle. Considering what had happened the last time they'd planned a wedding, she supposed it wasn't so extraordinary that this time he wasn't taking any chances. So she crouched uncomfortably on the stairs while her dress crept up her thighs.

"I bet you're all wondering why I called this meeting." Sonny's teasing remark went unnoticed by the group in the foyer. Even his presence only warranted a vague nod from Pop. Hillary and Sydney ignored him completely in favor of a closer examination of the infamous magic gown. Heather smiled politely, but Jake—damn his mischievous hide—greeted Sonny with a hearty "Hello, Harris. How have you been?"

Sonny's eyes narrowed, his jaw went slack, and his good humor faded into incredulity. "Daniels?" His voice cracked on the word like an adolescent boy's. "What are you doing here?"

"Social call," Jake replied amiably. "I was in the neighborhood and—"

"Well, you're on your way out of this neighborhood right now. I'll show you the door."

"Excuse me, Sonny, but the last time I checked this was my house, and if I want Jake to leave, I'll show him the door." Pop sounded all the more intimidating simply because he didn't raise his voice. "As it happens, he's agreed to stay with us until after the wedding."

Sonny looked properly appalled. "But he...he's..."

"Welcome to stay as long as he likes." Pop supplied the words Sonny wasn't searching for. "Don't worry, you won't even know he's around."

Sonny clenched his hands at his sides. "Wait until Gentry finds out he's here."

"Oh, she knows," Hillary said pleasantly.

"Yes," Sydney backed her up. "In fact, she was here just a minute ago."

"I'm sure she left rather than stay in the same room with her ex-husband."

"But he isn't her ex-husband," Heather explained. "They were never married."

"What?" Pop's voice went up like a rocket. "Who says they weren't married?"

"G-Gentry." Heather's answer wobbled a little in the wake of Pop's questioning. "She told us that Jake can't be called her ex-husband because the marriage was annulled. It never even existed."

"Oh." The thought seemed to please Sonny. "That's true, I suppose. An annulment wipes out any record, and if there's no record . . ."

"There's no ex-husband or wife. Now, why didn't I think of that?" Jake's amused gaze found Gentry, huddled by the bannister. "And since we were never married, I can be called a friend of the family and that clears the way for me to accept your hospitality.

Thanks, Charlie. I'd love to stay, if you're sure it's no trouble.''

"Of course it isn't. And Frannie will be so pleased to— Get your schnoz away from that, Cleo!'' Pop reached down and pulled the Labrador's muzzle out of the folds of ivory satin and pushed her away. "Go on. Get out of here.'' He looked at Jake. "You don't mind sharing the guest quarters with Cleo, do you? Frannie won't let her sleep in the house.''

"I'll be glad for the company,'' Jake replied, his laughing eyes seeking Gentry's once again. "I've never liked sleeping alone.''

Still crouched on the stairs, Gentry leaned her head against her hands, fighting the urge to wiggle uncomfortably as she tried to remain out of sight and still keep her butt covered...no small feat considering the creeping nature of the sequined dress. She must have made some revealing movement, however, because Cleo caught sight of her and bounded up the stairs, intent upon licking her ear. Gentry batted at the Labrador's delighted greeting, which only seemed to encourage more adoration. She cupped one hand over her ear for protection and pushed Cleo away with her other hand.

A mistake, she realized, as she teetered precariously, lost her balance and tumbled from stair to stair while the sequined train wrapped her in a cocoon of netting. Cleo, excited by the turn of events, began barking like a lunatic and played leapfrog over Gentry as she bounced from one step to the next. Arms pinned at her sides by the train, she landed on the foyer floor, rolled a quarter turn, then rolled back.

Sonny, Pop, Hillary, Heather and Sydney scattered as if they thought she might keep rolling and knock them over like so many bowling pins. Cleo, apparently believing she'd won the game, straddled Gentry's prone and sequined body to defend her prize against all comers, growling and barking at the onlookers who stood back uncertainly.

"I see you still like to make a dramatic entrance." It was Jake's voice she heard and his hand she saw, extending down, offering her quick, no-fault assistance. "Give me your hand and I'll help you up."

It was just like him to offer help when she was in no position to accept it. "I wouldn't give you my hand if you were the only thing standing between me and a hundred-foot drop."

"Strong words, considering I'm the only thing standing between Harris and a rather charming view of your breast."

"You're still a pervert, I see."

He shrugged as his gaze traveled her neckline with a familiar leer. Her head came up off the floor in a split second, but her arms were trapped at her sides and she could only lift herself far enough to see that the single shoulder strap of the dress had slid down her shoulder, exposing more of her than could be considered "charming."

"Don't move," she told him as she wiggled her shoulders in an effort to adjust the dress and get her hands free.

Pushing Cleo out of the way, Jake bent beside Gentry, still blocking the view. "If you keep that up, you'll wiggle right out of your clothes. Be still and let me help you." He scooped her up, set her on her feet and, with an artful brush of his hand, adjusted the drape of her neckline. His touch was a match to the flame of a thousand memories that swept through her with random disregard for where she was and who was present. It was just like Jake to remind her of the worst mistake of her life. Just like him to show up now, when he had no business showing up at all. She stepped away from him. Sonny approached, somewhat belatedly, and Jake looped the sequined train around and around her as if she were a maypole.

"You can let go of her now, Daniels," Sonny said, his arm slipping protectively around her waist. "I'll take care of her from here on in."

Jake held up his hands, letting the ethereal cloud of netting billow downward. "You're going to need a couple of full-time assistants," he said. "Gentry needs a lot of taking care of."

"Not that you would know anything about that." Sonny narrowed his eyes, facing down his rival. "Gentry is the most independent, perfect woman I know."

"Let's not get carried away." Sydney, always eager to stir up trouble, patted his arm. "I like Gen a lot, but I don't think she's worth fighting over."

Sonny shook off her hand. "What's the meaning of this, Gentry? What is *he* doing here?"

"Delivering a dress," Hillary said.

"Ben asked him to bring it over. And the dog, too." Heather's brown eyes went from Pop to Jake to Gentry to Sonny. "It's all completely innocent."

"Innocent?" Sonny repeated. "Innocent? Ha! He's about as innocent as that…that…" His frown turned to Gentry as he seemed to notice her dress for the first time. "What in the hell are you wearing?"

"I'm wearing the dress you had made for me," she said to Sonny. "The dress you asked your friend to design. The dress you want me to wear for our wedding.''

Words seemed to fail Sonny as he assessed the dress's faults. ''You can't wear that to the wedding. Especially not now that I've seen it. Besides, it isn't at all appropriate.''

''I tried to tell her that, myself,'' Hillary said.

''You and Hillary have a keen eye for fashion.'' Sydney clamped both hands around Sonny's arm. ''I've always said so. Pop? I think our bridegroom could use one of your famous Charlie North Specials. Can you make us all a drink?''

''Quicker than you can say 'down the hatch,''' Pop answered with pride. ''Head for the cabana and I'll mix up a pitcher.''

''Sounds great.'' Hillary looped her hands through Sonny's other arm and dazzled him with her best attention-grabbing smile. ''How was your golf game? You and I will have to play a round sometime. Maybe one day this week. I'm always looking for a partner.''

''I don't drink alcohol,'' Sonny protested as the two women drew him toward the terrace and a shot of Pop's own concoction—a mixed drink that changed colors, but not content.

Pop touched Heather's back, steering her toward the library, too. ''Luckily for you, Sonny, this is one drink you won't remember drinking, anyway.''

Like a cloud of dust, the bridesmaids swept through the library doors, leaving behind a dog, a dress and the only two people in the house who had no business being alone together.

Gentry looked at Jake, at the well-remembered smile in his eyes and on his lips, and she wanted, suddenly, to run into his arms as if the past two painful years had never happened, as if those years, like the marriage, could just be annulled, wiped out, forgotten and forgiven. But of course she couldn't do that, didn't know why the thought even occurred to her. So she stood there for a moment or two, while an endless line of questions trooped through her mind like soldiers marching to battle, knowing the question that overshadowed every other was the one she had too much pride to ask.

With a toss of her head, she scooped up the sequined train, turned on her heel and stalked up the stairs.

Chapter Three

Jake watched her retreat with an admiring eye and a knot of tension in his stomach. He'd known he would never completely recover from Gentry, but until he'd seen her draped over the upstairs bannister like a kid at Christmas, he hadn't thought the sight of her could still make him weak in the knees.

This trip had been a mistake, despite Ben's assurance that it was time to stop avoiding the entire Northcross clan because he didn't want to associate with one particular family member.

Who did he think he was fooling, anyway? He was here because he wanted to see Gentry. Anyone with half an ounce of discernment would know that. Anyone except Gentry, that is. He'd missed her. Missed her chin-in-the-air tenacity, her laughter, her energy, her passion for living, her smile . . . her temper.

He was an idiot to think she might have changed, that she might have missed him, too. She'd left him. Walked out. Run back to Sonny Harris and the ivory pedestal he kept her on. Oh, yes, Jake thought, he was an idiot, all right.

But since he was here . . .

Picking up the box containing the first Gentry Elizabeth's wedding dress, he headed up the stairs. His Gentry's bedroom was the second door on the left. He paused outside it, remembering the last time he'd stood here, so crazy in love he could hardly breathe. Taking a deep breath now, just as he had then, he shifted the box in his arms and knocked on the door.

"Sydney? Is that you?"

He meant to say no, to declare his presence with supreme indifference, but he accidentally bumped the door with the cardboard box and it swung open. Suddenly, his heart was in his throat and he couldn't have said a word if the fate of the world depended on it.

Gentry stood in the center of the room . . . he recognized her despite the fact that she had pulled the dress over her head and was trapped—half in, half out. Her arms were raised and extended through the neck opening while she tried, without success, to get a grip on the clingy fabric. Strands of red-gold hair looped over the top to curl like question marks on the iridescent sequins.

His gaze dropped to the hemline, which scooped at her waist in front and scalloped to just below her hips in back. Her legs stretched from here to tomorrow, and he admired their shapely length with a voyeur's pleasure. She would never forgive him for this, he thought. On the other hand, if he revealed his identity now, he'd never forgive himself.

"Don't just stand there, Syd. I need a little assistance here." Gentry struggled, but the stretchy fabric clung to her head and shoulders like spider's silk.

Shifting the box again, Jake gave the door a push with the sole of his shoe . . . on the not-so-outside chance that this encounter would end with an explosion of one sort or another. It swung to within a fraction of closing as he set the cardboard container on the bed.

"I can't get this silly thing off," Gentry complained from inside the dress. "Sonny's protégé didn't put in a zipper or a button or any other kind of closure. He probably thought it would detract from the flow of the design or something. Why don't you grab the bottom and I'll see if I can wiggle free."

A guy didn't get an offer like that every day. Jake moved closer, willing to lend her a helping hand.

"This is all Jake's fault, you know."

Not yet it wasn't.

"I can't understand why he would show up unannounced just before the wedding. It's obvious he hasn't outgrown that fiendish sense of humor, but I thought a couple of years would have made some small increase in his maturity level."

He admired her legs again as he looked for a handhold on the dress. If he so much as brushed a knuckle against her skin, she would realize he wasn't Sydney, but if he could pinch just enough fabric between his finger and thumb...

"Ouch!" Gentry jerked. "Take it easy. I'm underneath here, you know."

He was well aware of it as he surveyed the tight fit and looked for a propitious place to pinch.

"Ow!" She took a step away from his helpful fingers. "There has to be a better way to do this."

That would depend upon which side of the dress one was on, of course.

"Sydney?" The voice from inside the sheath sounded downright suspicious and he tensed, sure he was about to be discovered. "Do you honestly believe

Jake just *happened* to plan his vacation for this week?'' Gentry asked. ''And don't you think it's odd that he claims he didn't even get a phone call from Ben letting him know he should postpone his trip?''

''I think it was damned inconsiderate of Ben to forget about me just because he was off on his honeymoon.'' Grasping either side of the scalloped hem, Jake jerked the dress upward, pulling it inside out and off in a matter of seconds. Static electricity crackled and Gentry's hair stood out around her face like a weird science experiment. The sparks in her eyes had nothing to do with experiments, however. She was startled, shocked and furious... in that order and in increasing degrees.

Jake told himself not to smile—it would be the worst thing he could do at this point. No doubt about it. ''Gentry!'' He tried to sound as shocked as she looked. ''I didn't know it was *you* inside this dress.''

A blue norther couldn't have chilled the air more efficiently.

''What are you doing in my room?'' she demanded.

''Helping you with your dress.''

The startled look returned as she became conscious of her state of undress, then narrowed temperamentally in the split second before she turned her back to him. She grabbed a nightshirt from the foot of the bed and pulled it on over her lingerie. When she faced him again, it was only natural that his attention would be drawn to the message printed across the front of her shirt. It read Real Art Won't Match Your Sofa, and he smiled... despite his better judgment.

''What are you smiling at?'' Her voice pinned him like a tail on a paper donkey.

"Just admiring your nightshirt," he said pleasantly. "Let me guess . . . Sonny had that designed for you to wear on your wedding night."

Emerald anger flashed in her eyes. "What are you doing here, Jake? And don't bother repeating that nonsensical story about being in the neighborhood."

"I'm delivering a wedding gift, Liz." He motioned toward the bed. "At your brother's request."

"I don't believe you."

I don't believe you. Four simple words that carried their own history and hurt. And by employing them, Gentry had drawn the lines of a battle already fought and lost. His smile vanished as if it had never been. "Unlike some people, I take my promises seriously."

The corners of her lips tightened. "That is a matter of opinion," she said tightly. "I want you to leave."

"Pop wants me to stay."

"He loves an audience, you know that. I'll invite one of Sonny's friends to stay in the guest house and Pop will never know the difference. You're not welcome here, Jake."

"Get over it, Gentry. I'm going to stay a few days. I'm committed."

"Committed?" She stressed the one-word question. "That would be a first."

"Look, Liz, there's no reason we can't be civil to each other."

"We were married, Jake. Civility is a bit much to ask. I prefer that you take your *commitment* and leave."

"Ah, I see. You're afraid I'll upset your wedding a second time."

"As if you could." Her tenacious chin was aimed at him. "I'm immune to your backwoods charm. I've been inoculated. Nothing you do or say has the power to distress me. You've delivered the box, now go back where you came from."

"I will," he answered. "The moment my vacation is over."

"You can't possibly want to be here," she said, annoyed and openly perplexed by his desire to be present at her wedding.

"Maybe I want to stick around and see Ben. And meet his wife. Maybe, on the other hand, I just want to stick around and find out if you'll actually marry Harris."

"And why wouldn't I?"

Jake shrugged. "You didn't last time."

"The biggest mistake of my life."

"Not by a long shot."

"I suppose you think my biggest mistake was leaving you."

"No, I think your biggest mistake was running back to Sonny Harris. But then, that's just my opinion."

With a toss of her head, she dismissed his opinion, and he thought about kissing her until she admitted he was right. Which would only make him more of an idiot than he already was...although he would certainly derive some pleasure from the act.

"I realize this may come as a revelation to you, Jake, but I will marry Sonny Saturday afternoon and we will live happily ever after...regardless of your opinions."

Now that was a call to arms if he'd ever heard one. He moved to the bed, scooted the box to one side and sat beside it. "You won't live happily ever after, Gentry. Not without..." *Me.* The word hung in the air like the punch line of a familiar joke. Opening the box flaps, he pulled out layer upon layer of satin and lace. "A little magic."

GENTRY STARED AT HIM, grappling with a childish impulse to stamp her foot. She'd live happily ever after if it killed her. "Give me that." Moving quickly to the bed, she reached for the ivory wedding gown, intending to stuff it back into the box as quickly as he'd pulled it out.

Jake drew back, raising his eyebrows and giving her that Clark Gable look that used to raise her blood pressure and now just . . . raised her blood pressure.

"You want this?" he asked. "Why? You said you don't believe in magic."

"It isn't magic." She grabbed for it again and gained a handful of lace. "Now, let me have it."

"Too bad you didn't have it two years ago. It would have saved us both a good deal of trouble."

"It will save you a good deal more trouble if you'll—" she tugged on the lace "—let go of—" gathering more fabric into her grasp, she tugged harder "—the dress." He unexpectedly released his hold on it and she wobbled backward, nearly losing her balance. She regained her footing and flashed him a withering glance as she shook the heavy satin and smoothed the lace bodice. "You've delivered the dress, Jake. Now you can leave with a clear conscience."

"I see." He slipped off the bed with a lean, lazy movement that reminded her of the last time the two of them had been together in this bedroom. "You want to be alone so you can try on the wedding gown."

"I don't want to be alone, Jake. I just don't want to be in the same room with you."

He clicked his tongue in disappointment. "And I was so hoping we could be friends."

Folding the gown into thirds, she started to stuff it back into the box. "Friends are people you like."

"What was that?"

She paused to frown at him. "Let me think...could it have been a comment on your character?"

He stooped and looked questioningly at the floor. "I heard something fall."

"Maybe you heard my patience snap."

"You don't have any patience, Gentry. Something dropped on the floor."

Honestly. What did he think he'd accomplish with this delaying tactic? "This carpet is very thick. You couldn't have heard—" She heard a soft *plop,* and then another. *Plop, plop.* Like the first random raindrops of a coming shower. *Plop, plop, plop.* Still holding the antique wedding gown in her hands, she bent over to study the ivory-colored carpet. "I don't see anything," she said, half to herself.

He dropped to his knees and scraped his palms across the carpet. "You should be more careful with that dress, Liz. After all, it's a million-dollar... button." He held up a satin-covered object for her inspection. "You, my sweet, are losing your buttons."

She looked at the tiny bauble anchored between his thumb and forefinger. It was pale against the tanned, roughened texture of his skin, delicate as a pearl in the palm of a fisherman. Almost without conscious desire, she stretched out her hand to touch it...and then, coming to her senses, she snatched her hand away from a close encounter with his. "Good," she said.

"All the more reason to pack this garment away for posterity."

"You're just afraid to put it on, that's all."

"It's a dress, Jake. I'm afraid of snakes and big, hairy spiders, but clothes don't hold any terror for me."

He got to his feet. "Obviously. Otherwise, you wouldn't have worn that sequined creation in mixed company."

She shoved the satin skirt into the box with unnecessary force. "I'm going to wear it in public on Saturday...no matter what anyone says."

The door swung inward and Cleo trotted in. "Come in, come in." Jake reached down to scratch the dog's ear. "We could use an outside opinion. I say Liz is afraid to put on the magic wedding dress. She says she isn't. What do you think?"

The dog's tail wagged amiably.

"See?" Jake indicated Cleo's accord. "I had a feeling she'd agree with me."

Gentry tried to look properly impressed. "Amazing. How does she do it? Can she smell a mortal fear of satin in the room? Or does she detect the subtle scent of lace phobia? Then again, could it be she thinks you have a liver snap in your pocket?"

"Make fun all you want, but if this dog could talk, she'd tell you to stuff the new dress and wear the old one."

"Which is why I'm the bride and she's not. Take your psychic canine and go away, would you? You've delivered the dress...as promised. So now you can enjoy your vacation with a clear conscience. Just stay out of my way."

"I wouldn't dream of annoying you, Liz."

"Stop calling me that."

"Only if you'll try on the million-dollar dress."

Her gaze meshed with his in silent recognition of his challenge . . . and of her refusal to be baited. "What a shame," she said with facetious disappointment, "the buttons fell off."

"It won't take twenty minutes to sew them back on."

"That would depend on who's doing the sewing."

"Does that mean you still haven't learned how to thread a needle?"

"If I had, I certainly wouldn't admit it to you." She walked to the chest, opened a drawer and rummaged through the contents. Her groping hand closed around a small cloth jewelry bag. She dumped the silver earrings it held into the drawer before tossing the bag to Jake. He caught it . . . which really annoyed her. "You can put the buttons in that, if you want," she offered sweetly. "Then, if the mood strikes you, you can sew them on. I honestly don't believe anyone else cares whether the dress has buttons or not."

Jake tossed the bag in the air and caught it with an easy swipe. "Let's see, now. Charlie spent a million bucks on the wedding dress. As a rough guess, I'd say there's seventy-five to a hundred buttons on the dress, which makes each of them worth somewhere in the neighborhood of . . . oh, let's just guess and say a thousand dollars apiece." He tossed the bag and smiled as he caught it . . . again. "Yes, I think he will definitely care if some buttons are missing."

A good point, Gentry conceded, although she contrived to look skeptical. "You're his special guest, Jake. I know he'll consider your services as a seamster invaluable." She bent down, picked up a button near the tip of her shoe and lobbed it toward his head.

He swept it out of the air like a frog nabbing a fly. "One thousand," he said as he dropped it into the jewelry pouch with a flourish. There was a faint *ping* as it struck something metallic inside the bag.

Gentry stiffened at the sound, realizing just what she'd so casually handed over to him. Her wedding ring. A plain gold band she'd tucked away in a side pocket of the jewelry pouch for safekeeping. Of the dozen or so bags, pouches and boxes that contained her sentimental pieces of jewelry, how had she managed to grab the only one containing something she didn't want Jake to know she had?

Leaning over, he picked up a second button and dropped it into the pouch. "Two thousand."

She watched, helplessly listening for the pinging sound, which would expose her sentiment to Jake, and hoping he was too busy needling her to notice.

He winked at her as he picked up another button, then another. "Three thousand," he said, dropping it in. "Four. Five. Six thousand. Pricey buttons you have here, Liz."

"You always did overestimate the value of things, Jake."

He dropped in the last loose button, pulled and knotted the drawstring, then pitched the bag at the open cardboard box. Gentry breathed a sigh of relief. As soon as he left, she'd retrieve the ring and stash it somewhere else. Her relief vanished, though, as the pouch hit one of the cardboard flaps, bounced off and landed on the floor. Cleo's ears perked up and she gave the jewelry bag an inquisitive sniff.

"Leave that alone," Gentry warned the Lab.

The dog didn't even look up, but before Gentry could reach down and pick up the pouch, Cleo had it in her mouth.

"Drop it!" Jake ordered. "Drop it!"

The dog was on her feet and trotting toward the door before the command's final syllable.

"Cleo! Damn it! Come back here with that!" Gentry clapped her hands for emphasis, but the Labrador just increased her trot to a lope and kept on going...out the door, through the hall and down the stairs. Gentry glanced accusingly at Jake, mad at him because her wedding ring was on its way to God knew where. "If you'd just let go of the dress when I asked you to..."

"This isn't my fault." He fell into a quick step beside her. "You're the one who jerked the dress out of my hands and knocked off the buttons."

"I didn't knock them off. They fell off."

"You'll have to handle the dress more carefully from now on."

"If you'd left it in the box to begin with, there wouldn't have been any need to handle it, carefully or otherwise, and we wouldn't have to go chasing after Ben's stupid dog."

"I can't believe I've only been here for a half hour and already you're blaming me for everything that's wrong in your life."

"Not everything, Jake. Just everything in the last half hour." She glanced over the bannister as she started down the stairs. In the entryway below, Cleo scrambled on the tiled foyer, found her footing and then darted through the open library doors.

Jake passed Gentry, hopped over the bannister rail and saved a few seconds by skipping the last five stairs.

"I'll try to cut her off from this side. You go through the library in case she doubles back."

Gentry thought it sounded like a complicated plan for button recovery, considering she didn't really care if the dress was missing a few buttons. She had no intention of wearing the silly thing, anyway. If it wasn't for her ring, Cleo could have her fill of "magic" buttons. From the corner of her eye, she saw Jake lunge for the dog. He missed, of course, and Cleo quivered from ear to tail in a spasm of doggy glee. In the dog's view, the chase was on. With a playful twist, she jumped out of reach and tore across the entryway to the living room on the opposite side of the house. From there, she'd have a straight shot through the open terrace doors to the great outdoors and at least a hundred burial spots. Maybe burying the whole kit and caboodle was the best solution all around.

"She's heading for the terrace." Jake was after the dog like James Bond after a spy.

"For heaven's sake," Gentry said as he dashed past her in hot pursuit. "It's only a bag of buttons, not a matter of principle."

"Explain that to Pop," he called over his shoulder.

On second thought, it couldn't hurt to lend Agent 007 a helping hand. Gentry hurried after the man, the dog, the thousand-dollar buttons... and a plain gold band.

AROUND THE POOL, Cleo's entrance barely caused a stir. As Jake followed close on the Labrador's heels, he was greeted with a warm smile by first Sydney, then Hillary, then Heather. On the "brim" side of the cowboy-hat-shaped pool, Pop regaled the ladies with another of his behind-the-scenes stories about famous people he'd loved...or not loved, as the case might be. At the crown of the oddly shaped pool, Sonny stood with a glass in one hand, his other hand in his trousers pocket, talking with two men, one tall and blond, one slender and dark haired, but obviously listening to Pop's story with at least one ear, as well.

Jake acknowledged the men with a nod and the women with a smile and wondered if he could retrieve the bag from Cleo without having to explain where she got it, what was in it, and how he happened to know. Harris was spoiling for a fight, and Jake wasn't about to give him an excuse to start one.

Gentry bumped into him from behind. "Did you get it?"

"Not yet." He studied the dog with a disapproving eye. "Look at her. She trotted over to Harris and stretched out at his feet like she needed political asylum or something."

Going up on her tiptoes, Gentry looked over his shoulder at the Lab. "She's starting to chew on the bag, Jake. Go over and get it away from her."

"You go get it. Harris doesn't want to slug *you* in the nose."

"He doesn't want to slug you, either. *He's* a gentleman."

"*Gentlemen* are the worst. Especially when it comes to believing that their fiancée's first husband might not be the dastardly slob they've been led to believe he is."

"I never called you a slob."

"Why are you standing back there, Jake?" Pop interrupted his story to ask. "Pour yourself a glass of my rocket fuel and come on over and join the party."

"Don't even think about it," Gentry warned. "Go get the buttons. I'm going back inside."

He reached around and fastened his hand around her arm, holding her in place. "Oh, no, you don't. If I have to risk my nose retrieving your buttons, the least you can do is provide some moral support. Stay put."

"If Sonny sees me in this nightshirt, there's going to be a lot of explaining to do. I'd better just slip into the house and change."

"Since when have you shied away from setting a new fashion trend? Now, we're going to meander over to Harris, and while you distract him, I'll get the buttons." He took her hand—as if they were the best of friends—and strolled casually around the hat brim.

"Gentry!" Sydney caught sight of her and, troublemaker that she was, had to draw attention to her attire. "What are you doing in your nightshirt?"

Like a hawk spotting the tail of a mouse, Sonny's gaze zoomed in.

"I told you this was a bad idea." Gentry pulled her hand free and smiled brilliantly at her fiancé. "Sonny, I'm so wonderfully *happy* to see you!" Her voice rose on a note of artificial excitement. "I've been absolutely *dying* to know how you spent your day."

"Way to go, Liz," Jake muttered. "Now he's bound to think we have something to hide."

"We?" she questioned in a tantalizing and teasing aside. "Sorry, Jake, but it's every man—and nose— for himself. Darling..." She hurried to wrap her hands around Sonny's arm and kissed him, worshipfully, on the cheek. "You are the most devastatingly *attractive* man on the planet. I'm not sure I can *wait* until Saturday to be married to you."

Sonny's expression changed from gloomy to gratified in a split second, and Gentry, conversely, wished he weren't quite so easy to handle. "It's only a week, darling," he said with an adoring smile. "Even if it will seem like the longest seven days of my life."

"Oh, don't worry about passing the time, old man." Jake's approach was easy, irritating and completely assured, as if there were no place he'd rather be and no place he'd be more welcome. "The Four Horsemen—minus your beloved, of course, because she'll have to spend the week searching for yet another perfect wedding gown—will make sure you're properly entertained." His foot edged unobtrusively toward the jewelry bag safeguarded between Cleo's front paws. "You and I might even get in a golf game or two. Unless you'd rather go fishing." Cleo underscored the offer with a throaty and playful growl.

"I dislike everything about fishing." Sonny said it nicely, because he was a gentleman, but his meaning was unmistakable and very personal.

Gentry's eyes swung to Jake, hoping he wouldn't thrust his nose in front of Sonny's fist and create a scene.

"How about you two?" Jake turned his charm on the other two men as his foot edged toward Cleo once again. "Do you like to fish?"

"I do," said the tall blonde, extending his hand. "I'm Mitch McAlister, Sonny's best man."

"Jake Daniels." They shook hands.

"Lee Hess, one of the groomsmen." The dark-haired man introduced himself and Jake shook hands with him, too. "I've always wanted to try fly-fishing."

"Now there's a real man's sport," Jake agreed. "You'll have to visit the Two-Penny Lodge. I have a guide who can show you one of the best fly-fishing rivers in the country. In fact, there's one cabin on the property that is situated so perfectly, you can fish for days and not see another soul.''

Gentry knew that cabin well. She and Jake had spent some incredible nights there. And days. And they'd never gone near the river. "Well, there won't be any time for fishing this week," she said brightly, patting Sonny's arm affectionately, pretending she knew nothing about the Two-Penny Lodge and cared even less. "There's the party your family is giving for us at the country club tonight, and tomorrow we're all invited to a brunch at the Hamiltons'.''

Sonny adored her with a smile. "Don't forget you promised to attend an art gallery opening with me Wednesday evening.''

"How could I forget any promise I made to you?'' she said sweetly, stressing the words to annoy Jake.

"This is not the week for culture, Sonny.'' Jake stooped, and, acting exceedingly casual, he petted the Labrador. "Take my advice, a man should spend the days before his wedding kicking up his heels and letting the testosterone run wild. It's your last chance.''

"Mitch and I have been trying to tell him that.'' Lee nodded at the groom-to-be. "Without much success, I might add.''

Jake shrugged and scratched Cleo's ear. "If I were about to marry Gentry, I'd hope my friends would make certain those last days of freedom were well spent.''

"Since you're *not* about to marry her, maybe you should take your opinions and trot them over to the guest house.'' With a quicksilver change of expression, Sonny stepped closer, warningly standing over

Jake's stooped position. "Or maybe you could bury them in that isolated cabin in Arkansas."

"It isn't big enough for my opinions, Harris." Slipping his finger beneath the dog's chin, Jake made a grab for the jewelry bag. Cleo was on her feet in an instant, weight balanced on her front legs as she held tenaciously to the drawstring bag. "Let go," Jake said through gritted teeth. "Come on, Cleo, let go of the—"

The Labrador grappled for a better hold, losing ground and a good portion of the drawstring.

"What has that dog got in its mouth?" Sonny leaned over to assess the situation.

"Nothing." Gentry tugged on his arm, but Sonny would not be moved.

"If you must be so unsociable, you could at least do it on the other side of the pool so I wouldn't have to walk all the way around to bring you a drink." Sydney arrived at the crease of the hat's crown just as Cleo growled in earnest. "Pop sent me to tell you to mind your manners," she said to Gentry.

"Give me the bag!" Jake's voiced lowered to a frustrated threat.

"What's in the bag?" Sydney asked.

"Isn't that the pouch that came with those silver earrings I gave you for Christmas?" Sonny frowned. "How did the dog get it?"

Gentry knew she looked guilty. "I must have left it lying out."

"You should be more careful," was his response.

"Could somebody give me a hand?" Jake looked pointedly at Gentry and she reached for the end of the dangling drawstring, wanting to get the pouch away from the dog and Jake.

"Let me do it, darling." Sonny elbowed her out of the way as he caught the string and gave it a yank.

Cleo shifted her weight, holding her own against the dual, but uncoordinated, effort. Her wagging tail continued to flop rhythmically from side to side in canine delight.

"Are you sure there's nothing more than a pair of silver earrings in that pouch?" Mitch asked. "The way the dog's acting, there could be a fortune in gemstones inside."

"No precious jewels," Jake said tightly, digging in his heels and pulling steadily on the drawstring. "Only some very expensive buttons."

"Did you say buttons?" Pop and the others joined them in the indentation of concrete forming the hat's crease. "There're buttons in the bag?"

"On the count of three, Harris, pull as hard as you can. One, two, three!" Jake loosened his grip just enough to fool Cleo into shifting her balance toward Sonny. When she made a grab to get more of the cloth into her mouth, he seized the opportunity and jerked the drawstring. The bag ripped and buttons scattered like popcorn. The reflection of one shiny gold ring hit Gentry in the eye and she hoped against hope that she could get her hands on it before anyone else did.

Oblivious to anything but the game in play, tenacious Cleo pressed her sudden advantage, renewing her grip on the torn pouch even as she lunged to the side and took a broad jump into the pool. Jake let go the moment he saw her gather her haunches for her swan dive. Sonny wasn't so quick. The drawstring was still clutched in his fist when Cleo hit the water... and jerked him in with her.

Gentry had her head down, looking for the wedding band, when she felt a hand on her back and realized, too late, she was being propelled into the pool. Jake, she thought as the chlorinated water swallowed her whole. And sure enough, his was the first face she saw when she bobbed to the surface. There was no mistaking that devious grin.

She sputtered and pushed the straggly hair from her eyes before grabbing the crisp, starched crease of his jeans and yanking him off balance and into the pool with her.

Chapter Four

"I certainly hope we found all the buttons." Hillary wrapped a towel around her wet hair and twisted it, turban-style, on top of her head.

"If we didn't, it wasn't for lack of trying." Sydney leaned over the edge of the pool to wring out excess water from the hem of her blouse. "I'll never forget the look on Sonny's face when Cleo pulled him off balance and into the pool."

"You looked a little surprised yourself when Mitch picked you up and threw you in." Heather retied the wet laces of her canvas shoes. "I'm just glad no one got mad. Even Sonny eventually cracked a smile. I saw him."

Gentry had missed that. She'd been so preoccupied in looking for her wedding band, she couldn't say with any certainty what had happened after the bag tore, spilling its contents in twenty different directions. The gold ring had glinted in the sunlight just before it disappeared somewhere in the center of the hat-shaped pool. After she'd jerked Jake into the pool, she'd dived for the bottom to retrieve the ring, but Sonny had assumed she was being pulled under by the weight of her nightshirt, or something equally ridiculous, and in a burst of foolish heroics, he'd employed his Red Cross training to save her. By the time she'd convinced him she was merely trying to retrieve the scattered buttons, everyone else was in the pool, fully clothed, fully soaked, and full of the silliness prompted by an impromptu pool party. When the pool cleared some forty minutes later, the ring was nowhere to be found.

"He may have smiled at some point," Sydney commented. "But I'm willing to bet it wasn't voluntary. He wouldn't even play Marco Polo after Mitch persuaded him to get back in the pool. I hope you know what you're doing, Gen. Being married to Sonny isn't going to be very funny."

"You're such a poet, Syd." Hillary peeled off her sodden cotton vest and slung it over the back of a deck chair. "Frankly, I thought it was cute when he suggested we should all get out of the pool and change into our swimsuits."

"He was serious, Hillary. Couldn't you tell?"

"No." She considered that with a frown. "Are you sure he wasn't making a joke? Gentry? Didn't he mean that as a joke?"

"Of course," she answered, although she couldn't recall anything Sonny had said or done during the last hour. "How many buttons did we recover?"

"Jake said he counted eight, but Mitch thought there were only seven." Heather walked to the cabana, with a squishing accompaniment from her soggy shoes. She picked up the torn jewelry pouch and carried it to where Gentry sat at one of the cabana tables, pensively staring at the pool. "Why don't you count them again and see how many you come up with?"

"Thanks, Heather." Gentry took the knotted pouch absently, her mind on the missing ring, her silly heart absurdly grieved by its loss. "It doesn't matter. If we didn't find all the buttons, we didn't. I don't really care."

"But it's a million-dollar dress," Hillary pointed out. "Without all the buttons, it might not be worth as much."

"With or without the buttons, no one is ever going to wear it, so what difference does it make?"

There was a pause in which each of the women glanced at her and looked quickly away. With a frustrated sigh, Gentry squared her shoulders and told herself to buck up. It wasn't like she'd lost the five-carat diamond Sonny had presented to her—for the second time—when they announced their most recent engagement. Jake's wedding band should have been the first thing to go after she realized he wasn't going to come after her, wasn't going to call, or write, or want her back.

"I'm going in," she said with a decisive nod. "We have to be ready to leave in an hour and a half and it will take me at least that long to wash the chlorine out of my hair. Anyone else ready to go inside?"

"We'll sit in the sun another ten or fifteen minutes and dry out," Sydney said, confidently speaking for the other two as well. "You go on, take your time. You're the bride and you can be late, if necessary. Sonny didn't design a dress for you to wear tonight, did he?"

Gentry shook her head, unable to manage even a half smile in reply. "No. He bought a pearl gray sheath for me at that exclusive little boutique two doors down from the gallery. He saw it in the window and thought it would be perfect for tonight's dinner party."

"Doesn't he think you're capable of choosing an appropriate outfit?" Hillary asked with an edge of offended dignity. "Honestly, Gen, what's wrong with you? You've been dressing yourself since long before Sonny Harris took an interest in fashion design. You never used to care what anyone thought about your taste in clothing."

"I've matured," she said flatly. "Sonny has been wonderful, considering the way I treated him two years ago. I couldn't ask for a more understanding fiancé."

"You could ask for one with a little better fashion sense, however."

"Just because you don't like him, Sydney, is no reason to belittle his tastes. As a matter of courtesy, please keep your opinions about Sonny to yourself and don't feel you have to share them with me."

Sydney looked startled by the harsh tone, but Gentry was in no mood to back down. She was going to marry Sonny. The least she could do was defend his taste in clothing...even if she privately agreed that his fashion sense could use some refining.

"I'm sure you'll look beautiful, no matter who chose the dress." Heather tried to bridge the tension with a conciliatory cheerfulness.

"Wait a minute." Hillary's blue eyes brightened beneath the terry-cloth turban. "I have just the outfit for you tonight. That leather ensemble I bought at Neiman Marcus last month would look fantastic on you, Gentry. When Sonny sees the contrast of your red hair against the black leather, he'll forget he ever even saw another dress."

"I'm wearing the pearl gray sheath." Gentry tossed the remains of the pouch into Sydney's lap. "But if one of you wants to sew the buttons on the wedding gown, you're welcome to wear it. You know, if you rub the buttons, a genie might appear and grant you three wishes. Then you could all wear it."

"The gown was meant for you." Sydney offered the wrapped buttons to Gentry. "You're the one who should wear it."

"No, thanks. I've got all the magic I can handle. Dinner's at eight. Cocktails at seven-thirty. The Harrises are sending a limousine for us at a quarter past seven, so don't doze in the sun too long." With that, she turned and walked into the house.

"All right, fellow Horsemen." Sydney frowned thoughtfully at the lumpy jewelry pouch. "I say it's our duty as bridesmaids to make sure Gentry puts on the magic wedding dress. Otherwise, we'll have no excuse when she marries Sonny and turns into a red-haired replica of his mother. A pearl gray sheath, can you imagine?" She looked at the other two thoughtful faces. "Let's see a show of hands. Are you with me?"

Hillary thrust her hand in the air. "I'm in."

Two pairs of eyes turned expectantly on Heather, who wavered between a dislike of interfering and a steadfast belief in magic. "Do you think she'll get mad at us?"

"Probably," Sydney said. "But she'll get over it. Think of the alternative . . . do you really want to live with the knowledge that, no matter what you do or where you go for the rest of your life, there will always be a picture of the three of us wearing rose petal pink and standing next to a redheaded bride in sequins?''

Heather's hand shot into the air. "I say we steal her clothes and leave her with nothing to wear except the magic wedding gown."

Sydney's throaty laughter was replete with admiration. "For someone with such deeply held principles, you have a wonderfully devious mind."

"Thank you," Heather replied modestly. "Give me those buttons and let's get down to the details."

JAKE PACED TO THE WINDOW of the guest house and stared pensively across the precisely manicured lawn. If anyone at the Two-Penny Lodge had told him he'd be spending his vacation here, only a few yards from Gentry, he'd have thought they were fried to the tonsils. If he hadn't learned a long time ago to steer clear of hard liquor, he would almost believe he was in the midst of a delusional hangover himself. Bracing his arms against the windowsill, he turned his head to look at the old steamer trunk someone had refurbished and placed in front of the sofa as a coffee table.

For him, the only interesting thing about the antique trunk was the small gold band lying on its polished black surface. When the glint of gold, reflecting a ray of sunlight, first caught his eye, he'd thought it was an earring. Or a brooch. Some bit of jewelry left in the pouch that had spilled out with the buttons to sink in the pool's clear water.

But it wasn't some bit of jewelry. It was Gentry's wedding band. He'd known what it was the moment he spied it on the bottom of the pool, even before he checked the initials crudely scratched inside. What had him puzzled was what the ring was doing here. Oh, he knew how it had gotten to its position on the trunk. He'd tucked it in his pocket and brought it with him to the guest house after the wild, everybody-in-the-water free-for-all. He'd taken it from his pocket and laid it on the trunk before he showered and changed into fresh clothes. Then he'd sat and stared at it for a while. After that, he'd stared at it some more. And still he couldn't come up with a good explanation for its presence in Gentry's jewelry bag.

She'd dumped something out and into her drawer before she tossed the pouch to him. He'd watched her do it. So why hadn't she removed the ring? Had she meant for him to see it? Or had she forgotten it was there?

Turning from the late-afternoon sunlight beyond the window, he returned to the striped damask chair and stared at the wedding band again. She could have kept it as a reminder of the biggest mistake of her life, he supposed. But despite the brevity of their relationship, he knew her habits, and he didn't believe she would keep any reminder of the failure their marriage had been. Perhaps she'd put it in the drawer without thinking and forgotten about it.

Possible, he supposed, but not likely. She'd been angry when she left him. Since she hadn't bothered with a response to his reconciliation attempt, it had been patently clear that her anger had still been running strong at that point. And when Gentry was angry, she didn't forget. He found it hard to believe she could have tolerated the mere thought that any object connected with him was tucked away in her chest of drawers.

Picking up the ring, he slipped it on his little finger, where it lodged just below the first knuckle. Gentry had been as proud of that gold band as if he'd given her a diamond half the size of California. He'd promised to take her shopping for a more appropriate wedding ring as soon as the summer season at the lodge was over. She hadn't seemed to mind, had told him on more than one occasion she was quite content with her simple gold band...although she wanted their names and wedding date engraved inside. He'd obliged with the point of his pocketknife, etching on the inside of the band an imperfect *G* linked to a less perfect *J*. He supposed it had been his way of marking the plain ring as unworthy of her, his heavy-handed way of saying she deserved so much more. He wanted her to have more...the kind of diamond engagement ring and matching band she would have received from Harris, the kind of set she'd be proud to show off to her friends.

As if that had really mattered. By the time the summer was gone, so was Gentry.

But now, here was the ring. Like a souvenir given up as lost and then suddenly, unexpectedly discovered. And with its return, he faced an unsettling truth. He'd given up his marriage too easily, written it off as if it were a bad debt, said to hell with it, and conceded defeat without a fight. The fact amazed him now that he thought about it. Why had he let her leave? And why hadn't he done whatever it took to bring her back?

The answer eluded him, like a message held up to a mirror, with all the letters reversed and unreadable. Sitting back in the chair, he propped his feet on the glossy black trunk and held the ring up to the waning daylight. Maybe the why of it wasn't important anymore. Maybe the question he needed to concentrate on was what the plain gold band meant to him now. And what, if anything, it still meant to Gentry.

He glanced at the clock. Gentry and her entourage would be leaving for the party any minute now. Two years ago, Sonny Harris had unwittingly invited Jake to another party, not knowing that his gallery's newest customer had an ulterior motive in accepting the invitation. This time, Harris hadn't been so trusting. He'd made it unmistakably clear that Jake wasn't invited and wouldn't be welcome.

He glanced across at the other damask chair where Cleo was draped like a rag doll. She snored softly and her front legs twitched with her dreaming. "Hey, Cleo," Jake said. "How would you like to go to a party?"

The dog opened her eyes and her tail thumped once against the chair arm.

"We weren't invited, you understand, and crashing this particular party may involve some fancy footwork."

She lifted her head and her tail thumped with interest.

"Okay, then. Let's do it. Just remember who you came with and don't go sidling up to the first person who offers you something to eat."

Her tail stopped wagging.

"Well, okay, if all goes well, I'll make sure you get a juicy reward. Something with some meat on it."

She jumped from the chair and sat adoringly at his feet. As he reached out to pet her, the ring on his little finger stole a last ray of light from the setting sun and reflected it straight to his heart as hope.

Gentry's wedding band, her souvenir of their short-lived marriage, was the only party invitation he required.

"MAY THE YEARS BRING you happiness." The toast made the round of tables at The Silver Palm Country Club, which had been rented for the night by Mr. and Mrs. Milton Harris to honor their son and his bride-to-be.

"May the years bring happiness," the guests repeated in a random singsong, raising their glasses in yet another salute.

The ginger ale in Gentry's glass tasted flat. Or maybe the flatness was a result of the endless shower of happy wishes raining down around her. Sonny's family was overly fond of protocol, and there seemed to be an endless array of it surrounding the celebration of marriage. Each family member was delighted to propose a personal toast, often preceded by a "Sonny" anecdote, and always followed by a chorus of "hear, hear" and then the clink of glassware.

As she recalled, there had been a similar barrage of good wishes two years ago. That party, too, had been held at The Silver Palm, in this same room, with many of the same people, at almost the same time of year. Sonny had wanted it that way. He seemed to believe that if he could replicate the past and just rescript the ending, then her elopement with Jake would be erased from everyone's memory...especially his. He hadn't said that in so many words, but she knew. She wished he could have been satisfied to make a new beginning, but she was discovering that Sonny's forgiveness came with a price tag labeled Pride.

Uncle Alexander rose and tapped a spoon against his glass to gain the attention of his audience. "I'd like to propose a toast." He lifted his glass. "To Sonny and Gentry. Here's to your happiness...and a heartfelt wish that this time the wedding goes off as planned."

The toast was endorsed by a spurt of laughter and a round of applause. Even Sonny's mother laughed at the joke, as if it were too hilarious to think anything might interfere this time around. Gentry didn't laugh, but she managed a happy smile...at least a reasonable facsimile of one...as she clinked her glass to Sonny's. She ought to be enjoying the party. Sonny's family had gone to great expense to make it a memorable occasion, and she was ashamed of herself for not being more appreciative.

It was Jake's fault. If he hadn't appeared out of the blue today, walking back into her life as if he'd never been out of it, pretending Ben had imposed upon his friendship in extracting a solemn promise to deliver that silly old wedding dress... Oh, no, Jake had to accept responsibility for this disaster of an evening. It was entirely his fault that she couldn't stop thinking about him.

"You remember Aunt Dot," Sonny whispered close to her ear as a tall, kind-eyed woman with a generous smile rose to offer her good wishes. "When Sonny was only three years old..." Aunt Dot began.

Gentry's smile solidified. This was going to be a very long night.

Sonny swept Gentry around the dance floor to the tune of "You're Nobody Till Somebody Loves You." They danced well together, never missing a step, their movements flawlessly executed and as smooth as spun cotton. She and Sonny were a perfect match. Everyone said so.

Gentry couldn't understand why the song seemed to play on and on and on.

"Tired, sweetheart?" he asked, and she nodded because a more honest excuse eluded her. "We probably should stay at least another hour. I wouldn't want to disappoint everyone by leaving too early."

"I'm fine. Really." She offered a smile as proof. "I just need a little fresh air, that's all."

If he heard an echo from the past in her words, he gave no sign. She could hardly believe she'd repeated herself so exactly. *"I just need a little fresh air,"* she'd said at the party two years ago. But it hadn't been fresh air she needed that night. It had been Jake.

The song ended, and after a spattering of applause, another song began. Other couples moved from table to dance floor, and two of Sonny's cousins pressed forward to bestow more good wishes. As soon as they walked on, Sonny took her elbow again and started for the door.

Halfway there, Uncle Alexander stopped them. "You won't mind if I borrow Sonny for a few minutes, will you?" His skin was wrinkled from years of hard work and his eyes held the shadow of habitual worry, but he managed a cagey wink at Gentry before he took Sonny's arm and pulled him aside. "I know this is not the place to talk shop, but the manager you hired to oversee operations at the Alabama plant called me today and . . ."

Sonny's mouth tightened at the interruption, but he listened as the older man talked. Gentry eyed the walkway outside the floor-to-ceiling windows of The Silver Palm. When the club's restaurant was open to the membership, the walkway provided a buffer between the diners and other club activities going on at the same time. At private parties like this one, the windows could be removed completely, opening up the interior to the outside air. Tonight, tables were set up on the walkway to provide a place for private conversations or a respite from the noise and clutter of the party.

She could go out there alone. Sonny didn't have to accompany her. There was no need. Jake wasn't here. Not that it would matter if he were. Tonight, she wanted only a breath of fresh air. Nothing more.

Sonny caught her eye and motioned for her to go on without him. He hated to talk business at social gatherings. He didn't actually like to talk about it anywhere, but he was courteous to a fault. He was also conscious that Harris Manufacturing provided the funds for his art gallery. Lending a sympathetic ear to Uncle Alexander's latest concern was a small price to pay for the life-style he enjoyed.

Sonny Harris was a good man, considerate and kind, even if he did want desperately, and try too hard, to fit in. A minor flaw, she thought. Certainly nothing like Jake, who wanted his way or no way, who didn't care if he fit anywhere in the world outside the boundaries of the Two-Penny Lodge. He was the only man she'd ever known who had expected her to be more than she was, who challenged her to try harder, be stronger, grow up. His passion had energized and exhausted her, comforted and frightened her, and in the end, defeated her.

Two years ago, at a party nearly identical to this one, he'd asked her to run away with him. And she'd refused. Until he kissed her. Not far from the walkway she was approaching now. Out there, in the scent-sweet darkness of the summer garden, he'd slipped up behind her and whispered so softly she could almost believe he hadn't said the words aloud at all. *"I love you in blue... and every other color under the sun."* And then he'd taken her in his arms and kissed her until she would have gone anywhere with him.

The memory of those stolen moments made her shiver as she stepped out into the warm summer night. There was an eerie similarity tonight, a sense of déjà vu, of having felt this same hushed expectancy before. She shook it off with a tight shudder. Jake wasn't here. He hadn't been invited and she was sure he had no interest in tonight's celebration. But with just the thought of him, the memory of his kiss, came the illogical idea that he might be in the darkness, watching and waiting for her.

Gentry turned on her heel and walked briskly back inside.

"This party needs something." Sydney accosted her the moment she reentered the room. "A male stripper would do wonders for my attitude, about now."

"Not to mention what it could do for the blood circulation of Sonny's aunts." Hillary ducked behind a fig tree to take her place on Gentry's other side. She smiled and waved at Aunt Dot.

Gentry sensed mischief weaving toward her like a drunken sailor. "This party doesn't need anything except to be over."

"Aha, I knew you had to be as bored as we are," Sydney said. "Come on, Gen, let's have some fun. Spike the punch. Swing from the chandelier. Do a table dance. Don't shake your head at me. You deserve to have one last fling before you settle into a life brightened only by stories of Sonny as a precocious child.''

Gentry's suspicions formed a definite shape. ''Where's Heather?''

''Haven't seen her.''

''Me, either.'' Hillary's shrug was too pat, too quick. ''She could be in the bathroom, I guess. Maybe we should look for her.''

''Oh, no.'' Gentry backed away from their obvious ploy to separate her from the party. ''I'm not falling for that. If you're determined to embarrass me, you can just wait until the Hamiltons' brunch. At least they know what nitwits you three can be at times.''

Sydney gasped in mock offense and drawled in her finest imitation of a Southern belle, ''Why, Gentry Elizabeth Northcross, you can't believe that your dearest and best friends would ever do anything to put you to the blush. It would be so undignified, not to mention so unlike us.''

''Mmm-hmm.'' Gentry edged closer to Sonny's steady, no-nonsense presence. ''You forget I was with you the night you decided to drop a cherry bomb down the toilet of the Alpha Phi fraternity house as a grand and final last fling before graduation. If I hadn't convinced you how undignified that little prank would be, we'd have been expelled from the university for sure.''

''If only we could have gotten our hands on a Jiffy John that night,'' Hillary said with a sigh.

Sydney chimed in with a wistful sigh of her own. ''There was a good reason we were called the Four Horsemen in those days.''

''And a better reason we're not called that these days.'' Gentry knew these women as well as she knew herself, and when it came to mischief, she didn't trust them either in or out of her sight. "Whatever you two have cooked up with Heather for tonight is officially called off as of now. Sonny's family is not boring. Mingle a little. Find someone interesting to talk to. Aunt Dot, for instance, is a retired nurse. She ought to be able to tell some stories that will satisfy your thirst for excitement."

"Speaking of thirst..." Hillary reached across Gentry to nab a glass of red wine from a tray held by a solemn-faced waiter. "I'd like to make a toast, Gen. To true love."

Sydney barely managed to grab a glass of champagne before the waiter passed by. Lifting the champagne flute to Gentry, she clinked her glass with Hillary's. "To the *magic* of a true and lasting love."

Sonny turned, frowned at the sight of Gentry flanked by trouble on the hoof, and moved to intercept. "Having fun, ladies?"

Hillary giggled... and Gentry knew with a rueful certainty that whatever was about to happen would not be conducive to Sonny's happiness.

"Oh, look," Sydney said brightly. "There's Heather."

Gentry followed Syd's gaze to the doorway where Heather stood, partially in the room and partially in the foyer. Lifting her hand in an absentminded sort of wave, Heather leaned forward as if she were addressing someone much shorter. Her expression altered with amusement as she straightened and turned to someone just out of view.

"What is that dog doing here?" Sonny's tone was suddenly sharp. "You don't suppose she followed us all the way across town, do you?"

"What dog?" Sydney went up on tiptoe, trying to see.

Hillary, who was taller, looked over Sonny's shoulder. "It's only Cleo."

"Cleo?" Gentry repeated.

"How did she get—" Sonny's question tightened with anger. "I can't believe this," he said.

"Are you sure it's her?" Gentry tried to think of an explanation for the dog's presence. "It could be another dog."

"It is. It's Daniels," came his answer, and, with it, Gentry experienced a warm, rousing and embarrassing surge of excitement. Jake was here.

"What's Jake doing here?" Sydney turned a sudden frown on Sonny. "Did you invite him?"

"Of course I didn't. Did you?"

"Don't be insulting," Hillary said. "Inviting a guest to someone else's party would be rude."

"You don't say." Sonny took a step toward the door. "What about punching an uninvited guest in the nose?"

"Tactless and undignified."

"Just ask him to leave." Gentry put a restraining hand on Sonny's arm. "There's no reason to create a scene."

"You stay here." With that stern warning, Sonny headed for the door.

Gentry cast an accusing eye on her friends. "I don't know how you two convinced Jake to show up tonight, but it's your responsibility to make certain nothing happens to Sonny."

"What about Jake?" Sydney asked. "Don't you care if something happens to him?"

"Not particularly. He should have better sense than to show—" Gentry brought up her hand and, somehow, caught the suddenly too-close underside of Hillary's arm, knocking her elbow and sending the wine in her glass shooting into the air like Old Faithful. The bright red wine sparkled for a moment in the light and then splashed down . . . all over the front of the pearl gray sheath.

"Aaaah!" Gentry's exclamation wasn't loud, but it startled Sydney, who swung around with a jerk, which sent the champagne in her glass splashing across the wine stain already in place.

"Oh, Gen, I'm sorry." She brushed at the sheath with her hand and managed to spill the rest of the champagne down Gentry's leg and into her shoe.

"Quick," Hillary said. "What is it you're supposed to use to take out wine stains? Ginger ale or club soda?"

"Club soda," Gentry said.

"Ginger ale," Sydney answered, still rubbing at the spreading discoloration. "What are you drinking, Gentry?"

"Ginger ale, but—" Before she could clarify that she wasn't drinking anything at the moment, a glass on the nearest table was picked up and its contents applied full strength to the stain.

"Oh, way to go." Hillary took the empty glass out of Sydney's hand and set it back on the table. "That was not Gentry's ginger ale."

"Well, whose was it?"

"No one's. It wasn't ginger ale."

"Excuse me, but I was only trying to help clean up the mess you made by spilling your wine all over her."

"Oh, stop it." Gentry was torn between irritation with her friends and a pressing need to make certain a fight wasn't about to break out on the other side of the room. "I'll send the dress to the cleaners tomorrow."

"Oh, I wouldn't wait." Hillary's tone rose with alarm. "By tomorrow that stain will be set. You should probably go to the bathroom and rinse it out now."

"Rinsing won't work," Sydney warned. "You'll have to soak it in hot water."

Gentry frowned, feeling there was something in this conversation that had very little to do with the stain on her dress. "I'd have to take a bath in the sink to do that."

"No, you don't. We'll do it for you. Soak the dress, that is. And we can use the hand dryers to blow it dry. You'll be washed, dried and presentable in less time than it took Sydney to ruin the dress in the first place."

"I didn't ruin it, Hillary. You did. I was just standing there." Sydney took Gentry's arm and steered her through the crowd and away from the confrontation across the room. Not many of the guests appeared to be aware that anything out of the ordinary was going on. Maybe there wasn't. Maybe it wasn't Jake who'd been standing in that doorway. Maybe her friends had had one too many of Pop's special drinks today. Maybe they weren't acting strangely at all. On the other hand, her dress had had not one, not two, but three glasses of various beverages poured on it. That was enough evidence to make her extremely suspicious.

"I probably should just go home," she said.

Hillary disagreed with a shake of her head. "There's no need to do that. We'll take care of everything, don't worry."

"She's right." Sydney added her persuasive powers. "You don't want to miss the rest of the party. Not when you're having such a good time."

Like a white flag over Fort Apache, suspicion fluttered in Gentry's thoughts. It had looked like an accident, all right. But when it came to these two friends, there was always room for doubt. "I have a feeling I should refuse to go anywhere with the two of you."

"What's wrong with you?" Sydney's voice snapped with impatience. "You're beginning to sound paranoid. We're your friends, remember?"

All the more reason to worry, she thought.

It wasn't until some ten minutes later that she grasped the entire scope of their plan. By the time they reached the ladies' rest room, there was a consensus of two that Gentry might as well be comfortable while she waited for them to rinse and dry the dress. So, at Sydney's suggestion, she'd gone into one of the darkened offices, slipped off the pearl gray sheath and handed it out to Hillary. The dress was barely out of her grasp and the door closed behind it, when she caught a glimpse, an elusive twinkle, of bridal white hanging in a corner of the darkened room. She didn't know how they had gotten the wedding dress here without her knowledge, but here it was.

"You know, Gen," Sydney said on the other side of the door. "I'm afraid your pearl gray sheath is ruined, after all. But don't worry. I'm sure you'll find *something* to wear."

Footsteps clipped briskly down the hall and away, leaving Gentry undressed down to her undies and pearl gray heels, and alone with the magic wedding dress.

Chapter Five

Sonny was heading in his direction and Jake could see a cordial welcome was not on his agenda. Maybe crashing this party hadn't been such a hot idea.

"Bogey coming in at four o'clock," he said to Heather. "If you have any interception skills, now would be the time to test them."

"Most of the men I try to intercept go right past me," she said with a sigh. "You'd be better off sending Cleo."

"If only Sonny had the foresight to carry a rump roast." Jake patted the dog sitting politely beside him and watched his host's shoulders square with emphatic body language. "I certainly hope all the rumors about him being a gentleman are true."

"Even gentlemen lose their charm when threatened."

Jake glanced at Heather, but had no chance to ask if she thought Sonny Harris had good cause to feel threatened.

"What are you doing here, Daniels?" Sonny delivered the question like a security guard, all authority and demand. "And I'll warn you right now, it better not have anything to do with Gentry."

"Is she here?" Jake raised his brows in surprise. "I thought you didn't let her stay out past nine o'clock."

Sonny's jaw set. "Look, I don't want to cause a scene, but unless you leave as quietly and quickly as you came in, I'm going to punch your lights out."

Jake looked at Heather. "You were right, charm is definitely on the ebb."

"I'm asking you to leave, Daniels, as politely as I know how."

"And being darn civil about it, too. This may come as a surprise, but it wasn't my idea to crash this party."

"Don't tell me you have yet another package to deliver."

"Nothing like that. Cleo insisted I bring her. She is part of the family, you know, and she's been feeling pretty left out all evening. You really should have invited her along."

"Take your jokes and your dog and leave before I lose my patience. There are security guards on the grounds and they'll be happy to escort you off the property, if you think you're going to have any trouble finding your way out."

"I can find my way," Jake said easily. "I was at a party here once before."

Sonny clenched his fist and pushed up his sleeves. "That's it, Daniels. We're going to settle this once and for all."

"Not a good idea," Heather counseled. "Your mother looks pretty upset already."

Sonny glanced behind him and cautioned his more aggressive guests to stay back with an upheld hand. "Let's behave like gentlemen, Daniels, and take our disagreement outside where it belongs. Not everyone enjoys the sight of blood."

"Me, especially." Jake nodded agreeably. "You know, if I could only have a few minutes alone with—"

"Not a chance," Sonny interjected. "Gentry doesn't want to see you, alone or otherwise. You have no business being in the same country with her, much less in the same room."

"Don't be so quick to jump to conclusions, Harris. I was about to say, if I could talk to Charlie, I'll finish my business here and leave as quickly and quietly as I came. No blood. No upset mothers. No crying women. No trouble. You have my word of honor."

"Your honor isn't worth a fried potato to me. I'd much rather see your rear end going out the door."

"Eloquently put." Jake didn't blame the other guy. In his position, any man would be on the defensive. Two years ago, Jake had been feeling a bit desperate himself. "As I was saying, if you'd be so kind as to let me have a few minutes with my ex-father-in-law, I'll be out of here quicker than you can spit in my eye. Uh, that was just a figure of speech," he added quickly. "Where is Charlie, anyway?"

"I saw him a little while ago." Heather supported Jake's change of topic with a step forward and a concerted effort to look for Pop. "He may be outside. Or he could be in the kitchen. Or I suppose he might be on the dance floor. Do you see him, Sonny?" She craned her neck for a better view past Sonny, who never let his gaze stray from Jake.

"I'll find him." Sonny narrowed his eyes, issuing a silent warning. "You wait by the door."

"Jake!" Sydney rushed up and slipped her hand through the crook of his arm. "You scoundrel! Don't you know it's completely immoral to crash a party?

Hillary nearly fainted from the impropriety when she caught sight of you. She may not be able to speak for hours, she's so horrified.''

Something was afoot, Jake thought, noting the mischief sparkling in Syd's eyes and the breathy excitement in her voice. "There are social outlaws everywhere you go these days. She'll have to get used to it."

"Not tonight, she won't." Sonny glanced at Heather. "Would you escort Mr. Daniels to the door and stay with him until I can find my father-in-law?"

Sydney patted Jake's arm companionably as she tossed the other man a casual smile. "You're getting a little ahead of yourself, aren't you, Sonny? The wedding isn't until Saturday, you know. Pop won't be your in-law until then."

"A mere technicality, which will be remedied in a matter of days." The confidence in his voice was unmistakable and Jake wished he would sound slightly unsure of himself. "Now, Heather," Sonny continued, "if you please . . ."

"Why are we going to the door?" Sydney asked. "Why can't we sit at one of the tables over—"

"He's not staying long enough to sit anywhere," Sonny interrupted. "You're welcome to go with him, but either way, he's on his way out...even if I have to bodily toss him through the door."

"Good thing Hil didn't hear that," Heather observed aloud. "She'd be prostrate at the impropriety."

"Sonny?" Sydney's voice softened with persuasion. "Wouldn't it be better if Jake waited for Pop in a room somewhere? Then you won't have to worry about him bothering any of the guests. Heather and I will find a convenient place for him and make sure he doesn't come out."

Sonny considered that with a frown. "I don't care where you put him as long as I don't have to see him again. Be sure the dog stays with him."

"Oh, we will." Sydney performed a smart salute. "Your wish is our command." She turned her mischievous eyes on Jake. "You heard him, Heather. Sonny doesn't care where we put this party crasher so long as he isn't in here."

Heather shrugged and patted her leg. "Come on, Cleo. You're banished, too."

Turning Jake like a revolving door, the women marched him away from the party as if they were escorting him to the guillotine.

THERE WAS NO SUCH THING as a magic dress.

Gentry glared at the luminous ivory satin with its lace sleeves and lace-covered bodice. Out of curiosity, she checked the buttons, not really surprised to find none missing. Her bridesmaids wouldn't have overlooked that little detail and given her a valid reason for not falling in with their scheme and putting on the dress.

She stepped back and eyed it thoughtfully. Hanging there in the darkened meeting room of the country club, it looked ordinary enough, if a trifle fussy for her taste. She preferred more modest gowns, like the pearl gray sheath and the sequined ...

What was she thinking? There was nothing modest, or even attractive, about the sequined wedding dress. This antique gown was far more deserving of the term. It wasn't actually that bad. Maybe if Pop and Ben—and her ex-friends—hadn't been so determined to have her wear it, she might have tried it on. Just to see how it fit and how it would feel to wear something designed for a bride old enough to be her great-grandmother.

Her lips tightened with a frown. She was probably lucky the dress hadn't belonged to any of her descendants. Throughout her early adolescence, she'd believed she was actually the daughter of Libby Kirk. She'd found a scrapbook of the early days in Charlie North's career and secreted it away, poring over the publicity pictures and private mementos of that time in his life. Libby's name was underlined in every article, her face plastered throughout the scrapbook.

In her preteen years, Gentry had reached the romantic conclusion that she was a love child, born to her father's actress lover and subsequently adopted by his long-suffering wife. It was a wonderful story to tell her friends when they were sharing the deepest, darkest, most tragic secrets of their respective families. No one could top Gentry's tale of forbidden love, desperate passion, sacrifice and forgiveness. She had the charming, charismatic and extravagant father to lend the story an air of real possibility, too.

Then she'd turned fourteen and, in the scientific world of biology class, faced the inevitable realization that her Irish red hair and emerald green eyes had not come from Libby Kirk's brown-eyed, brunette gene pool, but from Frannie O'Kelley Northcross and a long line of ivory-skinned, green-eyed redheads. In some bizarre twist of psychology, which she had never understood, the knowledge ended her love affair with romance and shattered the image she'd created of her father.

Now, out of the blue, he wanted her to believe there was magic in an old wedding gown. He'd probably made up the whole story about the history of the dress, anyway. But Ben... She hadn't thought her brother would fall prey to any nonsensical notion regarding love and marriage. Obviously, though, meeting Sara had made him just as susceptible to romantic ideas as Pop. With a sigh, Gentry moved to the window and looked out at the shadowy greens of the golf course. Where was Sydney? How long were they going to keep her locked in this room before they realized she wasn't giving in to their blackmail and had every intention of remaining in her underwear the rest of her life if she had to?

Like a child drawn to a forbidden object, she turned slowly, bracing her hands on the credenza behind her, to look again at the wedding gown. Was there really any good reason to avoid putting it on, she wondered. What was the good of standing on principle, when it meant standing in your underwear? She could slip on the gown and leave the room. She could leave the building, for that matter. Go home. Change into something else and be back almost before she could be missed. If no one saw her in the dress, no one would ever know she'd had it on. She would know, of course, but she wouldn't have to tell anyone.

Almost without knowing her objective, she walked over and took down the wedding gown. The satin was heavy and cool to the touch and the lace as delicate and fine as silk. She could imagine how rich the material would feel against her skin, how the ivory lace would look with her coloring. On closer inspection, the dress was really lovely, old-fashioned and sparkling with the promises of generations past. Holding it against her, Gentry could almost visualize herself in another time and another place. Maybe the magic of the dress was like all other illusions...a reflection of something unexpected and unexplained. She could try it on and see for herself. There wasn't a mirror in this room, but the ladies' lockers were just across the hall and there was a full-length mirror there. Who would know?

If there was even a grain of truth to the magic dress myth, she'd see Sonny's image reflected with her own. Chances were, she'd see nothing more than a redhead in an old dress. With a twist of her hand, she fluffed the skirt to smooth out the wrinkles and still managed to hold the bodice in place while she swayed like a child playing dressup, humming the bridal march under her breath, imagining herself walking down a long church aisle, wearing a gown like this one.

When the lights came on, she blinked and, with a guilty start, let go of the dress. It pooled at her feet in a sigh of satin as she met Jake's blue eyes across the room. "Jake!" She ducked down, scrambling for a hold on the suddenly slippery satin. "For heaven's sake, turn out the light!"

The lights went out as quickly as they'd come on. "I'll be damned," he said. "I've found Fantasy Island."

"You're going to find nirvana if you turn on those lights again. Sonny will tear you limb from limb."

"I don't think it will matter to him whether the lights are on or not."

She shoved Cleo's inquisitive and cold nose away from her bare leg. "If the lights are off, no one can see in from outside. If they're on and someone in the clubhouse looks in this direction, everything is visible."

"Everything?" Jake asked. "Meaning you in your underwear?"

She covered her lack of clothing with an embarrassed and frustrated jerk on the dress. Holding the material across her breasts, she straightened and lifted her chin with all the dignity she could muster. "They might see that, yes. What are you doing here, anyway? I distinctly recall not inviting you."

"Like two pennies from the same mint, we just keep winding up together," he said. "Must be fate."

"Or at least one very bad penny," she suggested, conscious that the room had become uncomfortably warm and her cheeks uncomfortably flushed. "Now, just turn around and leave the way you came in."

"Can't. Hillary won't let me out."

"She can't keep you here against your will. You're bigger than she is."

"Also stronger," he stated modestly. "But that doesn't mean I'm a match for your friends."

"Are you saying all three of them coerced you into crashing this party and getting yourself locked into this room with me?"

"There was no coercion involved."

"I thought so."

"They were just trying to prevent bloodshed."

"Whose?"

"Let's just say your fiancé didn't exactly greet me with a kiss."

She adjusted the drooping bodice higher on her chest. "And that surprised you? Honestly, Jake, when are you going to figure out that around here you are the kiss of death."

"You didn't used to think so."

"I was young and foolish," she said in self-defense.

"Two years younger, but no less foolish than you are at this moment."

"I beg your pardon?"

He shrugged. "Begging isn't going to get you out of this mess, Gentry. You're going to have to take some action."

"And just what would you suggest?"

"Put some clothes on and let's get out of here."

"That's exactly what they want me to do."

He looked at her, new amusement edging his smile. "You are the strangest mix of contradictions I've ever encountered. Are you ever going to figure out what *you* want, Liz?"

"I cannot believe you have the nerve to say that to me." The dress slipped down as she sucked in an exasperated breath. "You, of all people."

"Who better?" he countered. "I happen to believe there's a wonderful human being trapped behind that facade of perfection. A woman who makes mistakes and, if I may say so, is about to make the biggest one of her—"

"You may not say so! In fact, you may not speak to me at all. I'm not interested in your opinions, and for your information, the *only* mistake I ever made was letting you into my life."

He looked at her long and hard, and then he pulled out one of the chairs and sat in it, putting his feet on the table and infuriating her with his silence.

"Well, haven't you got anything to say for yourself?" she challenged finally.

"Cleo," he addressed the dog. "Kindly tell Ms. Northcross I've been instructed not to speak to her."

"Don't bother, Cleo. I don't care to hear anything Mr. Daniels has to say to you, either." She let the dress sag and had to jerk it up again. She turned toward the windows and then, realizing she was only covered in front, turned hastily around and kept her eye on him as she cautiously edged back until her hips brushed the credenza. "Sydney stole my clothes," she said.

Courtesy of the moonlight that poured through the windows, she watched his gaze slide downward from her shoulders, tantalizing her with admiration, arousing every nerve ending to a shivering and all-too-familiar awareness.

"Don't look at me," she said.

"There's no reason to be mad at me. You're the one who's losing her valuables right and left."

Her heart skipped a beat. The ring. Had he found the ring? "I don't know what you're talking about."

His eyebrows rose with easy humor. "You've lost your clothes. Which is a pretty valuable thing to lose...especially when you refuse to wear anything else."

"What else?" She all but dared him to confess. Then she'd nail him with her utter indifference. "What else have I lost?"

"Now, how could I know that?"

He knew, damn it. She could tell by the lazy way he looked at her. "You couldn't," she said. "You couldn't know anything of importance about me."

"Of course not." Extending his arms over his head, he stretched, linked his fingers and brought down his hands to flex them like a wrestler before a match. "And I certainly don't know how this—" he pointed to the band of gold on the little finger of his left hand "—came to be on the bottom of the pool today."

There seemed little point in denying she knew it was missing. "Give that to me, please."

"Finders keepers, losers weepers."

"Fine." She gave a complacent little shrug. "I was only going to have it melted down and made into cheap costume jewelry, anyway."

"Really?" He held out his hand and admired the ring. "In that case, you won't mind if I keep it."

Once, he'd made her so mad she'd thrown a fish at him. A live fish. The biggest fish she could get her hands around. She'd hit him right between the eyes, too. It had been one of the highlights of her life.

"Where's a trout when you need one," he said, his grin slow and annoying.

"Can't I even have a thought of my own without you crashing it?"

"I always was able to read you like a book."

"Unfortunately, you're still reading at a seventh-grade level." Her lips tightened, and to her horror, she felt the sting of angry tears. This was not the way she was supposed to spend the week before her wedding. "Would you just leave?"

"I told you I'm not allowed to leave yet. I have to wait here for Sonny and Pop."

"Well, if you . . . what? Sonny's on his way? Here? To this room?"

Jake nodded. "That's my understanding. He's bringing Pop to talk to me."

"Why does Pop want to talk to you?"

"He doesn't. I said I wanted to talk to him."

"What about?"

"I didn't say."

She pursed her lips. "I've got to get out of here. If Sonny finds me here . . . with you . . ."

"He could conceivably jump to the wrong conclusion," Jake observed. "Since you're not exactly dressed for casual conversation."

Suspicion returned like a homing pigeon. "This is another trick, isn't it? Sydney and Hillary cooked up this whole idea just so I'd put on this stupid dress. And they sent you in here with some cock-and-bull story about Sonny bringing Pop to this room to add a little extra incentive. Oh, boy, when I get my hands on them . . ."

"If I were you, I'd put on the dress . . . on the outside chance it isn't a cock-and-bull story and Sonny is actually on his way."

"And give in? I think not. I wouldn't wear this wedding gown now if it were the only piece of clothing in existence. I wouldn't wear it if I thought Sonny's entire family was going to walk through that door."

"Okay, but I hope you know what you're doing."

"As opposed to trusting you and my so-called friends? Oh, I believe I know exactly what I'm doing." She paced toward the table, holding the dress in front of her, sidestepping Cleo on the floor, and kicking the satin skirt out of her way as she went. "I'm going to open that door, walk across the hall to the ladies' room and find my dress."

He put his feet down. "I wouldn't do that if I were you."

"Of course you wouldn't," she snapped as she headed for the door, seething at the chicanery of her friends . . . her trusted friends. "You'd go to the men's room."

"It isn't a joke, Gen. Sonny is bringing Charlie here to see me."

"Give it up, Jake." As she rounded the end of the table, he pushed to his feet. She wondered irrelevantly how she could have forgotten how tall he was and how broad his shoulders were, and how she loved to run her hands... "I don't believe you," she said. "When I open that door, Hillary and Heather will be standing there and Sydney will have a camera to snap my picture in the wedding dress... just so I can never deny having worn it. I grew up with these women, remember. To my shame, I've even helped them pull pranks like this on other people. The jig is up."

He stepped in front of her, blocking her path. "If you open that door, it very well could be."

Looking up, she nearly got lost in the midnight blue of his eyes, but she caught her heart before memory won it over. "How noble of you, Jake, to want to protect me." She lined the words and her expression in sarcasm. "Thanks, but no thanks. I can take care of myself." She shoved the wedding gown into his hands and pushed him out of her way. "There. You wear it."

Jake looked thoughtfully at the gown. "Sonny wouldn't hit a guy in a dress, would he?"

"If he could get his hands on a fish, he might." She jerked open the door and sashayed into the hall, expecting a camera flash and a burst of laughter at her expense.

Instead, she heard Pop's voice first, his deep, blustery vowels impossible to miss even at a distance. Frozen in horror, she watched as her father and her fiancé turned the corner at the far end of the hall and stopped dead when they saw her.

"Gentry?" Sonny looked like he'd run flat into a brick wall.

"Gentry?" Pop didn't look quite so surprised.

"Holy cow." She popped back into the room and slammed the door, her breath coming in hard, panicked gasps as she leaned against it.

Jake stopped contemplating the satin and lace in his hands to look at her. "Didn't the flash go off?"

"No flash. No camera." She inhaled sharply to catch her breath. "Sonny...and Pop."

Jake held out the dress. "I did warn you."

"How was I supposed to know you were telling the truth?" She took the dress in both hands, then shoved it back to him. "Get out of sight...and no matter what, don't let anyone see you. Got it?"

"Where should I go?"

She glanced around the room. No closets. No chairs big enough to hide a man of Jake's size. Beneath the table was nothing but open space. There was a rap on the door.

"Gentry?" Sonny asked. "Are you in there?"

With a tight frown, she jerked her head toward the shadows on the far side of the door, motioning for Jake to stand there. Holding the wedding gown, he moved with a rustle of satin to the indicated hiding place and whispered, "Never let them see you sweat."

With that in mind, she cracked the door and peeped out, intensely aware that Jake was watching her every move, his gaze like a spotlight on her bare skin. "Sonny!" she exclaimed. "I am so glad to see you. Would you find out what's keeping Hillary?"

"Are you wearing your underwear?" Sonny asked, not easily swayed from first impressions.

"Well, of course she is. Whose underwear should she be wearing?" Pop elbowed Sonny out of the way and bent to peer through the crack. "What are you doing in there, daughter?"

"I'm waiting for Hillary to bring my dress."

Sonny's eye appeared above Pop's. "Why aren't you wearing your dress?"

"For a young man, you're awful concerned about why she's not wearing all her clothes." Pop shook his head and shuffled his weight for a better position. "What happened to your dress, Gentry?"

"I spilled something on it and Hillary is rinsing out the stain. I think she's in the ladies' room. Would you mind checking to see how much longer it will be?"

"We can't go in the ladies' room," Sonny said. "Are you in there by yourself?"

"What kind of question is that?" she replied.

"Yeah, what kind of question is that?" Pop elbowed Sonny, then pressed his eye to the opening, trying to see past her. "You *are* alone in there, aren't you?"

"Of course." She added an extra snap of irritation to the words and ignored a strong impulse to glance at Jake and see if he was still watching her... as if she couldn't tell by the shiver trailing at random intervals across her shoulders all the way to her toes.

"You're sure?" Sonny asked. "You're sure Daniels isn't in there with you?"

"Who?"

"Daniels."

"Jake?" She stalled for time, hoping her friends would come through in the end and bring back her clothes. "Don't be ridiculous. He wasn't invited to the party."

"Well, that didn't stop him." Sonny replied. "He's here somewhere."

"He came to see me," Pop supplied, straightening with the soft *umph* of aging. "Are you going to let us in there with you or not?"

"Not. I'm underdressed for...casual conversation."

"Then we better locate Hillary and find your clothes."

"Good idea."

Jake shifted his weight and the satin dress he held rustled with the movement, sounding like a drumroll in the quiet.

"What was that?" Sharp-eared Sonny didn't miss anything.

"What was what?" She frowned through the crack in the door.

"That rustling sound."

"I shuffled my feet. My nylons make that noise. See?" She slipped out of one pearl gray pump to scuff her stockinged foot across the carpet. It was sticky with dried-on ginger ale and made no sound at all.

"I don't hear anything." Sonny's original skepticism returned.

"Exactly my point. Now, will you please..." The satin rustled again, and, behind her back, she cautioned Jake to be still with a fluttery wave. He caught her hand and held it wrapped in the warmth of his, robbing her of whatever sensible thoughts still occupied her brain. "Please," she said again, totally oblivious to everything except the memory of his touch, the times he'd fed her imagination with nothing more than a stroke of his fingertip, the way his hands had caressed her, the titillating whisper of his tongue on her skin.... She closed her eyes for a second and swallowed the knot of remembrance in her throat.

"What's going on in there?" Sonny asked.

"Nothing," she whispered, regretting the truth of that...for an instant. Only an instant. "What do you mean what's going on in here?" Her voice puffed with insult. "I'm waiting, uncomfortably underdressed, I might add, for someone to bring me something to wear."

"Here." Sonny stepped away from the door and began to pull off his suit coat. "Put this on and come out here."

Jake squeezed her hand, causing her to glance at him. He shook his head. Right. Like she didn't know why *he* didn't want her to cover up. She widened the crack another inch, then another, staying carefully concealed behind the door while she waited for Sonny to hand over his jacket.

Jake pinched her lightly on the arm and she thumped his shin with her foot. Pop cleared his throat. Then he cleared it again. Gentry met his eyes with a frown and followed his gaze to the floor behind her, where ivory-colored satin sparkled like the light of an infant star in a newly born night. Square in the center of the "star," Cleo sat in uncharacteristic calm, the tip of her tongue just visible between her teeth, as if she were about to blow a raspberry. Contrasted against the background of the wedding gown train, the black Lab couldn't go unnoticed by anyone looking in through the opening in the door...and Sonny would know immediately that wherever Cleo was, he would find Jake there, too.

"Here." Sonny thrust the jacket through the opening just as Gentry slammed the door.

Chapter Six

The howl on the other side of the door was thick with pain. Gentry gasped and turned, wide-eyed, toward Jake. "I think I killed him," she whispered.

"He couldn't make that much noise if you had." Reaching for the knob, Jake opened the door to view the scene in the hallway.

While Sonny clutched his hand and paced a few feet in front of the door, Pop followed him like an over-grown mother hen. "Would you stop moving around and let me have a look at that?" Pop said. "It might be broken."

"It might be, at that," Sonny snapped, his voice rough with injury. "But I don't know what you think you can do about it."

"Well, I could moan and groan for you while you look at it." Pop's tone picked up a degree of irrita-tion. He had little sympathy for injuries not involving blood or unconsciousness. "I once broke my wrist in three places doing a stunt and never missed a single day of shooting. Now, hold still and let me look at that hand."

Gentry picked up Sonny's suit coat from the floor, hastily pulled it on over her clothes—or rather her lack thereof—and stepped out into the hall. "I'm so sorry, Sonny. I wasn't looking and didn't realize you... Does it hurt much?"

"Of course it hurts, Gentry." Pop glanced at her. "Didn't you ever get your finger smashed in a door?"

"This is more serious than a smashed finger." Sonny grimaced as he moved his hand, then tried to look as if it didn't hurt too badly when he turned to Gentry. "Didn't you see my hand?" he asked her. "I was passing my coat through the..." His face became a thundercloud as Jake stepped into the lighted hallway. "I ought to punch you in the nose," he said.

Jake shrugged. "I'd be careful of that hand if I were you. You don't want to slam it into anything as hard as my head."

"Oh, yes, I do. The satisfaction would be worth the pain. Fortunately for you, I have more sense than to waste a good punch on a man of your ilk."

"My *ilk* and I are vastly relieved."

"Stop it." Gentry stepped between them and laid her hand on Sonny's uninjured arm. "This is not the way it looks, Sonny. Jake wasn't in there with me."

"I may be in pain, Gentry, but I am not blind."

"Well, yes, technically we were in the same room, but we weren't there by choice. This is all because my three humor-impaired bridesmaids thought it would be funny to force me to put on that old wedding dress that Pop—" she glanced accusingly at her father "—bought and convinced Ben to send to me."

"I fail to see how that explains what he—" Sonny scowled at Jake "—was doing in that room with you... especially in your state of undress."

"Trust me, Sonny. Sydney and Hillary will explain it all to you, just as soon as I get my hands on them.

Right now, though, I'm more concerned that we take care of you.'' She pried his injured hand away from his protective hold and turned it gently from side to side. ''Do you think it's broken, Pop?''

Charlie bent to study Sonny's swollen hand. ''Wouldn't be surprised. One way or another, he's going to have to have it looked at by a doctor. There's bound to be one at this shindig.''

''I'll find out.'' Jake stepped around Gentry, brushing her arm as he passed, arousing a host of contradictory feelings. He wanted to stay with her, he wanted to stay away from her, but mostly, he wanted her to stop touching Sonny with such tender concern. ''Pop,'' he said as he moved on, ''why don't you get some ice from the kitchen. For the swelling.''

''Oh, right.'' Pop fell into step behind him. ''Good idea.''

''Gentry,'' Jake called over his shoulder, ''take him into the ladies' room, immerse that hand in cold water and keep it there until we get back.''

''Jake?'' Pop asked as they rounded the corner at the end of the hall. ''What was really going on in that room between you and my daughter?''

''Nothing,'' he answered with genuine regret. ''Nothing at all.''

''NOT A DOCTOR, NURSE or paramedic on the guest list,'' Jake said as he entered the ladies' room.

Gentry looked up from the sink where she was holding Sonny's hand immersed in ice cubes. Relief filtered through her at Jake's return. Her fiancé wasn't turning out to be a very compliant patient. ''The swelling seems to be stopping, but it's not going away.''

"Hasn't Pop come back with the ice?" Jake asked.

"He's gone for a second bucket." Sonny's teeth chattered on the words, and one look at his pale face told Jake it was time to get him to a doctor.

Grabbing a towel from the counter, he held it draped between his hands. "Put your hand in this and let's go."

"Where are we going?" Gentry asked.

"I'm going to take him to a hospital. My rental is parked right by the side doors." He wrapped the towel carefully around Sonny's hand, then grasped his arm to lend support. Sonny didn't protest, which confirmed Jake's suspicion that the man was in no shape to make this decision for himself. "Get on his other side, Gentry, in case he needs to lean on you."

"There's nothing wrong with my feet," Sonny said, but he didn't shake off either helping hand.

Gentry frowned across Sonny at Jake. "Shouldn't we call an ambulance?"

"The truck will be just as fast and it's already here. Let's go."

"I'd rather have an ambulance," Sonny muttered.

"I'm not real crazy about giving you a ride in my truck, either." Jake kept moving, propelling Sonny and Gentry through the ladies'-room door and down the hall. "But what can I say? I'm a nice guy, Harris. You just never gave me a chance."

"Hey!" Pop's voice barreled down the hall behind them. "Where are you going?"

"The hospital," Gentry called back. "Tell Mr. and Mrs. Harris what happened and that I'll call them as soon as we've seen a doctor, okay?"

"Can you take care of Cleo?" Jake added as they reached the end of the hall. "I don't know where she went, but you might check the hors d'oeuvre table."

"Okay," Pop called after them. "But what about this ice? Don't you think you better stick his hand in here during the trip?"

"No!" Sonny yelled, showing surprising strength for a man who could have passed for a ghost.

IN THE EMERGENCY ROOM of St. Joseph's Hospital, Jake leaned forward in the uncomfortable waiting-room chair, rested his elbows on his knees and loosely clasped his hands. The ring on his little finger felt unfamiliar and he couldn't seem to keep his other hand away from it. Like a sore spot, it attracted his attention and called for more tactile investigation. As if he didn't already know the cool, solid shape of it. As if he needed a reminder that it didn't belong on the finger it now encircled.

Down a hall of curtained rooms just around the corner, he could hear random voices discussing individual injuries and treatments, and from time to time, someone pushed aside a curtain and scurried away. Medical personnel he recognized by the muted sound of their rubber-soled shoes. Patients walked more slowly, if they walked at all. So far, there had been twice as many whirring noises from wheelchairs as shuffling footsteps, and it seemed like hours since he'd heard the crisp *clip, clip* of Gentry's heels.

His finger touched the ring again, and in disgust, he pushed back in the chair and crossed his arms at his chest. What was he doing in this emergency room with Gentry and her fiancé? For that matter, what was he doing in California at all? He could have rearranged his plans, rescheduled his visit, gone home as soon as he discovered Ben was away. Arthur, Ben's butler, had offered to make a reservation for him at a nearby resort, apologizing for the inconvenience. But he'd wanted to see Gentry. Regardless of how Ben's invitation had been couched, regardless of how easily Jake had allowed himself to be persuaded to accept it, they both had known the underlying objective, and once here, there was no force on earth that could have changed his mind.

So you've seen her, Daniels. Now what?

The *clip, clip* sound of her shoes on the tiled floor brought his thoughts to immediate order, and he waited, watching for her like a soldier in a crowd, seeking the only face that mattered. She paused in the doorway, looking for him, and his gaze slid to her shoes before meandering up the incredible length of her legs to the tweed suit coat that covered just enough of her to be provocative. He'd never seen anyone with as much style as Gentry...no matter whose clothes she was wearing.

"They're taking him to X ray now," she said as she dropped into the chair beside him, bringing a warmth to the dreary waiting room, stirring a pleasured response inside him. "Then they'll decide whether to put him in a cast or not."

"Is he feeling any better?"

She shrugged and slumped down until her head rested on the back of the chair. "Who can tell? He's the strong, silent type."

"Are *you* feeling better?"

"About what? Sonny? He'll recover. Cast or no cast, he'll be ready to go home in another hour or so.

Can you wait that long or should I call Pop to come get us?"

"I'm already here," he said carelessly. "And it isn't as if I have a hot date waiting for me back at the guest house."

"It's a good thing, too. Cleo might get jealous."

He nodded, wanting to regain the easy camaraderie that had always come so naturally for them, not knowing how to begin. With a sigh, Gentry closed her eyes, and he wanted, desperately, to reach over and take her hand with his. But he didn't. "You look tired."

"Too many champagne toasts."

"It'll all be over soon. Only six more days before the wedding."

"Six days and three bridesmaids with time on their hands. A dangerous combination."

"As if you wouldn't be head mischiefmaker if it was one of them who was getting married."

Her lips curved. "Did I ever tell you what I did to Sydney when—no, forget I said that. If I did tell you, I shouldn't have, and if I didn't, I'm certainly not going to now."

"Let's see. I know you persuaded her to get hypnotized the night before high-school commencement, and during the solemn ceremony of graduation, you cued her to stand up and sing 'Suzy Had a Steamboat.' I know she was the prime suspect when a certain teacher's underwear mysteriously disappeared out of his locker and that you used the incident to blackmail her into using quotes from the *Kama Sutra* in her term paper."

"I never told you that," Gentry said with a lack of true concern. "You must have heard it from her."

"What makes you think so?"

"Because she thought up the term-paper thing on her own. All I did was loan her the book."

"And the boxer shorts?"

"It's a mystery to this day how they got up on that flagpole."

"Loyalty, the mark of a true friend."

"Syd and I have had our moments. Tonight not being one of the more memorable ones."

"Speak for yourself. I plan to remember it fondly and often. It's not every day I attempt to talk a woman into putting on a dress when she says she'd rather parade around in her bra and panties."

Gentry's eyes opened with a sparkle of disagreement. "I wasn't *parading* and you know it."

"We'll ask Sonny. He can cast the deciding vote."

"Don't even consider mentioning this to him." Her voice firmed for battle, and a well-remembered animation shimmered in her green eyes. "He thinks I'm very well behaved and I intend to make sure he never changes his mind."

"Won't good behavior be a little wearing on your nerves?"

"No. I have until Friday night to repay Sydney and Hillary for tonight's prank. After Saturday, I'll be as good as gold for the rest of my natural life."

"Which will last roughly until Sunday morning."

"My natural life or being as good as gold?"

"Don't change for him, Gentry. He shouldn't ask it of you, and if he does, you should refuse."

"Really?" The sudden chill in her voice caught him off guard. "Now, isn't it funny you should say that? I refused to change for you, Jake, and look what happened." Pushing up from the chair in a single lithe movement, she walked away, and he had to sit alone in the waiting room and listen to the angry *clip, clip* of her footsteps as she went back to Sonny...again.

"YOU TWO HAVE A LOT to answer for," Gentry said without preamble when she returned to the waiting room a short while later to find Sydney and Hillary ensconced on either side of Jake. Despite her annoyance, she was glad to see them. Glad, too, that their presence meant no more private conversations with Jake, no more opportunities for the past to pop up and punch her in the gut, no more looking at her ring on his little finger and fighting the impulse to ask for it back, no more watching him push the wayward dark hair off his forehead and remembering how often she had done that for him...and with such pleasure. Sitting beside Jake had been both comfortably reassuring and distressingly familiar—every glance, every movement, a reminder of all the reasons she had eloped with him two years before.

She moved to the unoccupied chair next to Hillary and sat down. "This is all your fault, you know."

Three pairs of eyes fastened on her and shared not a trace of guilt among them.

"Whose fault?" Hillary asked. "We weren't anywhere near Sonny when you slammed the door on him."

"You're not trying to blame us because you broke Sonny's hand, are you?"

"You know exactly what I blame you for and don't think we're going to have a good laugh about this later, because it isn't funny."

"No," Jake said. "It certainly isn't. Just ask Sonny."

Sydney looked at him and then sighed. "Well, it sounded funny at the time. I'm sorry, Gentry."

"Me, too." Hillary made a face. "It was Heather's idea, anyway."

"Mmm-hmm." Gentry knew Heather shared the blame, but it wasn't difficult to figure out who had made up the deciding majority. "What have you done with her?"

"Sidney and I offered to help, but you know Heather. Since she was the one who snuck the dress out of the house, bribed the limo driver to put it in the trunk, and managed to get the gown into the country club without anyone seeing it, she felt it was her responsibility to return it safely."

"Heaven forbid that any harm should come to that dress," Gentry said sarcastically. "How did you find it in the first place? I thought I'd hidden it especially well."

Hillary laughed easily, with the assurance of long friendship. "We know all your hiding places, Gentry. Just like you know all of ours."

"Obviously we know too much about one another."

"Not true," Sydney said. "There's one thing Hil and I don't know."

"And that is?"

"Did you put on the dress?"

Gentry lifted her eyebrows in triumph. "I never once considered it."

"Really?" Hillary asked. "Even when Jake came in?"

"Tell me the truth, Jake." Sydney patted his arm persuasively. "Was she wearing the wedding dress when you walked in?"

His mouth formed that funny little smile, the one Gentry found exasperating and endearing, the one that made her think something amused him, but nothing he would tell. "I'll plead the Fifth," he said.

"She was!" Sydney smiled broadly and leaned forward to look across the other two at Gentry. "You were."

"I wasn't."

"Then, what were you wearing?" Hillary posed the obvious question and then blinked in surprise at the obvious answer. "Gentry, you weren't wearing your underwear!"

"She was," Sydney said in disgust. "You are the stubbornest woman I've ever met, Gentry Elizabeth. Is that all you're wearing now, too?"

"I have on Sonny's suit coat, as you can see." Gentry stood so they could see exactly what she'd been forced to wear because of them. "It's not a precise fit, but it's adequate."

Hillary's forehead furrowed with a frown. "That depends on your definition of *adequate.*"

"But you were only in your underwear when Jake walked in, weren't you?" Sydney persisted.

"I closed my eyes," he said.

"Sure you did." Hillary called his bluff. "Tonight worked out even better than we hoped, Syd. I can't wait to tell Heather."

"Tell her what?" Gentry asked, a new irritation creeping into her voice. "You put Jake in the room with me, hoping what exactly would happen?"

Under Sydney's cautioning glance, Hillary lapsed into an uncomfortable silence.

"If you thought..." Gentry shook her head, unable to believe the expanding agenda her friends had developed. "Listen, you two, I am going to marry Sonny on Saturday. There's nothing you can do to prevent it and there's certainly no reason you should try. Jake has no more interest in me than I do in him." She looked to him for confirmation. "Tell them."

"Absolutely true," he said, and she thought it hadn't been necessary to say it with such swift conviction.

"See?" she addressed her friends. "If it wasn't for your pointless interfering, Sonny wouldn't be in the emergency room with a broken hand."

"Is it broken?" Hillary asked. "For sure?"

"We haven't heard yet." Jake stood and stretched, catching admiring looks from two nurses passing by.

"Stop that," Gentry commanded, forcing from her mind the image of how he looked when he did that without his shirt... or pants.

"What?" He looked down at her, clearly puzzled. "You want to see me writhing on the floor with a leg cramp?"

"I'd like to see that." Sydney scooted forward in her seat. "First the right leg, then the left, if you don't mind."

"Get a grip, Syd," Hillary suggested. "Looks like Sonny is ready to go."

A nurse's aide pushed Sonny's wheelchair into the waiting room. "Harris," she announced as if she were calling bingo, instead of his support group.

"Here." Gentry hurried over and knelt beside the chair, glancing first at the cast that reached from his knuckles to his elbow, then into his dilated and hazy-looking eyes. "Is it broken?" she asked.

"Smashed." His reply was a trifle slurred, his answer more than a tad accusing. "You smashed my finger," he said with a frown.

The nurse's aide set the wheels on the wheelchair so they wouldn't roll. "He has a couple of broken fingers and some nasty bruises. The doctor gave him some pain medication."

"Pills have no effect on me," Sonny declared with a sagging smile.

"He's pretty woozy," the aide explained. "I expect he'll sleep like a baby tonight. He may not even remember much of what happened."

"That's good." Gentry looked up to meet the woman's curious stare and smiled hesitantly. "Good that he won't have any pain, I mean. Will he need more medication later?"

"The doctor gave him a prescription." The nurse's aide tapped Sonny's shirt. "It's in his pocket. You may not want to get it filled, unless he needs it. Just check in with the cashier, and then he's free to go."

"Hey, babe." Sonny frowned up at the white-haired aide. "You can keep your perskripsh ... perskrtsh ... pills."

"Where's your insurance card, Sonny?" Gentry asked him, but received no response. She caught his face in her palms. "Sonny? Where is your insurance card?"

"I have a high tol'rance ..." He moved his mouth around the word, practicing. "Tall-rans. Tall-rans. I have a high tallrans for pain."

Gentry shook her head and rose. Jake touched her arm, drawing her aside. "I'll take care of the bill," he said. "You get Hillary and Sydney to help you take him home."

"They can't," she said, wanting to keep his dependable, reassuring support close at hand. "Hillary's car only seats two, and even if I borrowed it and you drove them home, I doubt I can handle Sonny by myself."

"Do you want me to deliver him?"

She did. She wanted nothing more than to go home and forget this embarrassing evening altogether. "I'd better stay with him," she said. "But if you'd drive us to the hotel, I'd be very grateful."

"You're sure you wouldn't rather have Sydney and Hillary do it?"

"They'd probably take his clothes and leave him wearing the wedding dress." She met his gaze and knew her motives were more complicated than she was willing to admit. "So, I can count on you?"

"Always." He held her gaze for another moment, until her heart caught on a sliver of regret. "You'd better rescue your fiancé," he said, nodding to where Sydney was in serious conversation with Sonny. "No telling what she's writing on his cast."

HEATHER FLIPPED ON the light and frowned when she saw the wedding gown in a hastily discarded pile on the floor. She should have known better than to play such a tasteless joke on Gentry. Of course, Gen could have put on the dress and not been so stubborn about it, but still, the whole plot had been Heather's idea. And now Sonny's hand was probably broken, Gentry was mad, the party had come to an abrupt conclusion, and she was left to pick up the gown and take it home. Some magic, she thought as she stooped to gather the ivory puddle into her arms.

The fabric flowed over her arms in a cool satin stream and escaped to the floor. Slippery stuff. She scooped the bundle into her arms a second time and straightened . . . and felt the dress slip out of her grasp to pool on the carpet in a whispery rustle.

With a frown, Heather rubbed her hands down the seams of her linen skirt before she stooped to pick up the dress once again. This time, she couldn't get enough of a grip on the material even to gather it into a manageable bundle. No matter how she gripped it, the material slid through her fingers like cornstarch, refusing to be bunched, clumped or otherwise crumpled.

This was embarrassing, she thought, and was glad Sydney and Hillary had gone to the hospital to check on Gentry and Sonny. If they saw her struggling to hold on to a dress, they'd never let her live it down.

Standing there in the meeting room, she decided she must be imagining the difficulty. How hard could it be to lift several yards of satin and lace off the floor? With renewed determination, she bent down, picked up one sleeve and held it firmly between her finger and thumb as she rose.

Success. The dress came with her, rising like a harvest moon from the dark-colored carpet. Smiling, she realized she'd only thought she had a good grasp on it before. After all, it was only a dress. But the moment she tried to gather the skirt into her arms, it poured through her hands like water over a rock. No matter where she grappled for a hold on the fabric or how securely she clenched her fist around it, the dress slid away from her and returned to the floor.

Frustrated, Heather braced one foot against the facing on either side of the doorway, bent from the waist and gripped the bodice of the dress with both hands. Taking a deep breath, she closed her eyes and did some mental imaging, preparing herself to get the silly thing off the floor once and for all. After she'd taken herself through the procedure in her imagination, she wiggled her shoulders and decided on the count of three that she'd jerk the dress into her arms in one concentrated move. With a wiggle of her hips, she tightened her grip on the fabric. "One...two... three."

"Could you use some assistance?" Behind her, a deep, husky voice broke the silence like a karate chop to the center of a brick.

Her heart leaped into her throat and she spun to face the speaker. Within the confines of the door frame, however, she had little room to maneuver. Her foot came down in the middle of the satin train, and just as she recognized Mitch, the dress slid out from under her and she landed on her butt, surrounded by the sneaky satin. She found herself looking up at the only one of Sonny's friends she had ever found even remotely attractive.

Who was she kidding? Mitch was drop-dead gorgeous. The kind of man women fought over. The kind of man who had his choice of women. The kind of man who dated tall, classy blondes like Hillary, not short, shy brunettes like her. He had a formidable reputation—a new love interest every four months, three a year with zero commitments. He was exactly the kind of man she avoided on principle, and precisely the type she secretly yearned after.

"Heather?" The sound of her name on his lips made her forget all the clever things she might have said, and even the inane reply she knew she actually would say as soon as she got her heart out of her throat. "Are you all right?"

She nodded in sheepish silence.

He extended his hand to her. "I saw you from the clubhouse," he said. "It looked like you might be having a little difficulty."

Swallowing her shyness, she determined to make some sort of vocal reply. "A little," she whispered.

"That's a beautiful dress." From a distance, his smile had fascinated her. Up close and personal, it was downright devastating. "What...uh...are you trying to do with it?"

She wished she had a witty answer, but her wits had deserted her...just when she needed them most. As if Mitch would remember anything she said, witty or otherwise. "I can't hold on to it," she admitted with a sigh. "The fabric is very slippery."

"Maybe if I helped, between the two of us, we could do it."

Heather wasn't sure she could stand on her own. Her knees felt rubbery and weak. "Maybe," she said.

"You want to give it a try?"

"Uh, sure." But she continued to sit on the floor, staring up at him.

"It might be easier to pick up the dress if you weren't sitting on it."

"Right. I wasn't thinking." Warmth flooded her cheeks with color. "You make me nervous."

"Well, you scare me to death, so we're even. Now, give me your hand."

She frowned up at him. "Is that your best pickup line?"

"I don't know," he said with a smile. "Is it working?"

"I'm still on the floor."

"Obviously, then, you're going to take a little extra effort."

She was flattered beyond reason, and determined not to let him know. He pulled her to her feet, but didn't let go of her hand. Heather stared at his fingers, long, slender and strong, curled around hers as if he were holding a delicate and perfect rose. When she raised her eyes to his, a sense of wonder made her heart skip a beat. "You're flirting with me," she said, surprised to realize it was true. "Nothing about me could possibly frighten you."

"You're the kind of woman who makes a man think he could spend the rest of his life just watching you walk, and talk, and laugh. For a guy like me, you're downright terrifying."

"I knew you could come up with a better pickup line if you put your mind to it." She stooped to gather the wedding gown into her arms, wishing she could be like Hillary and know just what to say, how to flirt with Mitch. As she straightened, the fabric slipped through her fingers like sand. Mitch grabbed for it...and it slipped away from him, as well. He laughed. So did she. They stooped together, in perfect sync, and as they touched the satin, something sparked...not as bright as a camera flash, but a definite twinkle of light...and the world stopped turning.

They stood, each holding a shoulder of the wedding gown, looking into each other's eyes and aware of something electric in the air around them. For what seemed like forever, they stood facing each other, united by several yards of satin and lace, a few feet apart, neither wanting to be the first to let the moment—or the dress—go.

Then, just as suddenly as it seemed to have stopped, the world began to turn again.

"Could we go out sometime?" he asked hesitantly, as if he wanted to get the words just right.

"Out? You mean, together?"

"Dates generally work better that way."

"Dates?" she repeated like a silly parrot. "You're asking me on a date?"

"Well . . . yes. If you want to. I didn't know if . . ." He looked uncomfortable and . . . nervous. Mitch McAlister, experienced and deadly with the opposite sex, was nervous about asking her for a date. "You're probably seeing someone else," he said. "I should have known someone like you wouldn't be free."

"I'm free," she said in a rush. "I'm really free."

He smiled again . . . and she wondered if love happened like this for everyone.

"What would you like to do?" he asked. "On our first date?"

"Anything you want."

"You shouldn't say things like that to guys like me. I might be tempted to take you at your word."

A new confidence spiraled up from her toes. "Oh, I know how to handle guys like you."

He shook his head. "I think I'm in serious trouble here. Maybe I should propose right now and get it over with."

"Propose?" Her confidence slipped and then surged to a new level. "I wouldn't even consider marrying you, Mitch. Not until after our first date."

Then, knowing it was the right thing to do, she let the magic wedding dress slip through her fingers as she

put her hands around his neck and drew his lips down
to hers.

SONNY'S SNORE was obnoxiously loud inside the cab
of Jake's truck. Gentry shifted her weight, scooting
closer to Jake, as her fiancé's sleepy head clonked onto
her shoulder. His heavy breathing stopped for a moment, then resumed with a vengeance, and she tilted
her head away from the noise...until she touched
Jake's shoulder and jerked upright again.

There were worse things than having Sonny snore in
her ear...like the electric awareness of being so close
to Jake...like the insistent knowledge that her body
distinctly remembered and craved the warm, muscu-
lar angles of the body on her left while it registered
only vague discomforts about the body on her right.
It wasn't fair, she thought. Sandwiched between the
man she was going to marry and the man she had once
been married to, she felt like a traitor to both.

"For someone who has a high tolerance for pain, he
seems to have taken a truckload of medication."

Gentry sighed and tried to adjust her position again,
drawing away from Jake and moving closer to Sonny.
"I'm sure they gave him a strong dosage," she said, on
the defensive for no good reason. "Sonny does have
a high tolerance for pain."

"He's clearly a man among men." Jake drove with
one hand draped over the top of the steering wheel and
one loosely curled around the side, and it reminded her
of the way he'd held her when they danced. So long
ago the memory should have lost its charm.

"There's no need to be snide," she said irritably.
"He's had a rough day."

"Yes, well, he isn't the only one."

They drove in silence for a few minutes. "Why did you come back, Jake?" she asked finally. "Why couldn't you have left well enough alone?"

He turned to look at her, the intensity of his expression making her very uncomfortable. "Well enough?" he repeated. "Is that what you've settled for, Liz? Well enough?"

"You know what I meant."

"Yes. The question is, do you?"

Sonny breathed in with a loud, low rumble.

"I refuse to engage in this meaningless dialogue with you, Jake. Every conversation we've ever had has ended in this *I know what you said, even if it isn't what you said* war of words."

"I remember several conversations that didn't end with *words* at all."

She couldn't believe he'd said that, and her gaze swung to his profile in surprise. "I can't believe you said that," she repeated her thoughts aloud. "But that's always been the trouble with you, Jake. You say whatever you think, whenever the thought crosses your mind, and you have no regard for whose feelings might get—"

"Hurt?" he suggested. "Have I hurt your feelings, Liz?"

"Lately? Certainly not. I only wish you hadn't delivered the wedding dress."

His laugh was ruefully short. "I knew this would all wind up being my fault. You haven't changed at all."

"I have changed, Jake," she said tightly. "I've learned I don't have to argue with you. Take the next exit and turn right."

He followed her directions precisely, and with a few more stilted instructions, he pulled the truck up in front of the Hotel Regency Pacific. Jake opened the door and stepped out. "You stay put," he said. "I'll get him inside and up to his room."

Ignoring his suggestion, she slid across the supple leather and scolded herself for noticing it retained the warmth of his body. "You'll need some help. He has a room key in his wallet, but it's the card type. I don't know his room number, and it doesn't look like he's going to wake up long enough to tell us."

"I'll manage." Jake tried to close the door, shutting her inside, but she caught the handle and held it open. When she slid from the seat to stand on the concrete pavement in front of the hotel, he stayed where he was and she brushed against him, entirely against her wishes . . . at least against her more sensible wishes. "You stay here, Liz. I'll take care of Sonny."

"If anyone should stay in the truck, it ought to be you." She gave the door a shove to close it and started around to the other side. Just as she reached the passenger door, her heel caught on an uneven bit of pavement and she had to balance against the side of the truck while she adjusted the fit of her shoe. She felt Jake's gaze sweep over her raised leg as he came up behind her to open the truck door.

Sonny's snore rumbled into the night air like a Mack truck as he slid into a semireclining position on the bench seat.

"We may not be able to pry him out of there with a crowbar." Jake glanced toward the glassed-in lobby. "Maybe I should ask the doorman to help me."

She followed his gaze to where the barrel-chested, stern-faced doorman stood just inside the front doors. "A good doorman would already be out here offering assistance," she said. "I'll just have a word with him."

"Don't do that."

She stopped in midstep. "Why not?"

He grabbed Sonny's ankles and pulled him forward, not even causing a change in the pattern of snoring. "Don't make me spell this out for you, Liz. Just get in the truck and let me deal with the doorman."

"Spell it out, Jake."

He pursed his lips in a frown, then canvassed the distance between her pearl gray high heels and the hem of Sonny's suit coat with a pointed gaze.

Gentry suppressed the impulse to bend her knees and make the coat seem longer. "You're surely not trying to imply that just because I'm wearing Sonny's jacket, I shouldn't go inside the hotel, are you?"

"You shouldn't go anywhere near a hotel looking like you do at this minute. A doorman could reasonably get the wrong idea."

"Because I'm wearing a man's jacket?" she asked in a sudden huff.

"That, and because you have a certain...shall we say, *tousled* look."

She cocked her head to the side, offended by the direction he was heading with this. "Are you saying I look like a tramp?"

"You *look* sensational. I only meant that Harris is very careful about appearances and he might prefer not to give the hotel management anything to talk about...if you know what I mean."

"No, I'm afraid I don't. Nor do I care to know. Now, wait here and I'll be right back...*with* the doorman."

JAKE WATCHED HER SASHAY up the hotel steps like a duchess, admiring her savoir faire, as well as her long, elegant legs. Her heels made saucy little clicks against the terrazzo tiles, and the vent in the back of Sonny's jacket parted with each step to reveal a tantalizing glimpse of derriere. Inside the lobby, a bellhop tripped over his own feet trying to bypass the scowling doorman and open the door for her.

Gentry opened the door for herself, and with her chin at a dangerous angle, she marched past the doorman and up to the registration desk. Although Jake couldn't hear what was being said, he could follow the conversation by the set of her shoulders and the toss of her fire red hair. When she put her hands on her hips, he groaned, knowing nothing good could come of that.

Within a matter of minutes, she was being ushered out the door by the scowling doorman, who seemed impervious to the demands she made along the way. As the door closed behind her, she stared in amazement at Jake. "They asked me to leave," she said. "I went up to the desk to report their slovenly doorman and to ask for Sonny's room number, and the clerk wouldn't let me finish a sentence before he advised me he would call security if I didn't leave immediately."

"Hmmm." Jake grasped Sonny's ankles and began to slide him out of the truck once again.

"Hmmm? That's it? That's all you have to say?"

"If you think I'm going to try to persuade the management of this hotel that you're appropriately dressed, you can think again."

"I was dressed like this at the hospital and no one asked me to leave."

''I don't believe the emergency room has the same problem with uh . . . solicitors . . . as the hotel does.''

Her swiftly indrawn breath signaled a brewing storm. ''Are you suggesting that anyone—excuse me, any *doorman*—would reasonably assume I'm a prostitute simply because I'm wearing an ill-fitting jacket in a hotel?''

Jake dropped Sonny's legs and turned around to face her. ''Could we please discuss this later? Although I'm sure getting booted out of a hotel lobby is hard on your ego, it really isn't a serious problem. Your fiancé, on the other hand—''

Umph. Jake whirled in time to see Sonny slide off the bench seat and crumple into a lazy L-shape inside the angle of the truck cab and the open door. His head drooped awkwardly onto his chest and he sagged against the truck like a rag doll.

''Aa-aa-aah!'' A woman's scream ricocheted out of the dark, somewhere off to the right. ''Help! Help!''

Jake spun toward the outcry, ready to race to the rescue, his muscles tensed for fight or flight. Gently, too, turned, backing unconsciously against his body for protection. In a split second, he processed a dozen different emotions—from fear to tenderness—and knew they were all centered on the woman beside him. Placing his hands on her shoulders, he moved her behind him. ''Stay here. Let me find out what's hap—''

''Help! Murder! Call the police! 911! Help, somebody help!'' The woman's voice rose like August temperatures, drawing the doorman outside to investigate, corralling the attention of a group of men who were leaving a supper club across the street, and acquiring quite a crowd with her frenzied cries.

Until the woman, who wore the uniform of the hotel housekeeping crew, stepped out of the shadowed portico and tossed her cigarette aside, Jake really thought she had stumbled onto a murder. But her pointing finger, though shaky, was dead-on, and he followed its indication straight to Sonny's limp and, to all appearances, lifeless body.

Oh, hell, Jake thought.

Chapter Seven

"Pain medication," Gentry repeated to the police officer for the third time. "I don't know what kind or how much he was given. I also don't know what is written on the prescription, but it is clearly a doctor's handwriting."

She was weary of questions. The policeman—his name badge read Sergeant P. Henry Orange—was openly suspicious of her, even though it was obvious she hadn't murdered Sonny, because it was obvious Sonny was still breathing. His snores practically rattled the crystal chandelier overhead in the hotel lobby.

If he'd made that dreadful noise when Mrs. Deets, one of the hotel's housekeepers, first saw him slide out of the truck, she wouldn't have mistaken him for a dead body. But Sonny had slept like a baby during those awful minutes when the crowd gathered and the accusing stares swung from Jake to Gentry...only to linger suspiciously on the skimpy length of her jacket. She had never been so embarrassed in her life.

"Now, where were the three of you going?" Sergeant P. Henry Orange asked again.

Gentry sighed audibly before she answered. "We were coming from the emergency room where, as I believe I mentioned, Mr. Harris was treated for a broken hand.''

The officer made a note. ''And how did he break his hand?''

''I shut a door on it.''

''Accidentally?''

She gritted her teeth. ''Of course it was an accident. I certainly wouldn't injure my fiancé on purpose.''

Sergeant Orange looked up from his notepad. ''Ah, but what if he wasn't your fiancé?''

''What if he wasn't my fiancé?'' she repeated with a frown. ''What are you getting at?''

''The facts, ma'am. Just the facts.''

She glanced across the lobby at Jake, who was being questioned by a second officer. Her frustration level rose considerably as she watched him stand and demonstrate a fly cast. ''Couldn't you go over and get a few of the facts from him?'' She pointed an accusing finger at Jake, but Sergeant P. Henry Orange merely scribbled more notes in his notepad.

''You seem angry.'' He glanced at Jake. ''Would you shut his hand in a door if you had the opportunity?''

''Of course not.'' She leaned back in the chair and studied her interrogator. Maybe she was going about this all wrong. ''Look, Sergeant Orange. I don't know what you think happened here tonight, but it's all very innocent. No one was murdered. Mrs. Deets admitted she never misses an episode of 'Murder, She Wrote.' She was taking her smoke break and she overreacted when she saw Sonny fall out of the truck. You could probably save a lot of time and paperwork if you'd call the hospital and have them verify that we left there less than an hour ago."

"Mmm-hmm." Sergeant Orange licked the blunt lead of his stubby pencil before he made another entry in his notebook. "It's my job to ask you questions," he said. "For the report."

"Do you have to write a report every time there's a simple misunderstanding?"

His glasses slid down his nose when he looked at her, and he jabbed them back into place with one finger. "What if it turns out not to be simple? What if he—" he nodded at the sofa where Sonny was sawing logs "—isn't your fiancé at all, but a guy you picked up tonight? And what if he—" he nodded across the lobby where Jake and the other policeman were chatting amiably "—is really your partner? And what if the two of you—" the nod swung to her "—were planning to rob him?" The nod returned to Sonny. "But the Mickey Finn you slipped him took effect before you could get him back to his hotel room, and you got caught in the act by Mrs. Deets. What about that?"

She stared at P. Henry. "I thought you were interested in the facts."

"There's facts, and then there's facts. I've spent twenty-one years on the force, ma'am, and believe me, I've learned not to take anything at face value."

"So what will it take to convince you that he—" she nodded at Sonny "—accidentally got his hand caught in a door? And that he—" she tilted her head in Jake's general direction "—drove us to the hospital. Which was where he—" she tilted her head back at Sonny "—was given some pain medication. And that put him into such a sound sleep that he didn't wake up when he fell out of his—" she nodded at Jake again "—truck."

Sergeant Orange pursed his lips, wrote furiously, then jabbed his pencil against the notebook to make an emphatic period. "What would it take to convince me?" He repeated her words in a considering mumble. "Now, that's an interesting question. You wouldn't, by any chance, be thinking you could bribe me, would you?"

She straightened in the hotel lobby chair. "I believe this is getting dangerously close to being harassment."

A faint smile tweaked the corner of his mouth. "Now, ma'am, let's stick to the facts. You posed an interesting question and I asked you what you meant by it."

Stoked by weary frustration, her temper flared. "I *meant,* I can't take this anymore. You've worn down my resistance. I'll tell you the whole sordid story. Just don't ask me any more questions!"

"Now we're gettin' somewhere." Sergeant P. Henry Orange flipped to a clean page in his notebook and poised the pencil lead above it. "Let 'er rip."

She did.

"How was I supposed to know he'd think I was confessing? He didn't believe anything I said up until then."

At the police station, Gentry and Jake sat side by side on a bench that was harder than it had been when they first were told to sit there. The room they were in was crowded, noisy and a good ten degrees warmer than it should have been. Across the room, Sergeant P. Henry Orange and two other policemen were sitting between two cluttered desks, having what appeared to be a rather heated discussion.

"It should have occurred to you that fabricating a crime might tend to annoy an officer of the law."

"You should have heard the fabrication he came up with," was her weak defense.

Jake's eyes met hers with the unspoken truth that her impulse had landed them on this bench, a mere step away from a night in jail.

"You can stop giving me that look now," she said.

"This look?" Jake narrowed his eyes accusingly.

"No," she answered irritably. "The one where you squinch your lips together and lower your eyebrows in that unattractive scowl."

"Oh, this look." He squinched his lips and lowered his brows. "Which one should I use for my mug shot?"

"I don't care. They're equally disagreeable." Her gaze followed a man in handcuffs as he was led past their bench, then she turned a worried frown to Jake. "You don't think they'll really put us in jail, do you?"

"Tough call," he said, seeing no reason to make her feel better just yet. If she'd only kept her cool in the first place, they wouldn't be in this predicament now. "You did confess to some pretty amazing crimes."

"Anyone who's ever been to the movies would have recognized the scene. I took it almost verbatim from Pop's performance in *Speak No Evil*. He won the Oscar, for Pete's sake."

"Just your luck to give an Oscar-winning performance to a policeman who believes *Dragnet* was the only good movie to come out of Hollywood in the last decade."

She slumped on the uncomfortable wooden bench. "I knew it was pointless to expect you to understand."

"I understand, Gentry, but I can't find it in my heart to offer you much sympathy. If you'd just kept a handle on your temper, you could have been in the hotel suite right now, listening to Harris shake the rafters with his snoring. And I could have been snug in my own bed, dreaming of a cure for deviated septums."

Her sigh was uncharacteristically regretful. "You're right, Jake. I have no right to complain when I dragged you into this. You were wonderful to stay with me at the hospital and afterward and... I'm sorry. I shouldn't have lost my temper, no matter what Sergeant Orange said to me."

He didn't think he'd ever heard that note of humility in her voice before. Maybe she really was sorry. "Would you repeat that, please?" he said. "I'm not sure I heard you correctly."

"I said, I'm sorry."

"No, not that. The part where you described me as... how did you phrase it... uh, *wonderful*. Wasn't that the word?"

She cut her gaze to him. "You must have misunderstood. I would never refer to my ex-husband as wonderful."

"I'm not your ex-husband, remember? That marriage was wiped out, expunged from the record, it never happened." He crossed his arms at his chest and leaned his head against the concrete block wall behind him. "So, you can describe me as *wonderful*. Unless, of course, you'd prefer to substitute something else, like, oh, let's say... *magnificent*."

A small, husky, hollow note of humor tripped from her lips. "Why am I laughing?" she said. "Nothing that has happened tonight is the least bit funny."

"Don't give up hope. The night isn't over yet."

Leaning back beside him, she drummed her fingers against her tweed-covered arm, unconsciously brushing his sleeve with each rhythmic tap, sending a ripple of quiet pleasure through him with her familiar nearness. "You know," she said slowly, "now that I think about it, there is something funny about what happened tonight."

He nodded. "You know, you're right. When Mrs. Deets put her ear close to Sonny's mouth to see if he was breathing, and he broke the sound barrier with a sudden snore, I thought seriously about laughing aloud. Probably would have, if the hotel doorman hadn't been frisking me for concealed weapons at the time."

Gentry shook her head. "No, the funny thing is that after all that's happened, I still don't know what you were doing at the country club. I'm not sure if my friends used you to try and trick me into putting on the wedding dress, or if you were there for some other reason."

"I had a sudden desire to apply for membership."

"Stick to the facts, Jake."

"Okay, Cleo had a sudden desire to become a member."

"She's already a member, by virtue of belonging to Ben."

"Well, there you have it, then. She wanted to play a few holes of golf. Practice her follow-through."

"They don't allow dogs on the greens."

"No wonder she wanted to wait until after dark."

"Tell me why you crashed the party, Jake, or I'll convince Sergeant P. Henry Orange you have facts you're trying to conceal."

"That isn't funny, Gentry. I knew Harris would have a detrimental effect on your sense of humor."

"Leave Sonny out of this."

"Believe me, I'd like to, but you insist on keeping him around."

"As if you care."

He turned his head to look at her, wondering if she regretted the abrupt way their marriage had ended. If maybe she, too, wished they hadn't given up quite so easily. "I care, Liz. I care very much."

Sighing, she closed her eyes and continued to rest her head against the gray wall, her hair a bright splatter of color against the dreary concrete blocks. "You know, Jake, when I left the Two-Penny Lodge that day, it never occurred to me you wouldn't be hot on my heels. Imagine my surprise when two weeks later, you hadn't even phoned to see if I made it home all right."

So, the breakup was his fault. The responsibility, his. If only he'd followed her... If only he hadn't been too proud to make a second conciliatory gesture... "Did it ever occur to you that the phone lines run both ways, Liz? You could, at least, have acknowledged my apology."

She opened her eyes. "What apology? You surely don't mean that cryptic little note you didn't even bother to sign."

"What note? I sent a package."

"No, you didn't. You sent a card that read '*Hasta la Vista*, Baby! Bon Voyage, Goodbye and Lots of Luck!' Sentiments courtesy of Hallmark. I thought at the time that the least you could have done was draw in a happy face."

"I didn't send a card, Gentry," he said. "And what makes you think I was happy when you left?"

"Oh, right. I remember what you said during that last fight."

"Well, refresh my memory, because I don't."

"I don't remember exactly, but it was something about how all I wanted was to change you into the kind of man you detested, that I expected you to make all the concessions and that only a spineless idiot would agree to the kind of life-style I was demanding, and that you weren't about to become a henpecked husband, and that I should stop trying to destroy your individuality and spend my free time learning how to cook a decent meal." She pressed her hands together, fingertip to fingertip, and brought the resulting pyramid to rest beneath her chin. "At least, I think that was the gist of it."

Jake didn't remember the quarrel quite that way, but in the interest of discovery, he decided not to offer his version. "So what part of it sent you packing? My defense of male individuality or the remark about learning to cook?"

"It was your untimely decision to go fishing. I decided, if you could run away from the problem, then so could I."

"And all this time I thought you left because you were too stubborn to admit I was right about your cooking." Her lips tightened at that and he bit back a surge of satisfaction. If she could still get mad at him, maybe... "In all honesty, Liz, I did not send that card."

"Then who did? And don't call me Liz."

"Don't be so touchy, Gentry. As for the card, I don't know who sent it. Maybe one of the guys at the lodge. Phil or Seth, maybe. You have to admit you didn't go out of your way to be friendly to them." Annoyance crackled in the gaze she turned on him. "Okay," he said. "So they didn't exactly roll out the welcome mat for you, either."

"I'm sure they were ecstatic when I was gone and the Two-Penny Lodge could return to its fishing fraternity atmosphere."

"It didn't. For better or worse, nothing was the same after you left, Gentry. Especially me."

A moment clipped past. Two patrolmen walked past the bench. Then, unexpectedly, her hand closed over his, a gentle touch, there on the hard wooden bench. "Why didn't you come after me?" she asked. "Were you too proud to admit you missed me?"

"I was too proud to go running after a woman who barely got my wedding band off her finger before she replaced it with another man's engagement ring. I couldn't believe it when Ben told me you were planning to marry Harris. Six weeks, Liz. You waited only six weeks before you were right back where I found you . . . planning a wedding to the wrong man." He withdrew his hand from hers. "I suppose that's one way to cover up your failures. Pretend they never existed to begin with."

A pay phone shrilled a few feet away. A stack of folders fell off a desk and spilled across the floor. Someone stepped on the papers, then stooped to pick them up. No one made a move to answer the phone. Gentry, he knew, wasn't going to answer him, either.

"What was in the package?" she asked finally, as if it mattered.

"A fish."

"A fish?"

He shrugged, somewhat self-consciously. "I figured you'd know it was my way of saying I'd rather have you hit me between the eyes with a trout, than be without you."

She laughed, but he detected the quiver of tears in the sound. "No wonder I never received it," she said. "That package was probably in the trash ten seconds after it was delivered. Didn't you think a fish might be a slightly smelly way to apologize?"

"I knew you'd understand. Besides, I packed that baby for travel. He should have been fresh as a daisy when the package arrived."

"Fresh as a daisy." She fell silent as she watched a harried-looking woman walk past, followed by a sullen teenage girl. "I'm glad you told me," she said with a sigh. "Even though it is all water under the bridge now." Her shoulder brushed across his upper arm as she shifted her position on the bench and tucked one long, graceful leg beneath her. "You still haven't explained what you were doing at the country club tonight."

He shrugged, the answer really no longer relevant. "Maybe I wanted to be there to toast your happiness," he said. "Or maybe I hoped I'd have an opportunity to kiss the bride."

"That's not done until after the ceremony."

"You don't honestly believe Sonny would let me get that close to you on your wedding day, do you? Besides, I'm not staying for the wedding."

"You're not?" Her voice registered dismay.

"I'm going back to the lodge tomorrow evening."

"But you wanted to see Ben and meet Sara." Her protest gave him hope, but not much. "You could stay until they arrive on Friday evening."

He shook his head. "I'll see them another time. I have no business hanging around here now. As Hillary would say, it simply isn't the proper thing to do."

"Since when have you cared what's proper or what anyone else thinks?"

"Since when have you changed your mind about the warmth of my welcome here? When I first arrived, you were adamant that I had to leave. Now that I'm prepared to go, you seem to want me to stay."

"It does sound that way, doesn't it." She wrinkled her nose with rueful self-honesty. "I guess it *is* that way, Jake. I don't want you to leave, but I don't want you to stay, either. You shouldn't have come here at all. Then, again, having this conversation was a good thing. I needed to know that, in your own offbeat way, you tried to apologize . . . even if it doesn't make any difference now. It's important to come to closure on past relationships. Don't you agree?"

He couldn't believe she said that so calmly, as if it were simply a matter of dotting an *i* or shutting a door. "Oh, absolutely," he said, repressed anger kicking in like a salesman's foot trying to keep a door from closing. Before she could fathom his intent and avoid it, he grabbed her shoulders, jerked her into his arms and captured her lips in a nonnegotiable kiss. A kiss he intended to demonstrate what he thought of the closure she wanted. A kiss he planned for her to remember long after he was gone. A kiss he would accept as final payment on the debt of pain she'd left him.

She sighed and surrendered, her hands softly slipping around him, her lips cleaving to his with candid familiarity. In an instant, the kiss ignited with raw, unbridled emotion, swiftly circumvented the safety net of his anger, and exploded with the passion he had kept too long suppressed. Closure? Who the hell were they kidding?

Gentry had no time to prepare, no time to blurt out an objection, no time to consider... as if time would have made a difference. The moment his fingers gripped her shoulders, she was turning toward him. Before his lips could descend on hers, she was lifting her face to receive him. Her body anticipated his nearness and curved eagerly to meet it. She was as helpless to prevent her response as she was to deny it.

With long-belated words, he had kicked out the supports of her self-absorbed anger. For two years now, she had nursed her resentment, fed her hungry heart the message that Jake didn't care where she was or what she did. He didn't want her back. Then, out of nowhere, he offered the truth. He'd sent a trout to offer his apology. A rather sweet gesture of conciliation no one except the two of them would understand. And she had answered with some nonsensical statement about bringing closure to their relationship.

She deserved the punishment in this kiss, had earned the anger that pushed against her and, paradoxically, pulled her closer. The noisy room, the phone that kept ringing and ringing, the activity, the people... all of it faded into fantasy as he became the only reality she knew. His lips moved over hers with absolute possession, refusing to accept less than her wholehearted response.

As if she had any other choice. Their passion was a two-edged sword, pushing and pulling at them as if they were magnets, drawn inexorably together in one direction and forced apart in the other. She was compelled by forces she could neither embrace nor resist, caught between the powerful pull of their attraction and the stubbornness that pushed them apart.

Regardless of what Jake believed, she hadn't left him because they'd quarreled. Nor had she walked out in a fit of temper because he had chosen to go fishing instead of discussing their problem. She had left him because she had seen her failures mounting in his eyes, imagined them stripping the love from his heart and replacing it with empty disappointment. She couldn't cook, didn't do housework, knew less than nothing about fish and how to catch them, didn't know how to talk to his friends or the guests at the lodge, and had nothing but time on her hands. Nothing she wanted to do was right, every suggestion she made was turned aside, her opinions weren't asked and barely noted when given. Jake had wanted her with him, but he didn't want her to make any changes in him or in his surroundings. So she'd grabbed the first opportunity to walk away while she still had the dignity to do so.

But dignity hadn't stopped her from missing him. She'd missed the feel of his mouth on hers, the sensual tango of their lips and tongues, the perfect oneness she felt only in his arms, the sense that if her heart stopped then and there, his heart would take over and beat for both of them. Maybe it already had. Maybe that was the reason she felt the rhythmic cadence and couldn't tell if it was his or hers.

His arms drew her closer, lifting her partially off the bench, fitting her body against his in a mutual and mind-altering embrace. She might have been anywhere. In a desolate cave or a busy jail. It might have been midnight. Or noon. She wasn't aware of time or place, or of other people approaching or passing by, or of the attention they might be attracting. She knew only three heart-stopping facts. Jake was here. She was in his arms. His kiss was everything she knew of heaven.

"I've heard that strange things go on at the police station, but I had no idea just how strange." Sydney's voice was like a splash of cold water on an overheated radiator, and Gentry jerked out of Jake's arms as if she'd been burned.

"S-Sydney." Her voice sounded guilty. "What are you doing here?"

"I thought I was here to comfort and support you through your miserable ordeal, but it appears you've already figured out how to reduce your misery."

Gentry felt the telltale flush heat her face. "I was...we were just, uh..."

"Yes," Sydney said. "I noticed."

Sergeant Orange stepped up behind her, pushed his glasses back on his nose and frowned down at Gentry. "Here's a question for you. If the guy back at the hotel really is your fiancé, how come you're playing kissee-face with this guy?" Hands on his gun holster, he seemed quite taken with this turn of events, supporting as it did, his original theory. "Now, which one of you is gonna crack first and tell me what's really going on?"

Jake looked at Gentry. "How many Oscars did Charlie win?"

"Four, in all. Two Best Actor, one Best Supporting and a Best Director."

"I'm going to snag one of his Best Actor Oscars right here." With a slightly wistful glance at her lips, Jake stood up. "Okay, Sergeant Orange, get your notebook, I'm ready to spill my guts."

"MY FAVORITE WAS the scene from *Cowboy Alley*. When you snarled and said, 'I always wanted to shoot the sheriff,' I swear P. Henry nearly wet his pants with excitement." Sydney closed the car door and started walking—in stockinged feet—with Jake toward the house, setting the locks and car alarm in an over-the-shoulder shot with the remote.

Gentry hooked her fingers in the heel cups of her pearl gray pumps and fell into step beside them. "That was a spectacular performance, Jake. Pop would have been proud of you."

"If I ever get tired of fishing, maybe I'll take up acting," he replied modestly.

"Don't even think about it," Sydney warned. "The only way I could convince Henry you weren't career criminals with sick, twisted brains was to promise him two weeks of private instruction in the art of fly-fishing."

"At the Two-Penny Lodge?" Jake asked with resignation.

"Well, you don't want to commute between here and there to give him a few lessons, do you?"

"What?" Gentry tried to look shocked. "Sergeant Orange accepted a bribe?"

Sidney sighed dramatically. "I'm afraid the two of you ruined a promising career tonight. He was on a straight path to the Cop-of-the-Year Award. It's tragic, you know, but he should have spent more time at the movies."

Gentry laughed, sharing in the giddiness that, when she'd been younger, had always accompanied a return home after staying out all night. Even Sergeant Orange's last words to her—"If I ever so much as see you step onto a street dressed like you are right now, it won't matter whose daughter you are. You'll be chewing the scenery from behind bars. Got that?"—seemed funny all of a sudden.

"Let's go for a swim," she suggested impulsively.

"In our clothes or out of them?" Sydney countered.

"Chooser goes first."

"Whoa, count me out." Jake stopped at the bricked path to the guest house. "I'm going to catch a little sleep before the sun gets all the way up. Thanks for coming to get us, Sydney. I'll call you later when I'm ready to go back to the hotel and pick up the truck."

"Sure thing, buddy. I'll be waiting by the phone." Syd blew him a kiss. "Call me," she sang. "Don't be afraid, you can call me."

Gentry frowned at her high-pitched rendition, and Sydney shrugged. "Can I help it if I have a song in my heart?"

Gentry took a last lingering look at Jake's backside as he walked to the guest house in the shaded light of early morning. "Why couldn't he have put on thirty pounds and grown thick and flabby across the rear?"

"Good genes." Sydney grinned. "You can spell that j-e-a-n-s, too."

"Clever." Turning, she headed for the house. "I guess I'd better skip the swim in favor of a shower, some adequate clothing and a return to the hotel before Sonny wakes up."

"Good idea. You don't want to take the chance one of the cleaning crew will mistake him for a corpse and call the undertaker."

"I'm sure he'll find the whole episode amusing...in retrospect, of course."

"Oh, of course. I expect he'll be vastly entertained, especially when he hears about the smacker you planted on Jake."

Her heart shuddered at the possibility. "I didn't do any such thing."

"You looked pretty firmly rooted to his lips when I saw you."

"You didn't see a thing," Gentry corrected her. "And you especially didn't see a *smacker*."

"So, you're not going to tell him about the kiss. You'd rather keep your guilty little secret, then." Sydney opened the back door and held it until they both could slip into the quiet house. "Wouldn't it be better just to confess, fight, make up, and get the whole thing out in the open? Secrets can come back to haunt you."

"Sonny and I believe in being totally honest with each other, but I'm not an idiot. There are a few secrets that ought to remain just that...secrets."

"Don't worry. I'm not going to tell."

Gentry stopped and Sydney bumped into her from behind. "You have to promise me you won't tell, Syd. Swear on your Blood Sister Oath right now."

Sydney made a face. "I would rather paint my toenails than cause trouble between you and your beloved. You know you can trust me, Gen. There's no need to drag out the BS Oath."

"Trust is the reason we invented it in the first place...and you're the main offender. Now, swear."

With an exasperated roll of her eyes, Sydney lifted one foot, raised her right hand and began to hop in a tight circle. "I, Sydney Jane Caroline Ryals, do solemnly swear that regardless of how many times I am tortured, beaten or horsewhipped, I will never reveal the secrets of my blood sisters." She put down her hand and foot. "There. Satisfied?"

"Do the rest."

Frowning fiercely, Sydney lifted her other foot, raised her left hand and made a counterclockwise hop. "I, Sydney Jane Caroline Ryals, swear that if I even think about breaking this sacred Blood Sister Oath, I will be cursed with bad skin, cellulite, halitosis and bad hair until the day I die." She stopped hopping and sighed. "I never realized what vindictive little brats we were in our younger days."

Gentry nodded. "We were so *dramatic* in our youth."

"As opposed to our adulthood, of course, when we act out scenes from movies in front of a whole squadron of police and kiss our ex-husbands in plain view of—"

Gentry whirled to face her. "You *swore*, Sydney."

"Well, excuse me, I thought you knew you kissed him."

"Don't mention it again."

They reached the stairs and walked quietly to the upstairs hall leading to the bedrooms. Stopping outside her own door, Gentry put her hand on Sydney's arm. "I almost forgot to say thanks."

"For what? Being there?" Sydney gave her a quick hug. "That's what friends are for." She took a couple of steps toward the guest room that was hers for the week, then backed up. "You do realize, Gen, that oath or no oath, you owe me big-time for this one."

"I'll be forever in your debt."

"You bet your butt you will." Sydney walked on down the hallway, humming a jaunty little tune that sounded a lot like "Suzy Had a Steamboat."

Chapter Eight

The Hamiltons' brunch in honor of Sonny and Gentry was supposed to be casual and relatively intimate. *Relatively* became the problem, however, when Sonny's family swelled the guest list and kicked intimacy out the window...or rather, off the terrace. Every last Harris aunt, uncle and cousin showed up, with a few friends. What should have been groups of two or three couples mingling around the pool became a crowd with groups of five or more couples centered around makeshift tables, hastily covered with cloths and decorated with platters of raspberry tarts. The remaining guests stood wherever they found space, balancing plates, cups and utensils, and defending their square foot of terrace.

At a center table, Gentry sat elbow to elbow with Sonny and Jake. Directly across from her, Sydney, flanked by Lee and Mitch, smiled as if she was in the catbird seat. To Mitch's right sat Frannie, Milton Harris, Heather and Sonny. To Lee's left was Pop, and next to him sat Tina, a young woman with short, spiky hair the color of black cherry Kool-Aid and contact lenses that turned her eyes into a disconcerting shade of purple. She got caught in the musical chairs shuf-

fle and ended up at their table, introducing herself as
"a friend of a friend of somebody's cousin." Next to
Tina sat Betty Harris. Hillary stood behind Frannie
and Milton, ready to pounce on the first available
chair.

Gentry had looked forward to this brunch for a
month, and now she was condemned to enjoy it while
Sonny seethed and glared across her at Jake, who was
hemmed in on his right by the cold shoulder of Sonny's mother. What a swell party this was turning out
to be, she thought.

How Sydney had gotten Jake into this small, *intimate* brunch was a no-brainer—she could have smug-
gled in an entire circus without the hostess being any
the wiser. And while it did cross Gentry's mind to
wonder how Jake had been persuaded to come, the
real mystery was how Sydney had maneuvered thir-
teen people and twelve chairs so that when everyone
was seated, Gentry was squarely in the middle of a war
zone.

Every time Jake sat forward, so did Sonny. If Jake
leaned back, Sonny followed suit. If Jake looped his
arm across the back of his chair, Sonny's arm snaked
around her shoulders to make sure his territory was
protected. Gentry tensed every time Jake opened his
mouth, because no matter who he spoke to around the
table, Sonny would suddenly find something to say to
the person sitting directly across, so that the two conversations canceled each other out and bombarded
Gentry with increasingly louder attempts to be heard.
When Jake offered his untouched raspberry tart to
Betty Harris, Sonny all but jumped across the table to

shove his in front of her first. Luckily, Gentry intercepted his plate before it tipped Jake's and dumped both of the tarts into Betty's ample lap.

Gentry might have had more patience with Sonny's behavior if he hadn't ignored her in favor of making sure Jake couldn't make contact with her. The most attention she received was when he apologized after accidentally hitting her with his cast, which happened nearly every time he touched her. Jake moved, Sonny moved, she received a *thunk* and a cursory "sorry." It was becoming quite annoying.

"So how did you two meet?" Tina asked Gentry, her purple eyes sliding appreciatively to Jake. "If I bet that it was love at first sight, would I win?"

"Yes," Jake answered.

"No," Sonny said at the same time, and then leaned forward to glare across Gentry. "What do you mean, yes?"

Jake's eyebrows lifted politely. "Tina asked me a question and I answered. Do you have a problem with that?"

"She asked *me*," Sonny snapped. "I'm Gentry's fiancé." His position clarified, he smiled at Tina. "We met through our mutual interest in art," he said, giving Gentry's hand an awkward pat.

"So did we." Jake smiled at Tina, too.

Another glare swept past Gentry. "I own an art gallery in Dallas." Sonny offered the information with yet another smile.

"That's where we met," Jake said.

Sonny stiffened. "That's where *we* met."

Gentry wished she'd never met either one of them.

"She came in to look for a painting," Sonny explained.

"So did I."

Sonny fired a warning glance at Jake across the neutral zone. "That's how we met," he said.

"Us, too." Jake nodded agreeably. "Except I was the one looking for a picture."

"Painting," Sonny snapped.

"Painting," Jake corrected himself.

Tina blinked her spiky eyelashes in some confusion and her purple eyes flicked to Gentry. "Are you going to marry both of them?"

"Fortunately, just one," she answered.

"That's me." Sonny shot a "so there" glance at Jake.

"He's right," Jake said. "We've already been married."

"Annulled." Sonny stretched his neck to deliver that one over Gentry's head.

Jake nodded concession. "Annulled."

Tina responded with another blink, and Gentry wondered if she could get out of here by crawling under the tables.

"Isn't this a lovely party?" Frannie said. "It's so nice all of Sonny's family could be here for the wedding."

Milton Harris shook his head in a skeptical, I-hope-he-can-pull-it-off-this-time manner. "After what happened at the last wedding, no one in our bunch wanted to take a chance on missing something this time around."

"This is nothing like the last wedding," Sonny insisted.

Milton looked pointedly at Jake. "Then what's *he* doing here?"

"He's visiting me." Pop's voice was pure John Wayne, daring anyone to make something of it.

"Just before the wedding?" Betty gave a short, humorless laugh. "That certainly seems odd."

If this had been a Western, Betty would have been the first one shot, Gentry thought. Pop was one of the good guys, though, and kept his six-shooters in his holster. "Nothing odd about it," he said. "I'm not the one who's getting married."

"Neither is he." Sonny leaned around Gentry to make sure Jake heard.

Jake's response was to lean back and drape his arm along the top of Gentry's chair, forcing Sonny to duck back in a hurried attempt to get his hand on her chair first. *Clunk.* The heavy cast struck the metal folding chair before it fell, *thunk,* against her backbone.

"Sorry." Sonny propped the cast on top of the chair again, edging Jake's arm out of the way. Gentry rubbed her backbone and counted to ten.

Jake shifted forward and laid his arms, hands clasped, on the table.

The dishes on the table rattled as Sonny's cast landed a second later, clipping Gentry's wrist on the outside. "Sorry," he said, and settled in the new position. Jake listened to a little of Pop's storytelling, then shifted in his seat and leaned back. Sonny caught the movement out of the corner of his eye and leaned back in his chair, too. A few minutes later, Jake scooted closer to the table. Sonny grabbed the edges of his seat as best he could with one hand and the chair hopped awkwardly. One chair leg nicked Gentry's foot in the process.

"Sorry," Sonny said. She raised her eyebrows and counted to twenty.

Jake lifted one arm in a slow stretch.

Thunk! Sonny's cast hit Gentry's shoulder in anticipation of Jake's next move...which didn't happen. "Sorry." Sonny resumed the arms-on-the-table, forward position.

Jake started to lean back. Sonny watched, warier now of leaping into action. Jake rocked forward. Sonny rocked forward. Jake rocked back, stretched out his legs and slumped a little in his chair. By the time Sonny got his slump set, Jake was back to the table with his arms crossed in front of him. Sonny followed, but no sooner got his arms positioned, than Jake straightened and draped his arm along the back of Gentry's chair. Sonny glanced over, realized he was out of sync and quickly corrected his positioning.

They reminded Gentry of two squirrels darting around the trunk of a tree, then dashing around in the opposite direction as soon as each one spied the other. Back and forth. Back and forth. She slapped her hands, palms down, on the table. "Would you stop that!"

The chatter around the table came to an abrupt halt and everyone looked to her for an explanation. She nodded pleasantly. "Sorry, I was just getting the kinks out of my system."

"Kooks, more likely," someone muttered.

She divided her irritable look between both men, turning her head to be sure they each got their fair share. "Now," she said, "if the two of you wouldn't mind, I'd like to enjoy the rest of this party without getting motion sickness. So, unless you have a life-or-death situation, *sit still*. Understand?"

"My fault," Jake said. "I was bored. No one to talk to and all. Sorry." He leaned past her and offered Sonny a handshake.

Sonny glanced from the proffered hand to his cast and scowled. "I don't know why you keep crashing these parties, Daniels. You're not walking off with Gentry this time, no matter what you think. She learned her lesson. She knows she made a mistake by not taking her vows as planned that day."

That was something of a misstatement, Gentry thought. She had taken vows that day...as planned. She and Jake had vowed their love and commitment in a motel room barely thirty minutes' drive down the road. The exchange of vows was theirs alone, communicated in long, hot, wet kisses and sweaty palms...and sweaty bodies...and bare chests and bare breasts and bare legs tangled in the sheets and each other...and in the erotic sounds of two passion-slick bodies coming together....

"Take a couple of deep breaths before you hyperventilate," Jake said, and then thumped her on the back.

Sonny jerked around in his seat. "Keep your hands off her, Daniels. If she needs a whack on the back, I'll whack her. I don't want you to touch her, understand?"

"Sonny, please." Gentry laid her hand on his cast. "What is wrong with you? You never make a scene."

"Well, it's time somebody did." Sonny's shoulders began to rise like an expanding balloon, his chest filling out like the north wind getting ready to blast the coast with a storm. He shoved back his chair, but it didn't move far enough for him to stand, so he hovered, somewhere between sitting and standing. "It's time somebody showed this coyote the door . . . and as Gentry's fiancé, it will be my pleasure to do it.''

"Sit down, Harris." Jake's voice was low, but forceful.

"Not until I've kicked your—"

"Would anyone like more tarts?" Frannie picked up the platter and passed it across the table, in the mistaken belief raspberry tarts would divert everyone's attention from the snarling going on around her daughter. "They're wonderful. Go ahead, have another."

Pop grabbed the platter and set it down. "Would you be quiet, Frannie? I don't want to miss this."

"Are you just going to sit there?" Sonny snarled at Jake.

"I was thinking I might, yes."

"You're not thinking too clearly, then. Get up or I'll haul you straight out of that chair myself."

Jake was clearly debating his next move. Gentry tamped down her complete disgust with both men and considered how to bring this embarrassing standoff to a conclusion with a minimum loss of face all around. She thought, somehow, this was her fault. She could have, should have, prevented the tension from reaching this point. Still, it was difficult to feel guilty when the testosterone levels were sky-high on either side. She shifted her focus to Sonny. "Sit down, Sonny. Contrary to what you might have been told in some smelly old locker room, I am not a prize you can win in a pointless brawl."

"I know that, Gentry." He patted her shoulder. "So I'll just punch him for my own satisfaction."

"Anyone care for more of this delicious punch?" Betty poured a little more into her glass before waving the pitcher around the table. "Who wants more punch?"

"Not now, Mrs. Harris." Hillary reached between Frannie and Milton, snatched the pitcher of iced punch and cradled it close against her, out of the way.

"Don't waste any more of my time, Daniels," Sonny challenged. "I want to know why you came back."

"I thought you wanted to punch me," Jake said.

"I changed my mind. First I want to hear you admit you came here thinking you could lure Gentry back into your bed...."

"Sonny!" Gentry grabbed his hand, but he shook it off.

"And ruin another wedding for us. *Then* I'm going to punch you."

Behind her, Gentry heard Jake sigh. "I never really wanted to shoot the sheriff," he muttered under his breath. His chair scraped as he pushed back.

Gentry shoved the table in her scramble to get to her feet and in between the two men. Behind her, like a baby learning to walk, the table wobbled, tipped and collapsed, dumping the platter of raspberry tarts indiscriminately as it fell. Glasses tumbled down the incline, throwing leftover punch in random splatters. Bullfrogs around a pond couldn't have leaped out of danger any faster than the people around that table. With squeals of surprise and gruff epithets, they jumped in all directions.

Betty got out of the way, then bent to grab her purse, bumping two innocent bystanders with one swing of her hips. Heather's foot caught in the rung of her chair and she fell sideways into Milton, who lost his balance, stumbled into Frannie, knocking her forward, then righted himself with an unstable turn, which put him on a collision course with Hillary. He threw his arms around her, but couldn't stop the momentum and they staggered together into first one table and then another, taking down three tables in one spectacular fall before they landed in a sitting position, upright and face-to-face, like rag dolls in an awkward embrace.

When the table tilted, Tina jumped onto her chair and then into Lee's unsuspecting arms. He caught her, but fell against Sydney, who pushed him upright and into a running walk, like a juggler balancing a broomstick on his nose. Mitch's flailing arms latched onto Sydney and dragged her backward in a reeling waltz that ended in a crashing finale.

Being the first on his side of the table to realize what was happening, Pop had jumped up and out of the way. He caught the edge of the table and attempted to hold it steady, but when Frannie tripped over his chair, knocking it backward, he made a grab for her, flinging the table into a cartwheel, that scattered another four tables like pins in a bowling alley. Knowing he was going down, Pop threw his weight to the side and fell against another guest, who lurched to the right and went down on top of the nearest table, which buckled under him, sending yet another group of sitting guests to their feet and into the chain reaction, which rolled over the crowded terrace like a synchronized wave through a crowd of sports fans.

Standing in the center of destruction, between Sonny and Jake, Gentry watched in wide-eyed disbelief as the anticipated brunch turned into a B-movie disaster. The guests went down like dominoes, one on top of another, in nearly every direction, and when it was over, the Hamiltons' terrace was strewn with overturned chairs and broken tables, and was littered with pieces of glass, scattered forks and raspberry goo. Not even the buffet tables had been spared, and the remains of the brunch floated like so much flotsam in the Hamiltons' pool. Everyone, it seemed, had suffered some damage, either a scrape, bruise or stain. Everyone, that is, except the three people still standing at center stage.

"Excuse me."

Gentry turned to see Hillary struggle to her feet— still carefully clasping the pitcher of punch, which she had miraculously kept from spilling—politely apologizing when she pushed, poked or stepped on anyone. "Pardon me," she said as she picked a path through the debris.

In all, there were four "excuse me's," six "I beg your pardons," and one "I'm terribly sorry for the inconvenience," before always-proper Hillary crossed the last fallen table and stopped in front of Gentry. Without a word, she held out the pitcher.

Gentry took it from her hands. "Thank you."

"You're welcome." Hillary stepped back as Gentry turned to Sonny.

"I believe you mentioned punch," she said, and then she upended the pitcher over his head.

"HEATHER?"

"Yes?"

On the lounge chair, Sydney fluffed a pillow and propped it behind her head before reaching for her magazine. "What are you doing in the closet?"

"Nothing." Like a whimsical thought, Heather's reply drifted through the adjoining dressing room and into Gentry's bedroom. "Just looking."

In the window seat, Gentry rested her chin on her knees and let her hand drop down to scratch Cleo's ear. "What's wrong with Heather today?" she asked. "She's been wandering like that ever since we got back from the Hamiltons'."

"You're in her usual place. Maybe she doesn't feel right sitting anywhere else." Seated at the lighted makeup table, Hillary sorted through a bag and withdrew a slim eyebrow pencil. "Some people are like that. Dustin Hoffman's character in *Rain Man,* for example. His bed had to be next to a window or he couldn't sleep."

"In my opinion, her current state of existence is closer to *Snow White* than *Rain Man.*" Sydney turned a page in the magazine she'd looked at the day before . . . and at the same, uninvolved pace.

"Are you saying she's a little *Dopey?*" Hillary managed to toss out the pun while she sketched a hint of color into one perfectly arched brow.

"*Happy* would have been my guess," Gentry said.

"I say you're both wrong. Listen." Sydney turned her head toward the dressing-room door. "Heather?"

"Yes?"

"Someday, my prince will come. . . ." Sydney sang the first line of the song and stopped. Heather's giggle followed like a puppy chasing a bouncing ball. Sydney lifted one shoulder in conclusion.

Hillary put down the eyebrow pencil. "Does that prove something?"

"Yes, Hillary," Gentry said. "Think back. When was the last time you heard Heather laugh like that?"

"Mmmm, the fraternity homecoming dance... No, that was you, Syd. Wait, I do know. High school. Senior year. Honors English. Mr. Rossinski. Oh, geez, she was so in love with him...." Hillary's voice trailed off in discovery and she turned around to share a look with the other two. "Oh, my gosh," she whispered. "She's met..."

"Mr. Right," they all said together and laughed. Gentry felt better. The disastrous brunch had left her moody and impatient, and wishing she and Sonny had eloped months ago. Planning this wedding had been a mistake, no matter what he said about rewriting their history. Maybe it would have been okay if Jake hadn't shown up to revise the history they were trying to rewrite. Maybe if he hadn't been there last night to sit with her in the emergency room or the police station. Maybe if he hadn't kissed her. Maybe if she hadn't kissed him back. Maybe if Pop had never read that article about the old wedding gown.

"Heather?" she said to the closet. "While you're in there, why don't you try on the wedding dress?"

"No, thanks." The dreamy reply drifted back, surprising Gentry with the refusal.

"But, Heather, it's a *magic* dress."

"I know. I didn't even have to put it on."

It wasn't easy talking to the closet, but Gentry tried again. "You can try it on now, Heather. Really, I wish you would."

"No, thanks." The refusal was a little less dreamy-sounding than the first, which made it even more surprising. Gentry caught Hillary's eye in the mirror and raised her eyebrows in a question.

"Come on, Heather," Hillary said. "Model the magic wedding dress for us."

"You do it," she answered. "I don't want to."

Clearly, Heather wasn't herself. Normally, she could be persuaded to try on clothes simply by a suggestion . . . and anything as romantic as waltzing around in a bridal gown . . .

"Why not?" Hillary asked, leaning toward the makeup mirror to check her eyebrow for imperfections.

"I already know it's magic. Someone else should try."

Sydney held up the magazine, opened to a page and showed it to Gentry and Hillary. "I'm thinking about changing my hairstyle. Do you like this?" She tapped the picture. "Short and sassy. What do you think?"

"I think you're sassy enough as it is." Gentry returned her attention to the closet. "Heather? I really want you to put on the dress. Please?"

"Oh, for heaven's sake, Gen," Sydney said. "If you want someone to put on the silly dress, why don't you do it? It is, after all, your wedding gown."

"It's not *my* wedding gown," she said firmly. "It's just a wedding gown. There's a difference."

"If it was just *a* wedding gown, you wouldn't be begging us to try it on."

"I'm not begging, I merely thought it would be fun—"

"For one of us to try on the gown and look in the mirror and let you know whether we see our true love's reflection." Sydney held up the magazine and frowned critically at the short and sassy haircut. "I think I might like my hair like this."

"I know whose reflection you'd see in the mirror," Gentry stated confidently. "Your own. Period. No matter who puts it on."

"Then what are you worried about?" Sydney cupped her hand at her nape and pushed her luxurious, dark hair on top of her head, trying to shape it like the pictured cut. "Put on the dress, look in the mirror and take your chances."

"I'm not going to let you or Pop or anyone else manipulate me into trying on that dress. It's a joke and I'm not going to fall for it. Besides, I have other things to do right now."

Sydney laid the magazine in her lap and frowned at Gentry. "Like what? You and your fiancé aren't exactly on everyone's favorite guest list after this morning's brunch. He's probably still washing punch out of his hair, anyway."

"Don't you dare forgive him too soon, Gentry," Hillary said. "Picking a fight with Jake is a stupid thing to do at any time, but to do it at the Hamiltons'..."

"I believe you made your disgust evident, Hil," Sydney said. "And I'm proud of you for not dumping the punch on him yourself."

"I wanted to, but it was Gentry's place to do it."

Gentry hugged her knees a little tighter. "I only wish I'd had a pitcher for Jake, too."

"At least he tried to avoid the confrontation," Sydney said, moving past the haircut. "He's leaving today, Gentry. Did you know?"

"He mentioned it, yes." Jake was leaving, which should make everything perfect again. She sighed without enthusiasm and put her chin on her hands. "Has he left already?"

"I don't know. Why don't you go to the pool house and find out?"

"No, thanks. I have better things to do."

"That's right," Hillary said. "Like trying on your wedding dress. This is an ideal time to put it on, to make sure it fits and that all the buttons are still on it. You want it to be in perfect shape for Saturday."

"I'm wearing the other dress on Saturday. It doesn't have buttons, and I already know it fits."

"Boy, does it ever." Hillary feathered her lashes with a mascara brush.

"Listen, Gen," Sydney said. "We're your friends and we can't let you wear that sequined sarong. I'm sorry, but this time you're going to have to defer to our better judgment. Go with the million-dollar golden oldie."

"Syd's right. Sequins aren't for you." Hillary met Gentry's gaze in the mirror. "Besides, Sonny saw you roll down the stairs in it, and now that he's seen it, wearing it would just be asking for bad luck."

"Also, it's *white*," Sydney pointed out.

"That's right...." Hillary began before she caught sight of Sydney's droll smile. "Well, it is white." She gave her blond hair a flippant little toss. "My opinion on that remains unchanged, regardless of what the rest of you think."

"And my opinion on the million-dollar dress remains the same, as well." Gentry put her hand in her lap and Cleo nudged her, requesting continued ear rubs. "Why don't you try it on, Hillary?"

"It would be bad luck," Hillary informed her as if she were stating a well-researched fact. "It wouldn't fit me, anyway."

"How do I look?" Heather pirouetted into the room and the conversation stopped. She wasn't wearing either of the wedding gowns. She was barely wearing anything at all.

Sydney's magazine dropped to the floor. Hillary's makeup bag spilled onto the counter. Gentry accidentally pulled Cleo's ear. Heather's softly curved body was nestled inside a red, ribboned teddy like chocolates in a valentine box. What it left to the imagination wasn't much, but it was enough. Just enough.

"My God, Heather," Hillary said. "Where did you find that?"

Heather bent in a graceful plié. "In Gentry's closet."

Two stunned glances turned to the window seat, and Gentry felt a blush steal across her cheeks. "I *was* married at the time," she offered in self-defense.

"So, can I borrow it?" Heather asked.

Sydney jerked the pillow from behind her head and sat up. "All right, Snow White, who is he?"

Heather giggled, sighed, and then sighed again. "He asked me to go ice skating tomorrow."

"Why don't you borrow some slacks and a sweater, instead?" Hillary suggested as she began picking up her makeup. "You're going to get very cold in that."

"I wasn't going to wear this then," Heather said. "And I can never imagine being cold again."

"Are you sure you didn't put on the magic dress and look in the mirror?" Gentry gently teased.

Heather's eyes shone like candles in a window. "I didn't have to. It worked, anyway. I touched it and he touched it and it was magic...." Her voice ebbed into the dream-filled smile.

"Who is he, Heather?" Gentry tried to pull the conversation down to reality. "Where did you meet him? When? What does he look like?"

Heather hugged herself, enjoying her secret for another moment. "*He* is Mitch McAlister. Sonny's best man. Do you remember when I came to visit you after Christmas? He was here, visiting Sonny. We were introduced then, but I didn't really know him. Then, last night...well, it just happened."

Sydney looked up with new interest. "You had sex?" She rounded her eyes. "Uh-oh. You know what that means, Heather. Now you can't wear a white wedding gown, either."

Hillary rose to the bait immediately. "It has nothing to do with virginity, Sydney. It's whether you've been married or not."

"We didn't have sex," Heather said. "Not that it's any of your business."

"No sex?" Sydney shook her head and picked up the magazine again. "Well, if that's not what *just happened,* I can't imagine what it was."

"Magic," Heather clarified, going dewy-eyed once more. "Magic and Mitch."

Gentry's stomach knotted with concern. Mitch McAlister came with a reputation for short-term affairs and an easy-on, easy-off kind of charm. On a scale of experience from one to ten, he was a fifteen, and Heather, a questionable three. Gentry shared her concern with Sydney and Hillary in a brief three-way glance.

"You can give each other that *look* all you want," Heather said with a confidence Gentry had never heard from her before. "This is different for both of us, and I'm going to trust my heart this time...and the magic wedding dress."

Gentry groaned. "I don't want to hear this. Heather, it's just a dress. There isn't anything magic about it."

"How would you know, Gen? You say that because you're afraid it is and that if you put it on, you might find out—" She stopped abruptly and refused to meet Gentry's eyes. It was clear what she was thinking, though. What every one of them was thinking, but would not say. If there was such a thing as a magic wedding dress, she might find out that she was about to marry the wrong man.

"Heather, we're all a bit concerned that Mitch McAlister may be a little more experienced—"

"I know his reputation," Heather interrupted Hillary. "We talked about that. What happened between us last night surprised him, too."

Sydney eyed her sternly. "What, specifically, did happen?"

"Okay." Heather could have passed for a schoolgirl giving a report... except for the red teddy. "As everyone was leaving the country club, I went to get the wedding dress to bring it home. Mitch saw me through the window and came to make sure I was all right and didn't need a ride home or anything. I know this part sounds kind of crazy, but I couldn't pick the dress up off the floor. It kept sliding out of my hands and then—this is the magic part—the dress sort of *twinkled*. I swear it really did make this kind of sparkle, and then we started laughing and talking, and well, then we kissed."

"And he didn't invite you to his bachelor pad to show you his etchings?" Sydney asked, and received a frown in reply.

"No. He asked me to go ice skating. He's never been and neither have I. Mitch said he wanted our first date to be something new and different for both of us."

"That outfit could fall in the same new-and-different category," Sydney observed dryly. "Aren't you making a pretty broad jump from Virgin of the Year to Boudoir Betty?"

Heather merely smiled. "Maybe I want to borrow this to take on my honeymoon trip."

"He proposed?" Hillary's eyebrows rose. "Before you've even gone out on a date?"

"No. But he will. And I'll accept."

Sydney smiled. "You sound very sure of yourself."

"Some things are right and you just know. It was that way for you and Jake, wasn't it, Gen?"

"That's the way it was." There was no reason to point out that some things didn't stay right, no matter how sure you were.

"And that's the way it is for Mitch and me." Heather did another pirouette, spinning happily in the daring red teddy. "Look, I'm twinkling. Can you see me?"

Sydney tossed the magazine aside, stood and walked through the dressing room and out of sight. When she returned, she had the million-dollar dress in tow. "Okay, one of us has to put on this dress and look in the mirror. Who's it going to be? Heather?"

"Not me. I'd see Mitch and then you'd tell me I'd made it up. You should do it, Syd."

Sydney pulled the dress against her and looked in the mirror. "No. Gentry wouldn't believe me, even if I swore on the Blood Sister Oath. Hillary?" She held out the dress. "You're it."

Hillary hesitated, glancing at Gentry, who tried to appear uninterested. "I don't know," she said. "I think it's too small."

"Come over here." Sydney motioned her into the dressing room and positioned her in front of the mirror. "Now, stand still while I measure this against you."

HILLARY FIDGETED as Sydney took the wedding gown off the hanger. She tried to catch Gentry's gaze in the mirror, but couldn't. This wasn't a good idea. She could feel the tension in the bedroom, even though she didn't fully understand it. Certainly it wasn't emanating from Heather, who looked a little like today's raspberry tarts, their filling bubbling over the crust, just as her body was bubbling over the red teddy, and her heart over a new romance.

Tension and Sydney were synonymous. She wore it like a medal of honor, always bringing a sense of energy and forward motion with her wherever she went. But this tension was different, and it made Hillary nervous and excited. "Are you sure you don't mind, Gen?" she asked.

"She doesn't mind." Sydney stood behind her, pulling, adjusting, fitting the bodice to her. "It might be a little short-waisted for you, Hil, but I think it will fit. In fact..." Stepping back, Syd looked at the dress questioningly. "Heather, look. If I didn't know this was Gentry's dress, I'd almost believe it was made to fit Hillary."

Heather bent to check the side seams against the width of Hillary's midriff. "It doesn't look too small to me. Maybe it hasn't been altered to Gentry's measurements."

In the mirror, Hillary caught a glimpse of movement and checked to see if Gen was paying attention. She wasn't. But something was stirring the air. Hillary felt a tightness across her chest. She felt light-headed and breathless and excited and scared. This was bad luck. She just knew it. "I don't think—"

"I think it will fit," Sydney concluded, nodding her satisfaction. "Take off your clothes and let's give it a try."

"This isn't a good..." Hillary couldn't finish the thought. She couldn't stop staring at herself in the mirror. She was only pressing the ivory gown against her body, but in the mirror, she was *in* it. The cool touch of the satin was all around her, as if she actually was wearing the dress. She closed her eyes, shutting off the illusion, but when she opened them again, the reflection hadn't changed. She was there, in the dress. Not Sydney or Heather, who were still in the room. Just her...and a shadowy image on her right. A shadow that took a shape and form she knew. As he came more clearly into focus, Hillary wanted to scream at him to get out of her fantasy. He didn't belong here. Not with her.

She felt the blood draining from her face when he winked at her and she let go of the dress, as if she'd burned her hands on the delicate lace. This was wrong. Something had gone wrong.

"Hil?" Sydney's concern reached through Hillary's frantic thoughts and calmed her. "You look like you saw a ghost in the mirror instead of Prince Charming. Are you all right?"

She glanced at the mirror and saw Gentry look up. Their gazes met and Hillary pulled herself together.

"I'm fine," she said, and gave a hollow laugh to confirm it. "I just felt dizzy for a moment. I should probably go outside and get some fresh air. Maybe go for a swim."

Heather put her hands on her hips. "Aren't you going to try on the wedding gown? We have to convince Gentry it's magic, you know. Otherwise, she's never going to believe."

Hillary bent toward the mirror and smoothed her eyebrows with a fingertip. "I'm tired of pretending," she said. "There's no such thing as a magic wedding dress. Why would anyone believe they could see their future in a mirror, anyway? Gentry's right. It's all nonsense." Then, before Sydney's skeptical gaze could probe deeply enough to reveal her secret, she walked into the bedroom and straight to the door. "If anyone needs me, I'll be at the pool."

Stepping into the hallway, Hillary closed the door behind her and leaned her forehead against it until she could get her bearings. It was nonsense, she thought. The dress was beautiful, but it wasn't magic. It couldn't be.

Because under no circumstances was Sonny Harris a part of her future.

Chapter Nine

"What's this about you leaving today?" Charlie pulled a chair from the table and sat down heavily. He eyed Jake with a purposeful gaze. "I invited you to stay the week."

Two years ago, Jake would have shifted uncomfortably under that look, but today he didn't have the energy. "It's time for me to go," he said. "I don't belong here. Not now."

"She tell you to go?"

There was no need to ask which "she" he was referring to. Gentry was the link between them, their love for her the only reason they knew the other existed. Jake smiled. "No. She doesn't know what she wants. But it isn't me."

"She's always been a stubborn little thing. I can remember when she was three, going on twenty-one. She'd put her hands on her hips and stick out her chin and there was no budging her. She might never know what she wanted or what she was going to do next, but I'll be damned if she wasn't a hundred percent sure of what she wasn't going to do... and that was whatever I had my mind set on her doing." Charlie smiled and surveyed the Stetson-shaped pool. "Frannie says she's just like me, but I don't see it. I always had the sense to know what I ought to do, even if I didn't do it.''

"Maybe she believes this is what she ought to do,'' Jake offered, although he didn't truly believe it.

"I kinda hoped you'd be able to change her mind.''

"Now, why would I want to do that, Charlie? She's hell to live with. Demanding, intractable, spoiled.'' *Passionate, exciting, intense.*

"She's a handful, all right. And I don't deny she's spoiled, but damn, son, have you ever seen anything else like her?''

That won Jake's reluctant smile. "No, sir. I never have.''

"So you'll stay the week, then." Charlie said it as if one statement logically followed the other. "Good, Frannie will be pleased.''

It was no wonder Gentry had turned out so stubborn, Jake thought. Charlie was like a bulldozer, and it would take a good-size rock to slow him down. "I don't know how Frannie has lived with the two of you all these years," Jake said. "She must have the patience of Job.''

"Frannie?" Charlie laughed. "That woman is hell on wheels. She's made me toe the line for thirty-some years, and this may surprise you, Jake, but that's not an easy thing to do." He ran his hand across the top of his head and through his silvering hair. "I'm not saying we didn't have problems. Still do. Big ones, too. We're both opinionated and mule-headed, but we get through them, somehow. Maybe because neither one of us has any place to run to.''

The message wasn't lost on Jake, and he pensively stroked a thumb along the line of his jaw. "You think I should have come after her.''

"Don't you?"

"I sent a fish to do a man's job," he said, half to himself, regretting the fear that had prompted that flippant attempt at apology. "I thought she needed some time, a little space to think. I thought she'd be back in a week."

"Not my daughter. She doesn't like to admit she made a mistake, and when you didn't come after her, Jake, she decided you had been the mistake."

"I was. She didn't belong at the lodge and we both knew it."

"She doesn't belong with the Can King, either. I know that and so do you."

"No, I don't," Jake denied. "They seem to be a perfect fit. I think they'll be very happy together."

"Time will tell, I suppose." Charlie stood, still a mountain of a man with a soft spot as big as the Rockies for the people he loved. "If you're still of a mind to leave, Jake, then so be it. You're welcome any time you want to come back, though. In case I never told you, I was mad as hell when you ruined the last wedding by skipping out with my daughter. But I got over it. Like Frannie said, it was only a wedding."

Jake wasn't sure what that meant, but he nodded as if he understood. "I'll be up to say goodbye before I leave."

Charlie turned toward the house, then stopped. He fished in his pocket and tossed something onto the table. It struck the glass top with a ping, and Jake cupped his hand over the object to keep it from bouncing off the table. "I found that by the pool," Charlie said. "Thought you might know where it belongs."

Jake watched him walk around the hat brim and up the steps to the terrace, waiting until Charlie was out of sight before lifting his hand. He stared at the tiny button a long time before he picked it up between his thumb and forefinger. It nestled there like a perfect pearl, ivoried with age, a bubble of an opening for the thread to pass through, imperfectly shaped, but lovingly made. As he stared at it, the button caught a ray of afternoon sun and reflected it in a startling twinkle that struck him right between the eyes.

With a blink, he closed his hand around it. Charlie was right. Jake knew exactly where this belonged.

As the bedroom door closed behind Hillary, Gentry sat up and exchanged a puzzled gaze with Sydney, who lifted her shoulder in a don't-ask-me shrug, although it was clear she was concerned, too.

"She must have a headache." Heather slipped the wedding gown back on its hanger and began to refasten the back buttons. "You know how she lets little things bother her."

Little things, yes, Gentry thought. But trying on a dress? And she hadn't seemed bothered before she stepped inside the dressing room.

"Do you remember the time Hillary was so undecided about what to wear to our first official junior-high-school dance, and so we took every stitch of clothing you owned, Gentry?"

"I remember that," Heather said with a laugh. "I wore Gen's new red-checked jumper and tore it on the bleachers. You three patched the material with about two rolls of duct tape and I spent the rest of the dance with my butt stuck to a chair. What did you wear, Syd?"

"I don't remember, but it was one of Gentry's best outfits, I'm sure. Hillary wore the taffeta dress you'd intended to wear yourself, Gen."

Gentry nodded. "I had to wear my mother's cocktail dress with forty dozen safety pins to make it fit. And, Syd, the first thing you said when you saw me was that I'd be a sure winner on 'Let's Make a Deal.' I never intended to speak to any of you again."

"But you had to," Heather said. "Because Brian Mahoney kissed you in the boys' locker room and you couldn't not tell your best friends about that."

The memory shifted focus, and Gentry shared it with Sydney in a perceptive glance. "I wish one of you had told me Hillary was hoping Brian Mahoney would notice her at that dance."

"She always said it served us right to be dressed to the teeth in your clothes, while you showed up in your mother's tacky brocade and got kissed by the cutest boy in the seventh grade... and she couldn't even get mad at you over it because it had been her idea to take all of your clothes."

"We used to have so much fun together." Heather sighed, missing the undercurrent of the reminiscence in her own state of bliss. "I think I'll change clothes and join Hillary at the pool. Anyone else want to go?"

Gentry shook her head, not in the mood for either sun or fun.

"I'm in," Sydney said, absently turning to take the wedding gown from Heather so she could change.

As Heather headed into the closet, she glanced over her shoulder. "What do you think about the teddy, Gen? Can I borrow it?"

"Of course," Sydney answered. "Seduction outfits don't transition well from one marriage to the next. If she's planning to wear that for Sonny, she might as well issue Jake an invitation to join them in bed.''

"What a scary thought that is," Gentry said. Just the combination of "Jake" and "bed" brought exciting, erotic images flowing through her mind with unsettling speed. Memory was such a traitor, tossing out the arguments and anger she ought to recall and filling her thoughts and senses with the passion, the laughter, the love. "Keep the teddy, Heather," she said quickly. "I don't want it."

"Thanks." Heather vanished into the dressing room and returned a minute later. "What about these?" From her outstretched hand dangled three more teddies, one black, one white, one a lipstick print.

Gentry caught Sydney's raised brow and dipped her chin in chagrin. "Keep those, too."

"Thanks." Heather vanished again, her pleasure in the gift drifting back in a soft, delighted giggle.

Sydney smoothed the folds of the million-dollar dress and laid the train over a second hanger. "Being married to a man with wild and rugged sexuality must have been a real burden to you, Gentry," she teased. "I don't know how you managed it."

She didn't know how she had managed without it. "I'll finish buttoning that if you want to go on and keep Hillary company."

"I wouldn't touch this dress if I were you," Sydney warned. "It's dangerous. It twinkles. It turns innocent virgins into killer vamps."

"Not to worry, Syd. I'm wearing my gold cross. No magic can hurt me."

"I hope Hil was as lucky." Shrugging, she turned away from the dress. "Heather? I'm going to my room to change. See you downstairs in a few minutes."

"Okay," Heather sang out. "Be there or be square."

Sydney rolled her eyes. "I think all this romantic stuff is giving me a headache."

"What you need, Syd, is a romance of your own."

"Bite your tongue, woman. If my life should suddenly become incomplete without a man in it, I'll get a dog and name it Mr. Right."

"Wish I'd thought of that," Gentry said as she took over Sydney's place and began buttoning the back of the wedding gown.

Her fingers paused midway to the neckline when Heather traipsed past, the teddies looped over her arm in a black, white and red-ribboned stream. "See you later," she called. "Thanks again for the stuff."

Then, finally, the door closed behind her and Gentry was alone. She stopped fussing with the buttons and stepped back to stare thoughtfully at the two wedding dresses hanging side by side on the dressing-room wall.

The skylight in the ceiling provided a steady stream of sunlight and the sequins caught every nuance of it, bouncing flashy rainbows off the ceilings, walls and mirror. Next to it, the old wedding gown hung in rich folds of ivory, absorbing the sunlight, enfolding it, guarding it, like a secret held in reverent and respectful silence.

Gentry touched a lace sleeve to assure herself it was just a dress. There was nothing magical about it. If the truth were known, Pop had probably found this costume at the studio and decided to have a little fun with it . . . at her expense.

Heather's account of a twinkling dress was easy enough to discount. Her imagination was always full of romantic fantasy, anyway. But Gentry had watched Hillary in the mirror as the gown was draped around her. She'd seen her eyes widen and then narrow in confusion, as if she really had seen a ghost, as if something actually had startled her.

It could be a setup, of course. Sydney and Hillary weren't above going to extremes to carry out a prank, and Gentry admitted she was overdue for a payback, even counting last night's escapade at the country club. She could imagine them coming up with this magic-dress scheme and carrying it out, possibly even under Pop's direction. Except that Hillary hadn't looked as if she were acting a part. Even if she were, why hadn't she done the obvious and insisted she had seen a man's reflection?

Dropping the sleeve, Gentry fluffed the skirt and watched the light ripple through the satin like a thread of gold. There was something mesmerizing about this dress, and there was no point in denying to herself that she was as fascinated by it as everyone else.

Lifting the hanger, she turned the dress face front and looked at it from another angle. Something about it beckoned her . . . probably nothing more than a normal curiosity. Pushing a strand of hair behind her ear, she decided there was only one way to satisfy that curiosity. She was alone. No one would know. And afterward, the dress would lose whatever strange attraction it held for her.

In a matter of minutes, she'd stripped off her shorts and shirt and pulled the dress over her head. It fell around her with a sleek rustle, and the lace sleeves slipped easily over her arms, a perfect fit. The dress all but buttoned itself, her fingers barely touching each button before it was tucked in its corresponding loop. She finished the left sleeve and was working on the right when she noticed that one of the buttons was missing. The last one at the wrist.

Gentry wished she'd checked the gown herself instead of being so careless. Either Heather had missed sewing one back on, or it hadn't been in the jewelry pouch with the others. Odd that Heather wouldn't have mentioned it, but then, she had Mitch on her mind, so maybe it wasn't odd at all. Gentry wondered if the button might still be around the pool. Chances were, though, it was gone for good.

She reached behind her for the headpiece and checked the mirror to center it on her hair. Then she waited, watching the mirror for a twinkle. But her reflection remained uncluttered and unaccompanied. Only a bride with bright red hair and bright green eyes and the bright idea that she would give this magic dress every opportunity to prove itself.

Giving the skirt a gentle twist, she admired herself in the mirror, feeling a little like a child playing dress-up. "Mirror, mirror, on the wall," she said aloud. "Stop fooling around and twinkle, would you?"

Just as she'd expected, nothing happened.

"Okay, magic wedding dress, you had your chance and blew it." Playfully, she stuck out her tongue before she whipped off the headpiece and tossed it behind her. Then she crooked her arms behind her back and reached for the buttons. One sleeve caught somehow in the lace and she frowned. Tugging slightly, she tried to pull it free. When that didn't work, she tried to reach her left wrist with her right hand. But no matter how she twisted and turned and stretched, the fingers of one hand barely touched the others.

It was quickly apparent she wasn't going to get out of the dress without assistance. If she didn't know better, she'd expect Sydney to come around the corner and snap her picture. But as much as she might wish this wasn't her own fault, Gentry knew the responsibility was her own. And she'd just have to buck up and bear the teasing....

With a disgusted sigh, she moved close to the mirror and pressed her shoulder against it, trying to get a better look at the snag. From the corner of her eye, she caught a movement and her breath stuck in her throat as Jake's image became clear and certain behind her. *Holy cow, it was magic!* was the first thought she had, followed closely by a second— *Could Jake's reflection get her unsnagged?*

His smile was the one that had stopped her heart the first minute she saw it ... and every minute after that, including this one. "Hello," she whispered, hoping the sound of her voice wouldn't shatter the illusion.

It didn't. His expression clouded with a faint surprise. Maybe she wasn't supposed to talk. "Is it okay to speak to you?" she asked, barely breathing the words aloud.

The surprise changed to a question, but he nodded.

So far, so good. She kept her eyes fixed on his in the mirror and tried to look reassuring. "Are you allowed to make contact?"

He clearly didn't understand that.

"Can you touch me?"

He appeared to consider the question carefully before he nodded.

"Oh, good," she whispered. "I didn't know how I was going to get out of this dress without someone finding out I tried it on."

"It'll be our secret . . . Liz," he whispered back.

"Oh. You can talk to me, too." The words were out of her mouth before she registered the changing tilt of his smile and the truth sluiced through her in a warm, mortifying wave. She looked over her shoulder and into his laughing eyes. "What are you doing here?" she asked.

"I'm trying to make contact."

"You should try knocking on the door."

"That's one of the great things about magic. No doors are needed. I can just *appear.*"

"In that case, you can just *dis*appear."

"Don't I get to make contact first?"

"I'll die in this dress first."

"That's a little drastic even for you, isn't it, Liz?"

"Don't call me that! Just go away."

"And leave you like this?" He shook his head. "I don't think so. People will say I twisted your arm."

She laid her forehead against the mirror, wishing it would swallow her whole. "This is the most embarrassing moment of my entire life," she said.

"Cheer up, kiddo." He stepped closer, took her by the shoulders and turned her around, so he could get a look at the snag. "I have a feeling you have more embarrassing moments ahead."

"Thanks. That makes me feel better."

"Good, because I'm about to make you feel worse."

"You can't."

"Let me give it a try. You're stuck."

She raised her head. "Stuck?"

"As in, the button is caught in the lace and I don't think I can get it out."

"Pull on it," she ordered. "Break the thread."

"I'm not breaking it. You do it."

"I can't. My arm is twisted."

"Then, you're going to be stuck like this until I can figure out a way to get you unstuck without damaging the dress."

"Forget the dress!"

"It's a million-dollar dress, Liz. You can forget it if you want to, but I can't."

She sucked in her breath, hoping it would loosen the bodice and let the button slip free. It didn't, and her temper crowded out her patience. "Jake, get me out of this dress, and get me out of it now!"

He frowned at her in the mirror. "Why couldn't you have asked me to do this when we were married?"

"I wasn't stuck in this dress then," she snapped.

"I don't remember you ever dragging me into your bedroom and demanding I get you out of your clothes then," he continued conversationally. "I might have had some incentive for ripping off your clothes then, but no, you have to wait until you're wearing a dress that cost—"

"A million dollars. We've covered that already, Jake. Will you concentrate on the button, please?"

"I'm trying." Grasping her by the shoulders, he turned her until her back was to the mirror. He high-stepped over a floor awash in satin and positioned himself behind her. "Now that I think about it, there were a few times you ripped off my clothes. You were always in such a hurry, Liz. Maybe you don't remember, but let me tell you—"

"I remember," she said tightly. As if she would ever forget the sexual hunger he'd aroused in her. Her body had craved his with an exciting, frightening and consuming appetite. Even now, the touch of his fingers at her back, the fresh, outdoorsy scent of him, snuck past her defenses, stirring up feelings she had to keep suppressed. Otherwise...

Otherwise didn't bear thinking about. She tried to see over her shoulder. "What are you doing?"

He took her shoulder and positioned it where it had been before. "I'm trying my best to tear off your clothes, and it would be a whole lot easier to get you undressed if you'd stop trying to see what I'm doing."

She stood still as long as she could. About fifteen seconds.

"Don't move your arm, Gentry," he said.

"I can't help it. This is uncomfortable."

"If you think it would be more comfortable, I'll be glad to go down and ask your friends to come up and assist you."

"No. I'd rather keep that for a last resort." She shifted her weight from one foot to the other and felt him draw back. "Sorry. I won't move again. It would be easier to stand still, though, if you'd talk to me and keep my mind off the fact that my arm is falling asleep."

His fingers closed over her upper arm in a gentle massage. Jake was always so good with his hands. Everywhere he touched her felt energized, warm and wanting. If he brought his arms around her, he could massage her breasts, her stomach... "That's much better," she said stiffly. "I thought you were leaving today."

"Tonight. I'm catching the red-eye flight."

"Oh."

"Isn't that soon enough to suit you?"

"That depends on how fast you get me out of this dress," she said, wanting badly to fidget. "I can't believe I got caught in this...." She smoothed the lace bodice at her waist with her unstuck hand. "Did you come to say goodbye?"

"No. I came to return something you lost."

"My ring," she said without thinking. "You brought back my ring."

His fingers lost interest in the snagged button and he leaned around her to see her face. "That would be the wedding band you were planning to turn into a piece of gaudy jewelry, wouldn't it?"

She realized she shouldn't have mentioned the ring. "I don't wear gaudy jewelry, Jake. I believe I said cheap. Cheap jewelry."

"I see." He returned to the snag. "You're not getting your wedding ring back, Gen."

"Fine. I don't really care one way or the... What were you coming to return?"

There was a startling knock on the outer door and Gentry stiffened. "Someone's here," she whispered.

"You stay here. I'll make contact with whoever's here."

She caught his arm as he started to step around her. "Are you crazy? You can't answer the door."

"Then you do it."

"Like I want anyone to see me in this outfit." She bit her lower lip. "Let's be quiet and maybe whoever it is will go away."

"You're the one talking."

She nodded. Another knock came, followed closely by another. Then a familiar *clunk*. "It's Sonny," she whispered hoarsely, turning to look at Jake. "What should we do?"

"Ask him in for cake and punch?"

"This time you could get punched."

"He doesn't know you're in here, does he?"

She shook her head no just as they heard the outer door open. "Gentry?" Sonny called softly. "I know you're in here."

Panic spiraled in her all over again. "Get in the closet," she whispered. "Quick!"

"Couldn't we just tell him I was only filling in for him until he got here?"

"Sydney said you were still mad about the brunch." Sonny's voice sounded stationary, at least. "I've come to make up with you."

Jake's eyebrows rose with interest. "See? He wants to make up."

"Will you get in the closet?"

With a shrug, Jake ambled to the adjoining doorway. "I think this is a bad idea, Liz," he said, but she motioned him on and he went.

"Gentry?" Sonny crooned, and she could tell he was coming closer.

"Go away, Sonny." She tried throwing her voice at him, but it came out sounding weak and uncertain.

"I'm sorry," he said softly. "Did I wake you?"

"No." Gentry looked around the dressing room, hoping some escape hatch would open in the floor. "Go away."

"Ahhhh. Were you crying?"

"No! I . . . Go away, Sonny. Please."

"I've come to apologize, Gen." His voice returned to the crooning tone. "Don't you want to make up? I've given you all afternoon to pout."

"I don't want to see you now," she said, giving her twisted arm a jerk, hoping to get it free, but merely succeeding in getting a cramp in her shoulder. "Ow."

His footsteps came farther into the room. "Where are you? Come out where I can talk to you."

"No," she called. "And I don't want you to come in here, either."

"You're being stubborn again. You know that makes me crazy."

"It makes me crazy for you to be in my bedroom. So go away."

His laughter said he'd misinterpreted her meaning. "Only five days to go, darling. Then it will be *our* bedroom . . . and a one-way ticket to paradise."

She glanced at the closet, thinking that if Jake so much as snickered . . . "I'm not dressed," she said in her best, I-can't-wait-to-be-with-you imitation. "Go downstairs and wait for me, please?"

"You're not dressed, huh? Maybe we could pretend this is already our bedroom. Preview a few of the rides in paradise. What do you say?"

"No!" That should stop him in his tracks. "I don't want to see you right now, Sonny. I want you to leave my bedroom right now. Is that clear enough for you?"

"Sure, but I don't know why you're so mad at me. The whole thing was Daniels's fault. All I need is one good swing, and he's history."

Glancing nervously toward the closet, Gentry hoped Jake wouldn't decide it was time to let Sonny take that swing. "You'd only hurt your hand," she said. "Is it feeling better?"

"The only thing that would make me feel better right now is seeing you."

She ran her hand down her midriff...and felt the perfect excuse. "I can't let you see me now because I'm wearing my wedding gown. I know how superstitious you are about that, and, well, I sort of panicked when you came in."

"You were beginning to make me nervous." His relief was evident in his voice. "I really need a kiss."

"I just told you, I'm—"

"I know. What if I just sit on the bed and wait while you take it off?"

"No, I...I'm not ready to, uh, take it off." She imitated Heather's giggle...badly. "It's a female thing."

"Oh. Well, then, what if I keep my eyes shut while you tiptoe out here and give me a kiss?"

"Couldn't I kiss you later?"

Dumb question, she realized, when he said, "I'll take one now and later, thank you."

"Fine." Maybe Syd had the right idea. Dogs had to be easier to care for. Gathering the skirt in her free hand, she eased the cramp in her shoulder with a shimmy, then walked across the dressing room to the doorway.

The first thing she saw was her fiancé, one hand over his eyes, his broken hand resting on the edge of the makeup table. The second thing she saw was Cleo, stretched out on the floor by the bed. If Sonny had taken another step into the room, he'd have seen the dog. Gentry said a little prayer of thanks for small favors and took a step forward...and then two steps back.

Frowning, she pulled the skirt into a tighter circle around her and took a firm step forward...and two firm steps back. This was not progress, she thought, and took her time making the next move. She reached the doorway again and, without a pause, stepped into the bedroom...and immediately found herself still in the doorway. She rubbed her eyes and promised herself a tall glass of Pop's secret formula as soon as she got out of this situation.

"Gentry?" Sonny called softly. "I'm waiting."

"Keep your eyes closed," she called back.

"I wouldn't peek for the world. I want to be surprised by the sight of you in your wedding dress on Saturday."

"You will be." But she could not get past the doorway. Confused, she lifted one foot and slowly, carefully, put it down outside the threshold. It settled easily on the bedroom side. Okay, that was good. She could do this. She repeated the process just as carefully, and found herself still in the dressing room. Her frustration level began to rise and she tamped it down. This was not difficult. True, kissing Sonny wasn't all that appealing at the moment, but she wasn't repelled by the thought, either.

This was simply one of those mind-over-matter deals. She was simply imagining the difficulty.

"I'm waiting...anticipating...." Sonny puckered and blew her an audible kiss.

Cleo's ears perked up.

Gentry gripped the outer frame of the doorway with her one available hand and took a deep breath.

"What are you doing?" Jake's whisper was right in her ear. "Do you want him to find me in your bedroom? Get out there and kiss him."

She tossed a glare over her shoulder and lunged through the doorway.

Jake caught her as she fell back against him, one hand clamped on her breast, one supporting her crooked elbow. He staggered but managed to push her upright. "Stop fooling around, Liz," he said into her ear. "This isn't funny."

As if she was having buckets of fun. "I can't get through the doorway." She turned so he could see her irritation as she mouthed the words.

"What?" he mouthed back.

"I . . . can't . . . get . . . through . . . the . . . doorway."

He looked past her, then back. "Why not?"

She rolled her eyes and tried poking her head through the opening. Apparently, that was allowed. "Are your eyes still closed?" she called to Sonny, even though she could see they were. "Don't peek."

"I won't."

Cleo sat up, yawned, stretched and shook herself.

"What was that?" Sonny asked.

"Just me," she answered as if she hadn't a care in the world. "I'm having difficulty with my, uh, bridal train. It seems to be caught on something."

"Do you need some help?"

"No! No, I'll get it."

She felt Jake's palms press flat against her hips. "You start, I'll push," he whispered.

"Wait," she snapped.

"Did you say something, sweetheart?" Sonny took a step toward her.

Cleo's tail began to wag a greeting.

"No," Gentry denied. "I was talking to the dress."

"I'll bet you look beautiful in it."

"Mmmm." She looked furious in it, but he didn't have to know that. "Just keep those eyes closed." Glancing at Jake, she nodded. She leaned into her first step as if she was entering a wind tunnel. And just as if there were a wind tunnel on the other side of the doorway, she made no progress whatsoever...even when Jake stopped pushing with his hands and put his whole body weight behind her. She sagged against the door frame, her arm pressed between her back and the frame. Tomorrow, maybe she'd tell Jake what a strange dream she'd had. Except tomorrow Jake would be gone. She'd never see him again. He'd be history.

"Gentry?" Sonny's croon picked up an edge of impatience. "Don't tease me."

Cleo's tail wagged faster.

Jake put his hands at Gentry's waist and stepped into the doorway with her, his body heat finding its way past the thick satin to arouse her body's interest. Then he moved past her into the bedroom. Her eyes flew to his in alarm, but he ignored her panic and got her arm in a firm, good-golf-club grip. He planted his feet several inches apart on the bedroom carpet and before she quite realized his intention, he jerked her into the room. She flew forward like a rock out of a slingshot, straight into Jake's arms, and they fell with a thud into a tangle of four legs, three arms and yard upon yard of innocent satin.

"Gentry?" Sonny leaned toward the sound. "Are you all right?"

She lifted her head and pushed against Jake's chest, ignoring the feel of his heartbeat beneath her hand, until she could raise herself enough to get Sonny in her sights. "Fine." She cleared her throat and said it again. "Fine. I just . . . dropped something."

"Must have been the set out of your engagement ring," Sonny joked with a smile. "Now, how much longer are you going to keep me waiting like this?"

She looked down at Jake and a totally inappropriate desire flickered in her eyes. She could tell because she saw his gaze drop to her lips in reply. "Give me a minute," she said weakly.

"No. I can't wait another minute for your sweet kiss." Sonny puckered again and made a series of kissing sounds. "Come here and give me a smooch."

So Cleo trotted over, put her paws on his chest and *smooched* him.

Chapter Ten

"Aa-aa-aa-ck!" Sonny yelled.

"Arf!" Cleo barked.

"I think I'm going to be sick." Gentry let her head drop onto her chest.

"Now would not be a good time." Jake put his hands at her waist and lifted her up and off of him.

She rolled onto her back on the floor, one leg tied to his by a lengthy twist of satin. From here she had a perfect view of the ceiling, until Sonny's head popped, upside down, into her line of vision.

"Gentry!"

"Sonny?"

"Daniels!"

"Harris."

Gentry managed a weak smile in the face of disaster. "You were supposed to keep your eyes closed," she said.

"So I wouldn't see *him*, I suppose?"

"No." Jake pushed up, bracing himself with his elbows. "So you wouldn't spoil the surprise."

"The surprise of finding you in Gentry's bedroom?"

"No, the surprise of seeing her in her wedding gown." Jake's tone added a distinctive *You idiot,* although he didn't say it aloud.

Sonny apparently heard it, anyway. "Get up, Daniels," he ordered. "So I can punch you into next week."

"Haven't you had enough punch for one day?"

"I've never hit a man when he was down, but you could be the exception."

"Stop it, Sonny." Gentry struggled to get up, but with one arm behind her back and one leg tied up with Jake's, it was a futile effort and she fell back. "Would it be too much to ask you to help me up?"

"Considering you sent the dog to kiss me, I'm not sure I want to help you up." Sonny's angry gaze swung from Jake to her.

It was terrible timing, but he looked so odd from this perspective, she smiled.

"It isn't funny," Sonny said. "She *licked* me on the lips!"

"Cleo!" Jake scolded. "I've told you not to French kiss on the first date."

Gentry closed her eyes, praying that when she opened them, she'd be alone.

"Your choice, Daniels," Sonny said. "I can take a swing at you whether you're sitting or standing."

"What about if I lie flat?"

"Let's find out."

"Sonny!" Gentry rolled onto her side and into a sitting position. "If you'll stop acting out your own version of *Rocky,* I'll tell you why Jake is here."

"One explanation comes readily to mind." Sonny scowled down at her, and all Gentry could think of was a line from a song. *A frown is a smile turned upside down.*

"That isn't the explanation." Jake got to his feet and Sonny took a swing at him. At the time, luckily, Jake was bending down to grasp Gentry's arm and help her up...and the punch sailed over him.

Gentry grabbed Sonny's arm and held on. "I never realized you were so violent," she said. "Will you stop and listen to me. There's a perfectly reasonable explanation."

He looked at her, his anger diminishing beneath the censure of her expression. "I'll listen," he said.

She relaxed a little. Sonny might not like it, but he'd believe her. He had no reason not to. "I snagged a button in the lace and Jake was only trying to get it free." She twisted at the waist, to show him that a button on her sleeve was indeed snagged in the lace at her back. "See, there's nothing to be upset about."

"I was only trying to help," Jake said.

Sonny still looked upset. "Did you call him to come over and help?" he asked. "Or did he just *happen* to show up at the exact moment you snagged the dress?"

"He came to return something I lost," she informed him crisply. *So there,* she thought.

"What?"

"What?" She repeated Sonny's question.

"What did you lose?"

"What did I lose?"

His expression turned suspicious again. "What did you lose, Gentry? What was Daniels returning?"

Gentry looked at Sonny, drew a blank and stalled. "What was he returning...?" *Rush in here with the answer anytime, Jake.* Finally, with a disgusted sigh, she turned to him and pointedly asked, "What did I lose, Jake?"

"You don't know?" Sonny said, incredulous.

Jake reached into his shirt pocket and extended his hand to show her the button.

"Oh," she said, pleased. "The missing button."

"What missing button?" Sonny leaned close, checking to make sure it really was a button.

"The missing button on this dress," she informed him, and held out her hand, turning it palm up, so he could see. "On the wrist."

"Where?" he asked.

"Oh, for heaven's sake, it's right—" She cut her gaze to her wrist, directing his attention to the single, unattached fabric loop that should have held a button, but didn't. Except now... it did. Every loop had a corresponding button. Not a missing link among them. Gentry frowned. "It must be the other sleeve," she said. "I only thought it was this one."

Sonny took her by the shoulders and spun her a half turn. A moment later, he spun her back. "No buttons missing there, either."

"Well, it came off of this dress somewhere." Jake took her by the shoulders, spun her a half turn and ran his finger down the back of the dress. "All there." He spun her back, picked up her hand and ran his eye along the buttoned sleeve, double-checking Sonny's initial inventory. His forehead furrowed with a frown. "Sonny's right," he said. "The buttons are all there."

"Then where did this one come from?"

"Which one?" Sonny asked.

"The one Jake's holding in his hand. The one he was returning."

Jake rubbed his jaw. "I gave it to you, Liz."

"No, you didn't. It was still in your hand a minute ago."

He held out his hands...empty.

"It must have fallen on the floor." She scanned the light-colored carpet.

"So," Sonny said. "To sum up, Jake came to your bedroom to return a missing button and had to stay because another button snagged in the lace and you needed his help to get it free. Right?"

That sounded like a fair account, and she nodded her acceptance of it.

"Only no buttons are missing," Sonny continued. "Except the button he came here to return."

"But you saw it."

He shook his head, his eyes cool with solidifying suspicion. "I'm not sure what I saw, but it obviously was not a button."

She could see this was not going well. "Don't jump to conclusions, Sonny. You can certainly see that my hand is caught, otherwise I wouldn't keep holding it at this awkward..." She tugged against the snag to demonstrate the strength of her testimony and her hand swung from behind her in a smooth arc, like a discus thrower winding up for the throw. She caught it with her other hand as it passed her waist, staring at it in surprise, then raising her eyes to Sonny's I-knew-it expression. "This is just a simple misunderstanding," she began, but he cut her off.

"Gentry, I think I'm quite capable of understanding what you've said...and what was obviously going on in this bedroom before I interrupted it."

Her temper flared into a low, don't-mess-with-me, I-only-did-it-for-you huskiness. "I didn't want you to know, Sonny, but since you've found out, I may as well tell you everything."

Behind her, Jake made a strangled sound, but she ignored him and kept her sultry gaze on her fiancé's face. "You see, it's just as you thought. Jake broke in here like a madman and began making wild and passionate love to me in my dressing room. I wanted to resist, but he can be so...convincing."

"Gentry..." Jake growled a warning, but she simply incorporated it into her improvisation.

"No, no, Jake. He deserves to know. You mustn't blame Jake, Sonny. It wasn't all his fault."

"That's a relief," Jake muttered.

"I should have screamed." She brought up her arm and laid her forehead against it. "Maybe I wanted him to kiss me, I don't know." The arm fell away. "But when you knocked, I panicked, and even though my closet was so close I could have reached in and grabbed a robe, I seized the nearest dress...which happened to be forty tons of satin with hundreds of tiny buttons, but I persevered because I wanted to protect you from thinking the worst. I quickly—because I knew how impatiently you were waiting—unbuttoned the dress and slipped into it. Then I quickly rebuttoned every button while trying to keep you from catching a glimpse of me in the wedding dress, because I knew that would be *bad luck*. Then I discovered one of the buttons had snagged in the lace, but I was so desperate to see you that, with one arm twisted painfully behind my back, I rushed to the doorway only to have some unseen force hold me back and prevent me from reaching you."

She paused to let her lashes flutter down to her cheeks, then swept them up to look soulfully into his eyes. "I struggled against fate, Sonny, truly I did. I know Jake will throw all of his weight behind mine when I assure you that only a force stronger than all of us could have kept me from fulfilling my destiny and giving you a *smooch!*"

For a moment, the silence in the room was similar to an audience's stunned reaction to an Oscar-winning performance. Then it was broken by a rhythmic *clap, clap, clap.*

"Bravo," Jake said. "That was magnificent, my dear. If only you could have given this performance for Sergeant Orange yesterday, maybe he wouldn't have held us in jail half the night."

Sonny's confused gaze stumbled to Jake, then returned to Gentry. "Jail?" His tone sounded dazed... or possibly numb. "You were in jail?"

"Not *in* jail," she clarified. "Just at the jail. It was a misunderstanding," she said. "Sort of like the one we're having now."

"But you were arrested?"

"No," she assured him. "Sergeant Orange wanted to arrest us... well, me, anyway... but there was no evidence. It was clear I hadn't committed a murder."

"Murder?"

"Actually, that was resolved before we left the hotel." Jake stepped forward to add his two pennies' worth. "Sergeant Orange was operating on the theory that he should do the city a favor and get Gentry off the streets for the night."

"He thought I was a prostitute," she explained. "Because I was wearing your jacket."

Sonny stroked his narrow mustache. "Where was I?"

"Dead—" Jake held Sonny's gaze "—asleep."

"The pain medication they gave you at the hospital knocked you out," Gentry told him.

"I was unconscious?"

"No," Jake said. "But you definitely weren't feeling any pain."

Sonny continued to stroke his mustache and stare at Jake. "I knew there was something I wanted to remember about you, Daniels."

They squared off like bulldogs, eyes wary, stance ready, all but drooling testosterone.

"What would that be, Harris? My admirable self-restraint?"

"No." Sonny moved his hand away from his mustache and smiled. "I want to remember how your nose looked before it got in front of my fist."

"Sonny!" Gentry gasped out a protest, but Sonny had drawn back his left arm and his fist was already on its way to connect with Jake's face. Luckily, Jake jerked back, his reflexes kicking in to save his nose. "You missed!"

At her relieved shout, Jake turned to frown at her. "What do you mean, 'You missed'?" he repeated just before the momentum of Sonny's windmill swing carried him all the way around and brought his right hand—the one with the cast—into direct contact with Jake's heretofore unbroken nose.

SYDNEY SLATHERED HER LEGS with tanning gel, then tossed the bottle over Hillary's prone body to Heather. "In my opinion, the situation is getting desperate. Jake's leaving tonight. If we don't do something, she's going to go through with the wedding as planned."

"You didn't really believe she wouldn't, did you?" Hillary's head rested, facedown, on her crossed arms, making her voice sound muffled and lethargic. "She's been planning this wedding for nearly two years."

"Four," Heather said. "If you count the time she spent planning the other wedding. Mitch and I won't have a long engagement, I'll tell you that right now."

"You're just anxious to wear those sexy teddies, Heather." Sydney adjusted her sunglasses and the angle of the deck chair. "I can't imagine what it's like for Gen to have to plan every inch of her walk down the aisle."

"She has Sonny to keep her centered," Hillary said.

"What does she see in him?" Heather asked. "I mean, he's nice enough, and steady as a stone, but... well, Jake is so much more her type."

"There's nothing wrong with being steady and dependable and... nice."

Sydney pulled her glasses down and looked over the rim at Hillary. "We're not saying there's anything *wrong* with Sonny Harris. He might be bearable, if he were with a woman who could temper his compulsiveness and give him some instruction on how to behave in a crowd. Someone like you, Hil, for instance."

Hillary's head came up with a jerk, but when her eyes met Sydney's, she quickly looked away. "Don't be ridiculous. He and Gentry are a perfect fit. Everyone says so."

"Except her best friends." Heather sat up and looped her arms over her knees. "I say we do something to stop this."

"Like what?" Hillary returned her head to her arms. "Kidnap her and keep her locked up until after Saturday?"

Sydney lay back, drinking in the warmth of the sun. "Hillary, you are brilliant. That is a terrific idea."

"Grow up, Sydney. We are not going to kidnap her. Even best friends should only go so far in pressing their opinions. Gentry is perfectly capable of deciding who she will or won't marry and whether she will or won't go through with this wedding."

"Feeling a bit peevish, are we, Hil?" Sydney asked.

"No," came the muffled but huffy reply. "I'm just tired of all these childish pranks. We should stop behaving like children."

"Hmmm. What do you think, Heather? Is it time to commit to a staid and mature existence?"

"She's kidding, Syd. Hillary will be last one of us to grow up. As long as she can raise a little hell with her friends, she can manage to be perfect and proper the rest of the time. Isn't that right?" She leaned over and dropped a piece of ice in the center of Hillary's tanned back.

Hillary swatted it aside with the back of her hand. "Why don't you two go play somewhere else?"

"Because we need your detailed planning ability," Sydney said, "in carrying out the kidnapping of Sonny Harris."

"Sonny?" Hillary raised her head.

"I thought we were going to kidnap Gentry."

Sydney shook her head. "Sonny makes a much better hostage. He's not overly suspicious of us and he has the advantage of being completely unnecessary for the next few days. We can say he's out of town on business and no one will be the wiser. It'll be a breeze."

"Won't Sonny be suspicious when we lock him away somewhere?" Hillary asked.

"We're not going to lock him away anywhere, my precious. You're going to persuade him to take a little trip with you. Heather and I will handle the rest from here.''

"And just how would I persuade a man I barely know to take a trip with me?''

"Your brilliant mind will think of something. I do adore scheming like this. If only Gentry could be in on it.''

"She'll never forgive us if Sonny doesn't show up for their wedding.''

"He will, Heather. We're only going to keep him a couple of days and let her think about the worst that could happen if he didn't show up. It'll be good for her.''

"Are you kidding? She'll kill us,'' Hillary protested.

Heather wavered. "Kidnapping is a federal offense.''

"For the last time, we are not kidnapping him. We're just going to get him out of the way for a while.''

"This is exactly the sort of adolescent prank I was talking about, Sydney.'' Hillary rolled over and sat up, her hands closing tightly over the edge of her deck chair. "It needs to stop.''

Sydney rolled onto her side and took off her glasses so she could meet Hillary eye to eye. "When our friendship reaches the point that we say 'to hell with it,' 'so what' or 'it's none of my business,' then we've written the last chapter in our relationship, because caring about one another, Hil, is what the four of us do best.'' She put her glasses on again and settled back. "Now, are you in or out?''

Hillary's sigh was as deep as the Grand Canyon. "I'm in.''

Heather smiled. "I'm in, too."

Sydney laughed. "So am I."

"I CAN'T BELIEVE YOU actually hit him!" Gentry paced her bedroom, annoyed with Sonny, irritated with Jake and furious with herself for being involved with them.

"He had it coming," Sonny defended himself while he held an ice pack on his hand. "You have to admit he's been asking for it ever since he got here."

"We're not talking about his behavior, Sonny. We're talking about yours. You shouldn't have hit him, no matter what he did, said or thought about."

"What about your behavior, Gentry?" He exposed her sore spot with one question and she paced some more.

"My behavior was..." She really hated having to admit she'd been wrong. "It left something to be desired."

"So you admit you should have insisted he leave and not let him run wild in your house like a tomcat on the prowl."

"Honestly, Sonny, you are so paranoid about Jake. I've told you he's history. I learned my lesson. How many times do I have to tell you I'm going to marry you before you finally believe me?"

He gave her a sheepish look. "I suppose I'll believe you on Saturday."

Saturday. Their wedding day. Gentry sighed, wondering if the curious lump in her stomach was anticipation or dread. "Maybe it would be better if we steered clear of each other for a day or two. Take our prewedding frustrations out on some of the other people in our lives for a change, instead of each other."

"You don't want to see me until the wedding?"

He looked hurt, and she wished she wasn't too upset to care. "I don't want to quarrel with you, Sonny," she said. "We've planned this wedding for so long, I just want it to be perfect. If we spend the week at each other's throats because Jake had the poor judgment to show up uninvited, then he's ruined our wedding again. Let's give ourselves some space. Okay?"

He stood and walked to the door, clutching the ice bag awkwardly with his cast. "All right, if that's the way you want it. Call me when you're ready to see me. I'll be waiting."

Gentry sank onto the love seat and put her head in her hands. He was such a martyr at times. All she wanted was a little time. A chance to catch her breath and look forward to the future. Jake's presence had stolen both. But he was leaving tonight, and tomorrow he'd be out of her life forever and everything would go back to being the way it was before. Perfect.

All she had to do was get through tonight. The rest would be easy. She could make it one night, knowing he was nearby. One night. Not even twenty-four hours.

She settled into the window seat and tried to amuse herself with thinking that Sydney, Hillary and Heather were probably plotting at this very moment to get her into the magic wedding dress. They could spin their devious wheels from now until Saturday, but she was never putting that dress on again. Now that she was out of it, she was sure she'd imagined the whole implausible afternoon. It had been a silly dream.

A silly dream about Jake.

She shut her eyes and leaned her head against her knees. One night. Just one more night.

HILLARY SPOTTED HIM in the hotel coffee shop, sitting alone at a table for two. Gathering her courage and every last ounce of her confidence, she approached him. "Sonny, hi. I was hoping I'd find you here."

He looked up from staring into a nearly full cup of coffee. "If you're here to tell me I'm an idiot for picking a fight with Daniels and breaking his nose, there's nothing you can say that will make me feel any worse."

Her eyebrows arched upward in surprise. "You broke his nose?"

"Yeah. This afternoon when I found him with Gentry in her bedroom."

"Really, hmmm." Hillary pulled out the chair across from him and waved away the approaching waiter. "What was he doing in her bedroom?"

"Returning a button, they said, but who the hell knows. They're both so...I don't know, frivolous, I guess. She makes up one story and he tells another. Gentry turns everything into a *drama*. She and her pop. Two of a kind."

Hillary considered that. "It's a very dramatic household," she said. "I don't understand why you look like you've lost your best friend, though. You broke Jake's nose. That ought to make you feel better."

"What?" He frowned. "I thought you were the primary reason I got sloshed with punch at the Hamiltons'."

"I detest public scenes," she said. "If you must fight, do it in private. That's my motto."

"I usually am a model guest. Daniels just rubs me the wrong way."

"I think we're all aware of that now."

"Gentry's right. I was clearly in the wrong. Physical violence is never a solution. I shouldn't have hit him."

She shrugged. "Get over it, Sonny. Everyone makes mistakes."

"I never used to."

"Sure you did. What are you drinking?"

"I don't know. Coffee, I guess."

With a laugh, she reached across the table and patted his hand. He wasn't so bad, she thought. Just a little too unsure of what people expected of him. With a little encouragement, he might develop into someone very nice to know.

He pulled his hand back. "I'm engaged to Gentry," he said, as offended as if she'd made a pass at him.

"I have a rule about my friends' significant others. You want to know what it is?"

"Okay."

"The rule is, no pass, no play, no promises. So you can relax, Sonny. I'm only here because I thought you might like to play a round of golf with me. Or we could just sit here and drink coffee and talk. Since you're going to marry one of my closest friends, you and I should probably get better acquainted."

He held up his cast. "Golf is out for a while. But if you don't mind drinking overbrewed coffee..."

"As a matter of fact, I do mind. I'm rather particular about what I drink. Do you like cappuccino?"

"If it's made correctly, sure."

"I happen to know where we can get the best in the world."

"The best?" He questioned her judgment with a skeptical smile. "It always makes me skeptical when someone says they know the *best* anything."

"You don't have to take my word for it. We can go there and you can decide for yourself."

"Now?"

"Do you have something else to do?"

He pushed his cup away and stood, tossing a couple of dollars on the table. "As a matter of fact, I'm free until Saturday. So where is this best cup of cappuccino in the world?"

"I'll have to show you. I could never explain how to get there from here. It's a long way from here, but I promise it's worth the trip."

"Then what are we waiting for?"

"I like people who know their own minds." She fell into step beside him. "Oh, I *was* wondering, Sonny... do you happen to have your passport with you...?"

Chapter Eleven

Gentry found the ransom note in her room that evening. The single sheet of notebook paper was stuck with tape to the center of the mirror in the dressing room and she pulled it off with a sigh. But when she unfolded the note, she had to laugh.

Cutout letters spelled odd-shaped words in between pictures cut out of magazine ads. Sydney's magazine would never be the same, and although Gentry couldn't say it had been sacrificed for a good cause, at least the note was clever and she could imagine the fun they'd had putting it together.

She scanned the note, pausing once or twice over a picture to puzzle out the meaning. HOLDING. A cutout yellow sun beside a picture of a man's hairy legs. RANSOM. A cellular phone was circled in red with a line drawn through the center and an arrow pointing to an ad for Florida orange juice. COME TO. A picture of a house with a pool. AFTER. Another smiling yellow sun, with an ad for a down comforter below it. OR ELSE. SIGNED. At the bottom, above a penciled-in signature line, was a picture of a wedding dress with a pasted-on cutout of Tinkerbell tossing magic dust. Glitter was glued all around the page and fell in a shimmering trail to the signature line. At the bottom of the page, big block letters spelled out P.S. BRING BEER!

Gentry read it again, aloud this time, laughing and shaking her head at the energy they'd put into this.

"*Holding...*"

"Sunburn, suntan, legs, suntanned legs... knees? Sun knees? Sonny!"

"*Holding Sonny ransom. Don't phone...*"

"Florida? Orange? Sergeant Orange!"

"*Sergeant Orange. Come to the pool after sundown. Or else. Signed, The Magic Wedding Dress.*"

She could imagine Sydney dictating the words, while Heather clipped the pictures and Hillary glued them neatly onto the paper. What they expected her to do was a little harder to imagine, but she suspected that if she went out to the pool, she'd find them there, pretending they had no earthly idea where the note had come from.

They would read it, ask questions, make up new interpretations for the pictures and deny ever having seen Sonny's legs.

"Are they missing?" Heather would ask with concern.

"You should check the emergency room," Hillary would suggest.

Sydney would, naturally, go straight for the bottom line. "Did you bring the beer?"

She was suddenly glad they were here for the week. Being with them was the best thing she could do for herself right now. After the incident between Sonny and Jake, she had wanted nothing more than to be alone, so she'd left the house, headed for her favorite stores and wandered aimlessly through the aisles.

She'd driven fast, put a compact disc in the player and turned up the volume. Anything to keep from thinking about Jake, wondering if he was all right, hoping his nose wasn't broken, thinking he had provoked Sonny's punch, knowing he didn't deserve a broken nose, deciding she wouldn't think about him ever again, and then running through the list again.

As she drove home, she had toyed with the idea of walking to the guest house. Just to check on him. Make sure...what? That she still loved him? Bad idea.

But now, here was an invitation from her friends, teasing her to come out and play. What would she ever do without them? She changed into her swimsuit and tucked the note into the folds of her towel, knowing they'd be eager to admire their handiwork. Then she headed for the kitchen to get the ransom for "sun knees."

JAKE DIVED INTO THE POOL, slicing his way through the cool, chlorinated blue until he reached the bottom, then turning to push off with his feet and shoot like an arrow to the surface. He had a picture of Pop's Stetson-shaped swimming pool hanging on a wall at the Two-Penny Lodge. It was something of a joke around the lodge that he had been Charlie North's son-in-law, and Jake wondered at times why he left the reminder in place.

But he knew the answer. The picture kept him centered. It had probably been the single, most compelling reason he hadn't put up a fight when Gentry left. For him, the pool represented everything she had been when he met her...cool, sophisticated, funny, intriguing, inviting, heated, sparkling, luxurious, exhausting, pampered...the list could run for pages.

Jake had grown up half a country away and never once imagined that such a pool... or woman, existed.

Gentry had blazed into his life like a fireball and he had been determined to have her, no matter the cost. He'd pursued her, romanced her, stolen her away, and then eagerly taken her home to a world he couldn't wait to share. But she didn't know how, or wouldn't make the effort, to fit into his world, and he soon discovered there was no more a place for her at the Two-Penny Lodge than there was for a swimming pool shaped like a Stetson hat. She didn't belong there, she didn't want to belong there, and he had been wholly responsible for her unhappiness.

Now he was just wholly responsible for his own.

He shouldn't have come here. No matter what Ben had told him. Gentry was going to marry Harris this time. It would be admitting too many mistakes to cut her losses at this point. One lapse in judgment could be explained away, wiped out, annulled, but to call off the wedding at the last minute a second time...

She wouldn't do that. He knew that as surely as he knew she wanted to. He'd known the moment he kissed her he couldn't stop her and shouldn't try. He'd waited too long, missed whatever window of opportunity he might once have had. Some mistakes couldn't be undone.

Feeling the curved side of the pool, he remembered the feel of her body stretched luxuriantly beside him in their bed at the lodge. Following close on the heels of that came the memory of this afternoon and Gentry in her dressing room, looking beautifully disheveled in the wedding dress, and trying to *make contact* with his reflection in the mirror.

He would treasure that image for the rest of his life.

Gripping the pool's tiled rim, he crooked one arm over the edge while he wiped the water from his face, being careful not to bump his nose in the process. He didn't want to get another nosebleed. It seemed to have taken forever to get that one stopped. He supposed he ought to be grateful Harris's cast-iron punch hadn't been delivered full face or full force, otherwise his nose would be flatter and fatter, and hurt like the dickens. As it was, he'd just gotten clipped, enough to make his eyes water like lawn sprinklers and give him one mother of a nosebleed, but narrowly missing serious injury.

He thought he might feel a little sorry for Harris...except that he couldn't find much sympathy for any man who could look forward to a future with Gentry in it. Even at her temperamental worst, she was pure, fascinating energy and he would have given ten years of his life to steal her away from this wedding, too. But then, as always, came the question he'd failed to ask before...once he had her, what would he do with her?

Shaking back his hair, he grasped the pool rim with both hands and pushed up and out of the water.

"Want a beer?"

His heart stopped beating and then rushed to catch up as he turned to see her sitting an oversize hat brim away. The moon was making a slow appearance in the darkening sky and the automatic lights around the pool flickered somewhere between off and on. She was sitting beside the round table where he'd sat with her father earlier in the day, her bare feet hooked on the edge of the chair, her legs drawn into a slender triangle, her arms carelessly draped across them. If he hadn't already been in love with her, he would have fallen head over heels right then.

"I'd love one. Thanks." He'd forgotten where he left his towel, so he wiped his face with his hands and finger-combed his slick hair, getting rid of as much moisture as he could before he walked around the pool to join her at the poolside table. His body, newly relaxed by the exercise, knotted with a tense and tight desire.

"Are you all right?" She peered closely at him in the semidark. "Don't you have to wear a bandage or anything?"

"No. I was lucky. I'll live to get punched another day."

"But I thought he broke your nose. The way you put your hands over it and with all the blood, I just assumed . . ."

"Just a nosebleed." Jake felt like a fourteen-year-old assuring his girl he was too much of a man to be felled by a bump on the nose. "It looked a lot worse than it was."

"I'm glad it isn't broken. I was always rather partial to your nose just the way it is."

"My nose and I are flattered. It's nice to know there's at least one thing about me you find appealing."

"You deserved that punch, you know," she said as if she'd thought about it a lot. "Except that no one actually deserves to be hurt. But you did do your best to goad Sonny into hitting you."

Jake wasn't sure there was a good way to defend himself on that, so he didn't try. "Did you mention a beer?"

She offered him the bottle and he took it, brushing her fingers in a touch that wasn't accidental and wasn't meant to be. She didn't jerk away from him, but she didn't respond, either...at least not that he could tell. He twisted off the lid and took a long, cold swallow from the bottle. Dropping into a chair across from her, he tried to think of something to say that wouldn't sound completely inane. "Did Harris hurt his hand?" Oh, great opener, Daniels, he thought.

Gentry lifted her brows, obviously sharing his opinion. "Not nearly as badly as I hurt his feelings after you left to take care of your nose."

"Did you beat up the bully for me, Liz?"

"Not for you. I couldn't believe the two of you were brawling in my bedroom. I made sure Sonny understood that it is not to happen ever again."

"It was hardly a brawl. He wouldn't have hit me at all if you hadn't distracted me by cheering him on."

"I wasn't cheering. I was glad he missed you...the first time."

"So was I. But then, I was glad when Cleo *smooched* him." Jake put his head back and laughed long and deeply.

"I did want to, uh, talk to you about that." Embarrassment was burned into every word, as if her voice were blushing. He loved it.

"You want to discuss *smooching?*" he asked in his best I'm-here-for-you-if-you-need-to-talk tone. "We could call Cleo in as a consultant, if you'd feel more comfortable."

She pressed her lips together, and he could all but hear her silently counting to ten. "Could we forget that part for a minute? I wanted to tell you...ask you, really, if... The thing is, something rather strange happened in my bedroom today and I..."

"Did you notice it immediately upon putting on the wedding gown or did it occur later?"

She frowned. "Later. It was an odd sensation and I... Maybe I imagined... Oh, never mind."

He cleared his throat and asked very seriously, "Are you referring to the moment our reflected images *made contact* in the mirror?"

Her eyes flashed to his in annoyance. "No. Honestly, Jake, can't you stop teasing me about that?"

"Stop?" He gave her a sympathetic smile. "This is the first time I've mentioned it, but if it bothers you..."

"It does. You're acting like there was really some sort of magic going on because of that silly dress. And it wasn't like that at all. I was distracted because of the button and—"

"Which button?" he interrupted her, as if it were a matter of grave concern. "The missing button? Or the missing button that wasn't missing? Or the missing button that wasn't missing that turned up missing after all?"

Her temper was rising. Jake even thought he could see her hair beginning to curl. "The button that caught in the lace when I reached behind my back to unbutton the dress."

She kept her consonants nice and tight. He'd always admired her articulation-under-fire skills. "Oh, the snagged button." He nodded. "Go on. You were distracted because of the snagged button...?"

"It isn't important."

"No, I really do want to hear about this strange occurrence that happened in your bedroom today."

Her discomfort was a thing of beauty and he watched her struggle with pure enjoyment.

"Okay. Well, when I was going into the bedroom, I felt... I mean, did you notice...? Was it my imagination or...?" She stopped and sucked in a breath of hard-won composure. "All right, I'm just going to say this straight out. Did I get stuck in the doorway between my dressing room and bedroom?"

He made her wait only a moment or two before he set her at ease with a nod of concurrence. "You were stuck, Gentry. You were stuck in the no-budge position until I stepped around you and pulled you through that doorway. I'm no therapist, you understand, but I think that what happened to you today is most likely a psychological phenomenon in which a person struggles with two conflicting desires... to go forward and to not go forward because the person fears what lies ahead." He paused just long enough to see her head dip in a nod of possible agreement. "It's called *Smooch-a-phobia.*"

He laughed so hard, he nearly didn't duck in time. The empty beer bottle soared over his head, with a mile to spare, and landed, neck down, on the lawn. "Liz? You missed me."

Her temperature hit the boiling point. "Jacob Daniels! You are the most annoying, exasperating, irritating—"

"Irksome," he suggested.

"Irksome, aggravating, irrepressible—"

"Irresistible."

"Irresistible, infuriating, maddening—"

"Magnificent."

"Magnifi—! Stop that. You know I hate it when you do that to me."

"I never could get you to work *magnificent* in. Tripped me up every time."

One foot began to swing back and forth as a mark of her irritation. "Sometimes I wonder how you ever persuaded me to run away with you."

"No, Gentry, it was the other way around. You persuaded me that I had to take you away with me."

"I did not. You begged me. You said you would feed me fresh raspberries and real cream."

"You misunderstood. I said you'd dine on baked trout and low-fat milk."

"You said you'd bring me breakfast in bed every day."

"I said, there would be guests to be fed every day."

"You said you couldn't live without me and that you would love me until the day you died."

Jake's desire to tease her fled. "Sometimes I say the damnedest things."

She met his gaze across the table and smiled, sort of sadly, he thought.

"Yes," she finally said. "Sometimes you do."

They sat quietly, letting the past slip back into the safe, manageable framework of memory. The moments whisked past one by one, linking hands to reach an uncomfortable silence. Gentry was the first to break it, and she chose the category called "regrets."

"You shouldn't have come here, Jake."

"I believe we've pretty well reached consensus on that, all around. If it makes you feel better, I wish I hadn't."

A faintly unhappy smile grazed her lips and was gone. "At last we've found something we can agree on."

"Don't be stingy, Liz. I bet we could list dozens of issues on which we see eye to eye."

"Name three and you can have another beer."

He tipped his head back and stared at the sky. "Rain, green and pasta," he said. "Hand over the beer."

"Wait a minute. Rain, green and pasta? What kind of issues are those?"

"Okay, maybe *issues* was the wrong word. But you said name three things we agree on and I did. So give me the beer."

She refused with a shake of her head. "That's cheating and you know it. I could as easily say we agree on snow, pink and potatoes. It doesn't mean anything."

He closed his eyes and breathed in the soft, sensual, familiar scent of her. "We agree we could never eat pasta too many times in the same week. We agree that green is a good color for a child's bedroom. We agree that rain is the most erotic setting for a kiss."

Her stillness drifted over him, sharing the bittersweet memories contained in three random words.

"Now, do I get the beer?" he asked quietly. "Or do I have to tell you why we agree on snow, pink and potatoes?"

"No." She picked up another bottle and held it out to him.

He took it with one hand, wondering why he hadn't left this morning, or yesterday, or anytime before now. "I'm going home tonight," he said, so he wouldn't be tempted to forget. "Catching the red-eye flight back."

"You mentioned that before."

"Did I?"

"Mmm-hmm."

He looked at the bottle in his hand and then at the ones still on the table. "Am I crashing another party here?"

Her gaze followed his to the evidence. "Oh, no. I was expecting to find my friends out here, but apparently I misinterpreted their plans."

"And here I was hoping you had come to kiss me goodbye."

Her short laugh was meant to scoff at the idea, but it caught a note of husky wistfulness in her throat and lost the intended effect. "That would be a stupid thing to do."

"Yes. And you're not stupid."

"No, I'm not."

"It would be a mistake to think we could find that *closure* you mentioned last night . . . at the police station . . . while we were sitting together on the bench."

She got the picture, as he'd meant for her to, and the memory of that angry, impulsive, passionate kiss joined them at the table like a guest who stayed on and on, not knowing the party was over.

She stood abruptly, unfolding from the chair like a long-stemmed rose, her body enticingly encased in a maillot. He admired her with a hunger born of deprivation and the same intense emotion he'd felt the first time he set eyes on her. He watched her take a running step and dive into the pool, escaping from him and the uncomfortable memories he'd brought with him.

If he had a grain of sense about self-preservation, he'd walk away right now.

But he set the beer on the table, followed her to the edge of the pool and dived in after her.

GENTRY DIDN'T KNOW why she was still running from Jake. But her impulsive plunge into the water was only another form of escape. Why had she stayed at the pool when she realized he was in it? Had she wanted to watch him gather himself and rise from the water like Poseidon? Did she need to see each drop of water kiss him in a caressing stream, bathing his hard body in glistening adoration? Was this her punishment for not being the wife he wanted? To see him one more time and know she would never desire any other man with the same intensity, the same aching need?

Maybe she was trying to postpone the goodbye she didn't want to say, running away from the moment when she would toss off a casual word of farewell, as if she didn't mind at all that she would never see him again.

The confusion flowed into her arms and legs and she set off across the pool to work it out, to convince her heart she didn't care. But she barely made a half lap before she felt his arm snake around her waist and pull her against him. She was ashamed she didn't summon the will to push him away, but what was the point? Her body would only have followed his, found some way to bypass the voices of reason and sanity to find the pleasure she had discovered so many times in his embrace.

Turning in his arms, she found his mouth and filled it with her tongue. From cool sensibility to eager intensity, she let the passion flood her senses like a drug, and they sank together, clinging and careless of any need but one. His hand tugged at her suit, found a way inside, and grasped her breast in a pleasurably painful massage. She dug her fingers into the taut muscles of his shoulders and clung to him until, inevitably, the kiss pulled them through a sea of regret to the incandescent twilight.

They broke the surface and the kiss at the same moment, splashing away from each other as if that would disguise the reality of the passion that drove them. Jake swam a lazy backstroke to the ladder, then climbed from the water. Gentry poured the tension inside her into long strokes, swimming the length of the pool, striving for exhaustion and forgetfulness. When her muscles protested the abuse, she pulled herself partially up onto the tiled rim and laid her head on her hands.

Her breathing was torturous and slow, as much a result of the intensity of that watery embrace as from the exercise. She tried to recover a normal rhythm— anything normal would be good. But then she heard the splash his wet feet made as they approached and her pulse soared out of control again. Touch me, she pleaded with him in silence, but kept her head down, embarrassed to let him see the desire in her eyes and know how badly she wanted him.

He stopped in front of her...she could feel the splatter of the water drops that dripped from his body to the ground...and then a pound of soft cotton towel dropped on top of her head. A moment later, a corner of the towel lifted and she opened her eyes to see him peering in at her. She couldn't do this. She didn't want to be here. To be so close to him and know they had never been further apart. "Jake, I..."

"Want another beer?" He sounded normal. As if they hadn't just shared a watery and erotic kiss.

She frowned beneath the thick cotton terry, unexpectedly annoyed by his casual tone. As if he were offering one of his buddies a cold brew after a successful fishing trip. "No, thanks," she said, pulling the towel off her head. "I've had one too many already."

Ignoring the offer of a hand up, she boosted herself out of the pool and gathered the towel around her, uncaring that he watched every move, but intensely aware that he did. She intended to leave then, but stubbornly, returned to her chair instead, unwilling to run away yet again.

"I don't know how to tell you this," he began hesitantly. "But your fiancé is being held hostage by a fairy."

She looked at his teasing smile and then at the ransom note open on the table, realizing she ought to thank him for forcing the tension to ebb beneath the comfortable pattern of their bantering. "I know," she said, searching for the light tone he would expect. "Three fairies, to be exact."

"Three fairies." He stroked his chin thoughtfully. "I was going to guess this was the work of the Tooth Fairy, but if she's not working alone... How many fairies are there altogether?"

"Well, let me think." With him so close, his body glistening with the interplay of moisture and light, it was difficult to concentrate, to hit the rhythm of their usual wordplay. "There's the Fairy Godmother, the Fairy Princess, the Queen of the Fairies, the Sugarplum Fairy, Woodland—"

"Okay, okay. Let's concentrate on one at a time." He pointed to the note. "Do you recognize her?"

"Yes, that's Tinkerbell."

"Is she from this area?"

Gentry twisted her rope of wet hair into a thick knot on top of her head and noted the level of her tension by the erratic tapping of her foot. "Haven't you been to Disneyland, Jake? The *Magic* Kingdom?"

"I thought Tinkerbell lived in Never-Never Land."

"Only in the off-season."

He picked up the note and scanned it, then had to brush the glitter from his fingers. "What's all this sparkle stuff?"

"Magic dust."

"Oh." Impressed, he looked more closely at his fingers. "Does this mean I can fly?"

She couldn't think of a response, much less a witty one, so she just sat there, her body begging for his in a mute, hopeless silence, as her foot tapped and tapped....

"I can see you don't believe in magic dust, Liz." His tone sounded a little forced as well. "But if you ever want to see Sonny again..." He looked up. "I suppose you do want to see him again?"

She made a rueful face and nodded.

"I was afraid of that." He sighed and looked at the ransom note again.

Was it her imagination or did the paper tremble slightly in his hand?

"How did these three fairies convince Sonny to go peacefully? Did they sprinkle him with magic dust? Give him a couple of painkillers? Get him punch-drunk?"

"If I had to guess, I'd say they overpowered him with their combined charm and talked him into doing something he will regret in the morning."

"Hmmm," Jake murmured. "I'd like to meet these fairies myself."

And that was the last turn of the screw. Gentry jumped up, gathering her towel, picking up the remains of this unbearable tension, forcing herself to talk normally, move normally, act normally.

Don't think about the fact that he's leaving in a couple of hours. Don't think about never seeing him again. Don't think about kissing him goodbye. Remember how you failed. Remember how unhappy you made him. Remember how unhappy you made yourself.

"Well, I've got to go. Have a safe trip. You should visit Ben and Sara sometime. Maybe the five of us can get together. Play golf. Go fishing. Wouldn't that be grand? It would be—"

Then she was pulled fiercely into his arms and his mouth was on hers, his tongue tasting hers, his body hard and demanding against hers, and the tension inside her snapped, uncoiling like a spinning reel, releasing the passion, the hunger, the love.

In seconds, their hands sought remembered territory, their lips claimed new possession. His desire was the rough thrust of his tongue in her mouth. Hers, the frenzied search of her hand beneath the cool, wet cling of his swimsuit. His deep moan of pleasure filled her senses as his rigid desire filled her hand. He fumbled at her breast, gave up trying to push aside the maillot and took her in his mouth. She kissed his shoulder, his neck, caressed every slick, hot part of him. Their passion was like a separate entity, awakening at a touch, whipping through their bodies with no thought for any need but its own. Taking, probing, reaching...until it exhausted their energy, and simply stopped. She was almost grateful when Jake took the initiative to pull back and let her catch her breath.

She was shaking when Jake gathered her gently against him; trembling as he held her, touched her hair, whispered words—just words—to her racing heart; quivering as his lips bathed her in soothing, calming kisses. When she finally caught her breath, she lifted her face for his kiss, wanting him to immerse her confusion in a numbing embrace that would annul her failures and wipe away her mistakes, and leave her, finally, whole.

Jake cupped her chin in his hands and looked into her eyes. With excruciating tenderness, he stroked her cheek with his thumb and brushed aside a strand of her still-damp hair. "You are the most tempting woman I've ever known, Liz, and I want you so much it's a constant, aching hunger inside of me."

"That's the way I feel, too." At this moment, she would do anything, say anything, to have him. "Let me go with you, stay with you, be with you. This time I'll get it right. We'll get it right. I won't be so demanding. I won't insist on having my own way. I—"

His thumb stopped on her lips, stilling her plea. "Gentry, if I believed there was a chance in hell you meant one word of that, I wouldn't let go of you until sometime in the next century. And I know without a doubt that an hour from now, I'm going to be kicking myself from here to town and back again, but I'm saying goodbye. Right here, right now. I'm going to walk out of your life because you and I are not a perfect fit...and we're never going to be. Sometimes, you have to know when to cut line and move on. That's what I'm doing, before I ruin your life again."

His words took her completely by surprise, and before she could form a coherent protest, he brushed her lips with a softly poignant kiss. "I've probably seen a thousand movies with really great exit lines, but not one of them comes to mind. So, I'll just leave you with my for-what-it's-worth opinion. On Saturday, wear the million-dollar wedding gown. It'll make your pop happy. You look like a million dollars in it. And if there should be such a thing as magic and happily-ever-after... Hell, it can't do any harm to wear the silly thing.''

She watched him walk away, disbelieving, hurt, irritated, and getting angrier with every step he took. He probably thought she'd go running after him, assure him he was wrong, that he wouldn't, couldn't ruin her life. Well, he was wrong. There was such a thing as dignity.

''I'll show you, Jacob Daniels,'' she said softly, over the lump of pride in her throat. ''I'll show you. I will live happily ever after... without you.''

The only problem with that, Gentry thought, was that he would never know if she succeeded.

Chapter Twelve

The wedding dress poured over her in a bath of cool satin and fine lace. Slipping her arms through the sleeves, Gentry drew the bodice in around her in a close and perfect fit, and then, one by one, she touched each button, nudging each into its corresponding loop. She didn't look at the mirror, wasn't even tempted to turn and see if Sonny might be hovering like a shadow waiting to appear in the reflection with her.

"Gen?" Sydney tapped on the dressing-room door. "Need any help?"

"I can manage, thanks. Is he here yet?"

"I don't know. Heather?" Syd's voice faded as it was directed away from the door. "Any sign of them yet?"

Heather's reply was too muffled to distinguish inside the dressing room, but then Sydney's voice returned, happy and excited. "Not yet, but he should be here any minute now. You sure you don't want some help getting into that dress? I could get a shoehorn and wedge you into those sequins in nothing flat."

"I'm already in my dress," Gentry called. "Be out in a minute."

There was a quiet rustle of silk as Sydney moved away from the other side of the door and the murmur of voices as she spoke to Heather and was answered. Gentry smiled a little at the thought of how many times she had planned this day.

Her wedding day.

She and Syd and Hil and Heather had gathered in her bedroom dozens of times over the years to plan their weddings, dreaming about what they'd wear, what everyone else would wear, what colors they'd choose, what music would be played, the candles, the flowers—even the vows were subject to change. They had imagined all the little details...except the groom. In their make-believe *"at my wedding, I'm going to have..."* he was a stick figure in a tux of whatever color they liked at the time. He didn't get to speak or do anything but wait for her at the end of the aisle. Gentry had always felt he should look like Barbie's Ken...tall, handsome, smiling and plastic. The perfect man.

She fastened the last button—they were all in order, not a missing one among them—and fluffed the satin skirt. When she turned to check her appearance in the mirror, she didn't look for misty images or allow herself to remember Jake's wonderfully roguish grin looking at her, eager to *make contact*. Her cheeks were a little flushed...either with excitement or the memory of how easily she had accepted the idea that his would be the face she saw...if there was such a thing as a magic wedding gown.

Which, of course, there wasn't.

"Gentry?" It was her mother's voice, her mother's quick tap on the door, and then Frannie entered. "Oh..." The clasp of hands, the instant tightness of lips, the shimmer of tears in green eyes just like Gentry's own, made the ageless connection between mother and daughter. "You look . . . lovely."

With a smile, Gentry invited her mother into the dressing room and got ready for an adjustment. She stood patiently, facing the mirror as Frannie adjusted the fit of the wedding gown, the drape of the veil, an uncooperative strand of hair, a smudge of makeup, a smudge on the mirror, her own dress, hair, hat, shoes. Somewhere there was probably a mother's handbook in which the rules were laid out so that the ritual of adjustment could be completed. Frannie finished in record time, her anxious energy turning to the arriving guests, locating the photographer, checking on the caterer and the florist, keeping Pop from rearranging the seating, and all the other details that would take her through this ceremonial rite of passage.

Gentry breathed a sigh of relief when her mother left, and with a passing glance at her reflection, she opened the dressing-room door. Her bridesmaids were gathered by the window in a huddle of rose petal pink and curiosity as they watched the arrival of guests and activity going on outside.

"Gentry!" Heather saw her first and her brown eyes widened with pleased surprise. "Oh, I'm so glad you decided to wear that dress."

Hillary turned, affection shining in her blue eyes. "You look beautiful, Gen," she said.

Sydney scanned her from head to toe and nodded. "Wise choice. I wasn't looking forward to explaining why I allowed you to get married in a sequined Slinky."

"I changed my mind," Gentry said. "I knew Pop would be happy if I wore this dress, and as Ben pointed out, it isn't every bride who has a million-dollar wedding gown."

"You changed your mind." Sydney shook her head in surprise and repeated, "You changed your mind. We have spent this entire week trying to get you into that wedding gown. We ruined your pearl gray dress—"

"No great loss to the world of fashion," Hillary commented with a sorry-but-it's-the-truth shrug.

"We locked you in a room with nothing else to put on. We tried bribes, coercion and finally took poor Sonny hostage—"

"At considerable expense of my time and pocketbook," Hillary pointed out.

"Promising to return him only when we had a picture of you in the dress. Throughout you were your normal, stubborn self, not willing to bend an inch or cooperate with your devoted friends in any way, shape or form. And today, you just *changed your mind.*"

Gentry smiled. "I'm the bride. I can do that."

"If we'd known you'd decide to wear this dress, we wouldn't have had to take the other one to the— Ow!" Heather stopped to rub the arm Hillary had just pinched. "She would have found out what we did, anyway."

Hillary sighed. "We took the other wedding dress to the cleaners . . . and it, unfortunately, shrank a little."

"Just enough to keep me from wearing it?" Gentry asked, loving the idea that her friends would go to such lengths to save her from what they considered a serious fashion mistake. "Lucky for you I decided on this one. Otherwise, you'd be spooning me into the sequined creation with Sydney's shoehorn."

"You look just beautiful in that, Gentry. I've never seen you in anything else so becoming." Heather came closer to admire her. "And it fits you like it was made exactly to your measurements." She glanced at Hillary. "It's a good thing you didn't put it on, Hil. It wouldn't have fit you at all."

Hillary turned—too quickly—to the window. "Look, there's Lucy Pendrax. Would you look at the belly on her? She must be having triplets."

"Let me see!" Heather ran to join Hillary in the window, her rose petal bridesmaid's dress hitching up in back as she kneeled on the window seat.

Gentry's gaze cut to Sydney's, sharing a common concern for Hillary. Ever since the day she'd held the dress against her and looked in the mirror, she had been jumpy, nervous, given to lapses in attention and wistful sadness. Even the two-day kidnapping stunt hadn't helped. She'd been the designated kidnapper and had, insanely, coerced Sonny into a round-trip to Paris, just to introduce him to the "best cup of cappuccino in the world"—his words, not hers. Gentry still couldn't believe Sonny had gotten on the Concorde with her, spending the better part of forty-eight hours en route to and from a coffee bar. Sonny had had nothing but good things to say about his time as a hostage. He had nothing but praise for the coffee bar...and Paris. He was thrilled that, finally, her friends liked him.

Sydney lifted one shoulder in a slight shrug, as if to say, *Whatever's wrong with Hil, she knows we're here. She'll let us know when she's ready.* Gentry nodded, hoping that was true.

"The bridegroom has arrived. Oh, there's Mitch!" Heather squealed the words, almost bouncing up and down in her excitement. "Hi, Mitch!" she called, although he couldn't possibly hear her. "He's getting out of the limo," she reported. "The women are swooning because he's so handsome. They're crowding around him, screaming for his attention. But he isn't interested. He's looking around for his one true love." She glanced over her shoulder at Gentry and Syd. "That's me."

"Oh, look," Hillary said dryly. "He's grabbing that blonde. Now he's tossed her over her shoulder and he's beating his chest like Tarzan...."

"Shut up, Hillary." Heather returned to the window with a complacent sigh. "You're just making that up."

Gentry laughed and put her hand on the door frame. Looking into the bedroom, she wondered when the four of them would be like this again, if it would ever, really, be like this again, if perhaps it shouldn't be. Their friendship had changed before. It would change again. She was going to go forward and the first step was through this doorway. Bracing herself for resistance, she stepped forward. No unseen hand pushed her back. No force pulled her from behind. The dress moved with her like a childhood lullaby, softly sweeping the floor in a low rustle of sound.

So whatever had happened to her the other day had been a psychological thing, a resistance to entering the room where Sonny waited, when Jake was there in the room behind her. It wasn't so strange, she told herself. Jake wasn't here now to hold her back.

The bedroom door opened and the ever-smiling wedding coordinator looked in. "The photographer is on his way up," she said. "Everybody ready?"

From that moment on, Gentry was surrounded with wedding traditions. Posing for pictures, receiving wishes from friends and relatives who "couldn't wait to get a peek at the bride." Ben and Sara, newly returned from their honeymoon, came in to say hello and offer best wishes, but there was no chance for private conversation, no opportunity to ask them if the dress was really magic, to discover if it had worked that magic on them. As if their obvious joy in each other could be called anything else.

Pop came and went, had his picture taken, left with the photographer, returned some time later, realized the photographer had missed the traditional shot where Pop dropped a penny in her shoe for good luck, and hurried off to find the poor man and drag him and his equipment back upstairs again to get the picture. Frannie popped in twice...to make sure the *girls* were ready and didn't need any motherly adjustments.

Gradually, music wafted up from below and well-wishers drifted down to take their seats, and the bedroom cleared of everyone except the bridal party. Then, suddenly, the coordinator was there, moving Heather and Hillary into the hall, reminding them to wait for her cue, telling Sydney to be ready, asking Pop to straighten his tie.

"You look beautiful, Gen," Sydney said as she waited by the door. "Are you sure you want to do this?"

Gentry nodded, feeling as though she were being pulled through a looking glass into a place she didn't want to go. "Are you kidding?" she said. "This is it. The happily-ever-after we all dreamed about."

Sydney's gray eyes questioned her, but when she spoke it was only to say, "We didn't really shrink the other dress. We just took in the seams a little."

"Don't give it another thought," Gentry said. "This dress is a better choice. I mean, who am I to argue with magic?"

The wedding coordinator waved Sydney into the hallway. Syd made her usual I-can't-believe-I'm-doing-this face before she walked from the bedroom in a whisper of rose petal pink. Gentry decided it was true . . . pink really wasn't her most flattering color.

POP, UNUSUALLY QUIET, waited for Gentry at the top of the stairs and she slipped her arm into his. "You're sure you want to do this?"

"Not you, too," she said while the wedding march swelled around them and they waited for their cue. "Sydney just asked me the same thing."

"Smart girl, that Sydney."

Gentry nodded. "Yes, she knows when to keep her opinions to herself."

"That's her job as your friend. I'm your father. My job is to give you my opinion whether you asked for it or not."

"Okay, Pop," she said with a sigh. "Give it to me straight."

"My opinion is, you're the most beautiful thing I've ever seen. You're the very best parts of your mother and me put together, and from the minute you rushed into my world, screaming at the top of your lungs and threatening me with your little balled-up fists, I've been your most ardent fan."

She had to blink back a mist of tears as she leaned over to kiss his cheek. "Thanks, Pop. I love you, too."

He nodded and cleared his throat. "Now, you want my advice?"

"Sure."

"When we get to the bottom of these stairs, I'm going to open the door and you run like hell."

She laughed. "Why would I do that?"

"Because it's the right thing to do."

At the base of the stairs, the wedding coordinator watched Sydney's measured steps turn onto the satin material that marked the aisle leading through the house to the terrace and the flower-draped arbor where Sonny waited for his bride. Gentry looked down at the guests seated on either side of the aisle and then at the front door. The thought of running like hell was appealing. She could keep on running away, she supposed, every time she doubted her decisions, every time something didn't feel quite right. She'd run away from her wedding, from her marriage, from the man she really loved. She'd run from the idea that love could hurt, could make her angry, could expect her to compromise, to change.

The music sounded a fanfare and Pop led her down the stairs. He paused when they reached the last step and asked her the question with his eyes. *Do you really want to do this?* they asked. *There's still time to run away.*

The door looked tempting, but it was time she stopped running away and faced herself and her future. Marrying Sonny felt like a mistake, but she wasn't going to leave him standing at the altar again, leave him to deal with the sympathetic pity of his family and friends, leave him feeling like he'd failed her, when all he'd ever done was try to be the man she wanted him to be. She met her father's eyes and shook her head.

Then the aisle was before her, stretching through a sea of murky faces and happy expectations, and at the end Sonny waited, handsome, perfect, Barbie's Ken doll in the flesh. Except he wasn't smiling. She supposed if she had been the one jilted before, she'd be feeling a little nervous at this point, too.

Her grip on Pop's arm clenched convulsively. "Pop," she whispered. "What if I make him miserable?"

He patted her hand and whispered from the side of his mouth, "What do you mean, *if?*"

She pinched his arm and he winced ... but never missed a step.

"Don't worry, Gentry. There's a good chance Sonny won't notice how miserable he is."

That was really encouraging. Here she was, walking down the aisle to her groom, thinking about his inevitable misery.

"Did you want to run away from your wedding?" she asked Pop.

"Yep. So did your mother."

Okay, then, so this was normal anxiety. Wedding jitters. Sonny would smile any minute now and she'd be fine.

The aisle was getting shorter, the distance to her happily-ever-after diminishing. There was still no change in Sonny's expression. Maybe when she got there, she'd find out he *was* Ken, that he really was made out of plastic.

"There's still time," Pop said. "I can have you out of here and on your way to Jake in a snap of my fingers."

"I already made him miserable," she said. "And he noticed."

"Marriage is probably always going to be a roller coaster for you, sweetheart. Whether you're on the kiddie ride with Sonny or the thrill-seeker with Jake."

There were only a few more steps, only a few more yards of white satin aisle. "I failed at one marriage already. This one looks safer."

"You didn't fail, Gentry. You just quit trying." Pop put his hand over hers and squeezed reassuringly.

And then, there was no place to run. The aisle ended with Sonny. She stood beside Pop, waiting for him to speak his lines about giving her away and then offering her hand to her bridegroom. Sonny still hadn't smiled and Gentry began to feel nervous. The minister began the prepared ceremony. "Dearly beloved..." he began.

This was a bad idea, she thought. She didn't want to marry Sonny. He was a perfectly nice man. But he didn't deserve to be miserable. Only Jake deserved that kind of misery. So okay, what did she do? Turn around, tell a joke, say she'd just discovered she had made a terrible mistake. She looked at each of her bridesmaids in turn. They looked awful in pink. If she called this off now, they'd be the first in line to murder her.

So, she'd just say nothing and let the ceremony proceed as planned and then... Then she'd be *married*.

"If any man has cause why this man and this woman should not be united in Holy Matrimony..." the minister intoned.

Gentry swallowed nervously. She had cause. Good cause. The bride loved another man.

"Let him speak now or forever hold his piece."

Forever was a hell of a long time. So Gentry opened her mouth to speak.

FROM THE BACK OF THE ROOM and through a rosy wash of color, Jake watched Gentry walk down the stairs with his heart in his throat. The million-dollar wedding dress seemed to be a living thing, full of warmth and life and sudden twinkles of light. Gentry had infused it with her energy and had been touched by its magic, and the resulting combination was enchanting. He had never seen her look so confident, so sure of who she was and where she was going.

He had never been so sure he was a fool for thinking he could stop her from making another mistake.

She passed the row in which he was sitting, incognito, wearing borrowed glasses with tinted lenses, an ill-fitting suit and a hairpiece the wig-shop owner had assured him made his full head of hair appear *"magnifico."* He didn't know what he was doing here, other than he had regretted walking away from her from the very minute he did it. In all the minutes since, he hadn't been able to think of a single reason why he should have to be noble. He was miserable without her, and, damn it, she was miserable without him. And he knew without question that Sonny Harris was going to be miserable with her.

So here he was, watching her walk down the aisle through rose-colored glasses, desperate to stop her, and scared to death that if he did, she'd never forgive him.

"If any man has cause why this man and this woman should not be united in Holy Matrimony..." the minister intoned.

Jake took a deep breath of courage. He had cause. Good cause. The bride loved another man, who loved her with every beat of his not-so-noble heart.

"Let him speak now or forever hold his piece."

Forever was a hell of a long time. So Jake stood up to speak.

"Wait!"

Mouth open, the words ready to spill from her lips, Gentry almost choked as she realized the voice that had stopped the ceremony wasn't hers. The solemn quiet changed into a low buzz of surprise as the guests shifted in their seats, exchanged puzzled looks with other guests and cast suspicious glances at the odd-looking man who had popped from their dignified midst like a broken spring and now stood in his place as the room settled into a collective hush.

Gentry heard the scrape of a chair and registered the intrusive noise. Her over-the-shoulder glance registered a familiar shape standing in the back of the room . . . a tall man with a rooster's comb of dark hair and bad glasses . . . but she could only deal with one shock at a time.

"What did you say?" she asked Sonny.

"I said I can't marry you, Gentry."

"You can't?" She had the strangest feeling, as if she were light enough to fly. "Or you don't want to?"

"Would you like to speak to each other in private?" the minister whispered with an eye on the attentive guests.

"Shh," Pop told him.

Sonny had lost his usual sheepish expression and he didn't look away from her question. "Does it make any difference?" he said. "I'm sorry, Gentry. I thought it would be best not to make a scene, but as you were walking down that aisle, I knew I couldn't marry you because..." He looked over at Hillary, standing as still as a statue, then took a deep breath and squared his shoulders. "Because I've fallen in love with somebody else."

"What do you mean you've fallen in love with somebody else?"

Gentry and Sonny and Pop turned in unison to see who was yelling at them from the audience. They stared at the man as he lunged through the seated guests to reach the aisle.

"Who is that?" Sonny muttered

Pop squinted. "Elvis?"

"Jake," Gentry said and laughed. "What are you doing here?"

"Don't ever ask me that again," Jake said, walking purposefully toward the arbor. "Why would any man be here with you unless he was so besotted and so much in love with you he wasn't able to think straight?"

She considered that possibility. "Well, Sonny's here and he's not in love with me."

"I heard," Jake said, a note of annoyance in his voice. "If it wasn't to my advantage for you to be jilting my wife, Harris, I'd punch you in the nose right here and now."

"Why are you wearing a wig?" Sonny asked.

"I was afraid if you found out I was here, you'd make a scene. So I wore a disguise."

"Very clever, Jake." Sydney gave him the A-OK sign with her thumb and forefinger. "Can I borrow the glasses?"

He pulled them off and tossed them to her. She dropped her maid-of-honor bouquet to catch them. "Thanks."

"You're welcome. Now, I'd like to make a suggestion, if no one objects."

"I object," said the minister.

"Save it for later," Pop told him.

"I suggest that we take a thirty-minute break and then begin this wedding over again. Only this time I'll be the bridegroom."

"This is really very irregular," the minister began.

"Shh!" the bridesmaids hissed.

"Gentry…" Jake turned to her and took her hands in his. "I made a big mistake the other night. I tried to be noble, to insist you make a choice instead of running away from your commitments." His smile was confident, but wary, as if he weren't at all sure of her response. "I really thought you'd come after me," he said with a shrug, "and that we'd be able to stop this wedding before it reached this highly public arena. But once again, I underestimated your stubbornness. It won't happen again."

She could fly. She just knew it. "It will, too," she said, putting her hand to his cheek and absorbing the miracle that had brought him here, the wonderful knowledge that he had come after her. Two years late, but he had finally come. "But probably not today."

"Wait a minute," Sonny said. "You're not angry, Gentry, because I ruined the wedding? I figured you'd chew the scenery. Even though I knew deep down you'd be relieved."

She smiled into Jake's wonderful eyes. "I'm so glad you spoke when you did, Sonny. I was getting ready to say something when you said it first. I never wanted to hurt you."

"As it turns out, my heart's still beating." His gaze slipped past Gentry and she followed it to see Hillary—perfect, proper Hillary—crooking her finger at Sonny like a vamp intent on his seduction.

"I've known this was a mistake almost from the day I persuaded you to take my engagement ring back. Not long after the day I intercepted a rather smelly package from Arkansas and substituted a good riddance card."

"You swiped my trout?" Jake said incredulously. "If I wasn't such a forgiving guy, I'd have your fishing license revoked."

"I can't believe you did that, Sonny." Gentry wondered if she had ever really known him well at all. "Whatever possessed you to open a package addressed to me? And how could you have known it was from Jake, anyway?"

"I figured any communication from the Two-Penny Lodge was bad news for me." His gaze tracked its way back to Hillary. "And since all's fair in love and war, I did what seemed right at the time. I thought if we could do it again, plan the wedding again, get everything perfect..." He couldn't quite pull his gaze back to Gentry, though he kept talking to her, even as he edged his way toward Hillary. "I guess perfect isn't always possible."

"Sometimes imperfect is a much better fit." Uncaring of the watchful eyes of the audience, her family and friends, Sonny's family and friends and cousins, Gentry went into Jake's arms, pulled off the wig and tossed it in the air. Then she grabbed the back of his head and pulled his lips down to hers.

"Excuse me," the minister said hesitantly. "The kissing is supposed to come after the ceremony."

"Shh," the audience said in a collective whisper.

Jake managed to pull free long enough to ask, "I take it, Liz, that you're agreeable to my suggestion?"

"Not necessarily," she said, eager to reclaim his lips. "I'm not sure I like the idea of a thirty-minute break."

"I'm willing to compromise. We'll make it fifteen."

"Ten," she corrected him against his lips.

"Okay, five."

Pop turned around. "I think you should keep your seats for the moment. When the negotiations are over here, we'll let you know what time this wedding will resume. In the meantime, enjoy the music...." He glanced behind him at the rather passionate clench involving his daughter and soon-to-be son-in-law again and shrugged. "Hell, you may as well enjoy the show, too." He took the seat next to Frannie and slipped his arm around her shoulders.

A ray of sunlight caught on a button of Gentry's dress and splintered into a dozen tiny sparks that scattered over the room like fairies on the loose, sprinkling their magic dust on Gentry and Jake.... Sonny and Hillary... Heather and Mitch... colliding at last to shower down on Sydney and her new, rose-colored glasses. *A twinkle here. A twinkle there. Magic, magic, everywhere.*

Epilogue

There were three very good reasons not to get too close to the wedding gown, Sydney reminded herself several hours after the wedding. Gentry, Heather and Hillary. All three of them had been dazzled by the magical gown and blindsided by true love. Sydney had looked on good-naturedly throughout the entire week, thankful that *she,* alone, had had the good sense not to buy into the whole idea of a magic wedding dress.

Of course, she was alone now... her friends gone with their new significant others to their respective "happily-ever-afters," leaving her to spend one last night in Gentry's abandoned bedroom. All alone with her thoughts... and the wedding dress. It hung on a hook on the dressing-room door, tantalizing her with its provocative gleam. Not that she believed the occasional twinkles of light were anything more than stray moonbeams catching in the satin; but, still, they were enough to distract her from the magazine she was trying to read.

Oh, who was she kidding? She had no more interest in that magazine than she had in going for a late-night swim. She was interested in only one thing: putting on that silly dress and looking in the mirror.

It was the height of nonsense, of course, and she didn't expect to see the man of her dreams. But how could she pass up her last opportunity to see herself in the wedding gown? No one would ever know, and she hated thinking she might look back someday and regret not trying it on just this one time.

Action followed the thought like a rainbow after a storm, and she had barely gotten the dress off the hanger and over her head, before a sensation of happiness warmed her from head to toe. Odd. If anyone had asked, she'd have said "happy" was her predominant emotion of the entire week. But this was different. It was as if the warm glow of the ivory gown began inside of her and was merely reflected outward by the satin and lace. Not bothering to button either the back or the sleeves, Sydney held the bodice together and spun toward the mirror.

As if the dress had been impatiently waiting for her surrender, the image she saw was immediate and astonishing. Sydney knew she had never worn anything so breathtaking or looked so beautiful. The wedding gown gleamed, almost preening with satisfaction in the reflection, and she couldn't help but admire the lovely bride she saw in the mirror. She supposed she should be watching for her "true love" to appear, but it seemed more likely this was merely a vivid dream . . . or the work of an overactive imagination.

But she didn't turn away, not even when a man suddenly appeared beside her in the mirror. Especially not then.

She recognized him, although she couldn't say how or why. He was as familiar as a warm breeze, as anonymous as a distant melody. Straining to make out his features in the too-brilliant light, Sydney leaned closer to the mirror.

The reflection vanished, leaving her with a light-hearted sense of expectancy. Ordinarily, she would have been as frustrated as hell at being denied the knowledge she sought. But this was all right, some-how. He was out there. In her future. She wasn't des-tined to spend the rest of her life alone. Or with a dog named Mr. Right. Love awaited her in its own good time and it would find her. Just as it had found Hil-lary and Heather and Gentry.

Satisfied, Sydney slipped out of the gown in a rus-tle of satin, thinking that from now on she would be searching every face for her Mr. Right. Wasn't that the ultimate practical joke on her? She, who had always professed her immunity to romance. She, who had al-ways proclaimed independence to be far superior to a love relationship. Yes, this was a prank worthy of her three closest friends. And to think they hadn't had a thing to do with it.

Other than leaving her alone with the magic dress, knowing she'd be unable to resist trying it on.

The scoundrels. They had planned this. She just knew it. Well, she'd show them, Sydney thought as she hung the bridal gown back on the door. She'd have the last laugh. She would simply find her own true love and live happily ever after, too.

This time, when the wedding dress twinkled at her, she knew it wasn't moonbeams at all. It was magic.